# CAROLE MONDRAGON

*DEDICATION*

To Emma, The Light in Our Lives

And to Bridget Egan

## COLCANNON

Did you ever eat Colcannon
When twas made with yellow cream
And the kale and práitaí blended
Like a picture in a dream
Did you ever scoop a hole on top
To hold the melting lake
Of the clover flavored butter
That your mother used to make

An old Irish Poem

DECLARATION:

This is a work of fiction and although some of the places named are real, none of the characters are. Any resemblance in name, character, or description to any person, living or dead, is purely chance and unintentional.

Mykel the donkey and Beauty the pony were not only real at the time of writing, but most of the events described here that involved them were true.

Copyright © 2021 Carole Mondragon

www.CaroleMondragon.com

**ISBN:** 9798-4548-3752-5

All rights reserved.

CONTENTS

PROLOGUE
CHAPTER ONE | 1
CHAPTER TWO | 9
CHAPTER THREE | 25
CHAPTER FOUR | 35
CHAPTER FIVE | 45
CHAPTER SIX | 63
CHAPTER SEVEN | 77
CHAPTER EIGHT | 101
CHAPTER NINE | 111
CHAPTER TEN | 123
CHAPTER ELEVEN | 135
CHAPTER TWELVE | 151
CHAPTER THIRTEEN | 157
CHAPTER FOURTEEN | 173
CHAPTER FIFTEEN | 187
CHAPTER SIXTEEN | 195
CHAPTER SEVENTEEN | 211
CHAPTER EIGHTEEN | 223
CHAPTER NINETEEN | 233
CHAPTER TWENTY | 241
CHAPTER TWENTY-ONE | 257
CHAPTER TWENTY-TWO | 265

EPILOGUE | 271

GLOSSARY | 273

ACKNOWLEDGMENTS | 275

OTHER BOOKS BY THIS AUTHOR | 277

# The Irish Heirloom

# PROLOGUE

Breath catching in her throat, Bridget hurried her step. She passed several gráigeanna where, instead of the comforting welcome of turf fires curling up from each cottage, she was met only by an eerie quiet.

Some cabins and cottages looked as though they had been pulled down, their occupants gone. One such abode had been burned, smoke still emanating from its ruined state. Above all, there were no people that she could see as she evaluated her surroundings.

Riddled with alarm, Bridget began to run towards her own village. She urged herself on until at last, she stopped at the hazel trees and knew she was home.

Panting loud and puffing from the physical exertion, Bridget looked about with wild eyes. 'Where is everyone?' she wondered.

Heart in mouth, Bridget proceeded cautiously, dreading the unknown yet desperate to know the state of the place.

As she entered the street, she was shocked to see that most of the homes had been demolished to some degree so that the walls were not complete. Not one had its thatched roof intact.

She was transfixed by the scene. The hair on the back of her neck stood up in response even as her brain slowed down. She could not make sense of what was before her, nor could she move for several minutes.

The lack of childish laughter chilled her. No voices called out to each other. No pots were clanged in the making of the morning porridge. No old men sat in the winter sunshine and no chickens pecked in the dirt at their feet. The village was not only deserted but desecrated by what appeared to Bridget to be an unseen force.

She wondered if her parents were safe. This thought freed her body from its paralysis, and she began to run faster than before, desperate to see them.

Skirts flying about her ankles, she followed the track that led between the cottages toward the end of the village where the stream ran.

"Mam," she screamed as she splashed through, uncaring of the icy water as it dragged against her skirts. "Da, where are you!?"

That the cottage was empty, she could see before she arrived, for there was no door.

Bridget all but flew inside and looked in the corners as if by doing so, she could make her parents appear from the dust that gathered there.

Exhausted and disoriented, Bridget sat in the frozen mud at the entrance to her home. Tears ran down her face as sobs jarred her frame. She had no idea of what to do or how to make sense of it all.

At a sudden noise, she listened with head turned. Scrambling to her feet, Bridget ran toward the sound.

In one of the cottages, she found a man turning over the few belongings left within.

She stopped in the doorway, bringing a shadow across him. He in turn, fell back in shock at the sight of her.

Bridget could see the man was ill. He was emaciated with a haggard face and eyes that stared. She pulled the piece of cheese and bread from her pocket that Cook had insisted she bring to sustain her on the journey. She held this out to the man who grabbed it with trembling hands.

Stumbling to the corner of the cottage, he pushed the food into his mouth and swallowed piece after piece, not bothering to chew first. His eyes closed as the last of the food disappeared until Bridget feared he had fallen asleep.

She moved to rouse him. "Please!" she begged. "Where is everyone?"

The man opened his eyes. After a huge sigh, he merely raised an arm and pointed, indicating the direction that led out from the other end of the village.

In her grief, Bridget cared nothing for the discomfort of the poor man but lunged forward and grabbed hold of his coat. "Eileen and Joe Egan. Where are they?" She shook him hard. "Where!?" she demanded.

Tears flooded Bridget's eyes as she waited with bated breath, hoping his next words would still her fear...

## Chapter One

Melody, laughter, poetry, and a touch of magic with the slight hint of an American accent and all of it stirred into a rich stew. That was the pleasure of hearing great aunt Maggie's Irish. Magic was the ingredient Erin cherished most out of that musical stew.

As a child, Erin had spent her summers in Ireland. During the long, lazy evenings which were often interspersed with dull Irish rain, she recalled enchanted hours at the feet of her Great-Aunt Maggie, affectionately known as Gams.

With the beloved aging face smiling down at her, Erin would sip at steaming hot chocolate accompanied by thick-sliced butties, comprised of bread with a layer of butter and another of jam. With this delicious treat, it was always acceptable to dip the butties into the hot chocolate for an extra special combination.

In this delightful setting Erin was introduced to mischievous faeries, from as tall as herself to so small they could hide under mushrooms to shelter from storms, or leprechauns for whom the word mischievous didn't even come close. "To be sure the rapscallions are downright divilish!" Aunt Maggie would laugh.

These memories filled Erin's mind as the plane began its descent over Ireland. Coming down from the clouds, the windows flooded with sunshine, catching the auburn tints in Erin's long brown hair while spreading a warm yellow radiance throughout the cabin until every part of the interior glowed. Dark lashes closed momentarily over blue-gray eyes against the unexpected brightness.

When she peered through the porthole, Erin could see clouds above and the expanse of the blue sky they had just entered.

She gasped in surprise as the island of Ireland unfolded in its own cheeky way, offering an extra tantalizing moment of mystery before gifting its charms. Instead of the expected view of the land below, an additional layer of cloud hung there, so that Erin felt she was suspended between the two layers in anticipation of the grand reveal.

For a long moment, the plane explored its way through the fluffy blue tunnel before banking slightly to the left as the pilot began descending into the lower cloud. A sea of faces turned toward the port side windows for their first eager glimpse of Ireland.

As they dropped through the gray-white blanket, a velvet carpet of sparkling landscape revealed itself in hues of green and gold. It was so magical that all the passengers released a communal "Ahhh!" of delight.

Erin turned to share the moment with the woman sitting next to her who said, "Sure it's a lovely sight when you're coming home."

Erin agreed, her face lit in a happy smile. Surrounded by the soft lilting burr of Irish accents for the journey across the Atlantic, Erin had enjoyed the sense of returning to a beloved place even though it was in the sadness of Great-Aunt Maggie's loss.

"It must be magical, living here," Erin said to no one in particular.

The woman in the next seat over chimed in with an omniscent smile, "You know, I've been to many places in this world. My children are scattered to the four winds, wild geese every one of them. Sure I can tell you, the places where they are now, the land does not sing to them the way it does here in Ireland." She placed a finger on the side of her nose and lowered her voice as if sharing a secret with Erin, "Their ancestors are from here, do you see. This land, this soil, this is where the land sings to their souls. And if it's home you're returning now, the land will sing to you also."

Erin looked at her astonished. She opened her mouth to speak but closed it again as something Gams had once told her began to surface in her memory.

At that moment, the passenger door was opened to admit cool Irish air. Erin lost her train of thought as the scent of fresh fallen rain pervaded the cabin.

The woman stood up and pulled her hand luggage from the overhead compartment. With a final wink at Erin, she bustled down the aisle ahead of others who were still gathering their belongings.

Distracted for a moment by one passenger calling out, "Home at last!" Erin turned her head to follow the responding cheers. When she looked back, her travelling companion had disappeared from view.

Erin stretched her curvy five-foot six-inch frame and joined the line of tourists and Irish passengers gathered in the aisle. Their gentle smiles and quiet chatter told of an expectation for peaceful satisfaction ahead, a different life altogether from the fast-paced metropolis many had left behind in North America. Seeing this, Erin couldn't help but feel guilty for leaving work on a moment's notice. She knew that it was for a good reason, that it's perfectly acceptable to take time off when a loved one dies, but the job felt like a big part of her identity at this point.

She had worked hard to get to the position she was in now, and she didn't know much else. Even when she was off work, she was answering calls as to how to fix the machines, ordering food items that had run out, as well as staff members not showing up, and sometimes all of the above in one day.

To see the relaxed and cheerful atmosphere of the Irish, in an airport of all places, was to her, a sight to behold. Considering this contrast in pace, she thought about her last day at work before leaving.

*****

Erin was the morning manager at a thriving specialty cafe back home and often ran around multitasking with a skip in her step. Truth be told she enjoyed the chaos of the weekends and the long line of customers. She felt a sense of accomplishment in being able to juggle multiple orders and tasks simultaneously.

Although short-staffed that day, Erin found her flow with her co-worker Janey. Together they sent out drinks faster than the transaction of ordering them, thereby keeping the customers happy.

Erin had been pouring coffee in a cup the size of a soup bowl when her cell phone rang. The country code clearly marked the caller as located in Ireland and that meant only one thing.

A rush of thoughts competed in Erin's head ranging from delight to guilt, for it had been several months since she had spoken to Gams.

The customer tapped her credit card on the counter in a bid to regain Erin's attention. Summoning a quick smile Erin placed the coffee on the counter, ran the card and handed it back.

"Hey Janey, I have to take this call!" she waved her phone urgently, "Take over, will you?"

Janey glanced at the long line of customers waiting to be served. "Make it quick, okay?"

Erin put the phone to her ear as she pushed open the back door of the café and blinked as she stepped into the bright sunshine.

"Hello! ... Gams?"

"Miss Egan?" a distinctly Irish voice asked. "Erin Bridget Egan?"

"This is she," responded Erin, unconsciously adopting the formal manner of the caller.

"Would you be the Erin Bridget Egan who has an aunt here in Cuilrecool by the name of Margaret Bridget Egan?"

"Great." Erin raised a hand to fiddle with an earring.

"What's that now?"

"Maggie Egan is my Great-Aunt."

"Right so," the caller gave a polite cough. "My name is Orla Hanratty. I'm calling about your aunt ... Great-Aunt."

"Is she sick?" Erin interrupted, standing up straight, preparing for bad news.

"No .... No .... Ah now, there's no easy way to say this so there isn't," Orla Hanratty coughed again. "I've to inform you that Margaret Bridget Egan has passed away."

"She's ...?" Erin could not finish the sentence.

"Now, there's the matter of the will."

Erin's eyes blurred with quick tears, "Gams is ... dead?" She slumped against the wall.

"I'm afraid that's the case. I'm sorry for your loss, so I am." There was a brief pause before Orla Hanratty continued, "You'll be here for the funeral?"

Erin struggled to catch her breath. "When is it?"

"We've five days before the internment. The wake will be held in the parish hall."

"Okay," Erin's voice came out in a squeak.

"Would it be convenient to meet the day after the wake, so?"

"Erm …"

"Can you be here for the tenth?"

"Of this month?"

"Well yes," Orla Hanratty's tone became urgent, "there's the reading of your Great-Aunt's will."

Erin fought to control herself from breaking down, with the result that the words came out as a question rather than the intended statement, "And I need to be there."

"Aren't you her only relative now!" The voice went from apologetic to a distinctly disapproving tone, "If you're coming, we'll be expecting you on the tenth."

The call ended abruptly.

"Hello?" Erin looked at the phone. The screen was blank, and the caller gone. She pushed a hand through her hair and looked around as if for help. A door slammed in the distance, a car engine started and drove away down the alley, other than that, no-one was in sight.

Erin looked down at the blank screen on her phone and burst into noisy tears.

A few minutes later Janey opened the door and hissed, "Hey! You said you'd be quick. It's crazy in there!" She paused as Erin turned to face her with heavy black eye makeup smudged halfway down her pale cheeks. "What's going on? Are you okay?"

"I just-- I can't talk right now." Erin began to walk inside.

Janey raised a hand, like a stop signal. "You can't go in there looking like that." She nodded toward the restroom, tutted in sympathy, and headed back into the cafe.

In the restroom, Erin cleaned her face as best she could and quickly applied fresh mascara. Eyes still red from tears, she squared her shoulders and walked into the cafe.

She couldn't face having to serve customers at that moment, so she swapped places with Janey, focusing on making the drinks while Janey took orders.

The café was crowded. Erin tried to bury her heartache as she methodically poured coffee and frothed milk for lattes.

Fortunately, customers were content to wait in line because they could spend the time ooh-ing and aah-ing over a glass-covered display case filled with an assorted variety of rich cakes topped with icing or fresh cream.

As the rush quieted Janey approached Erin, concern on her face.

Erin wasn't ready to open up just yet, fearing that she would start crying again and this time she wouldn't be able to stop.

"I'll be downstairs if you need me," Erin gulped, and headed for the back stairs to where the daily baking took place.

The baker was not one for idle chatter and merely nodded at Erin who was no stranger to helping out in the basement.

In this solitary environment, Erin eased herself into the steady rhythm of pouring and mixing ingredients, then listened for the bell that indicated when the cakes were ready to come out of the big ovens.

To prevent the guilt from settling in, she reasoned that it was foolish to think of going to Ireland right now. She told herself she had a job to consider. Only a few years ago she had started as the dishwasher and was now manager of one of the most popular cafes in the state.

Managing a coffee shop was a step toward the larger goal of owning her own place where she planned to run events that centered around her community. She hoped these would draw a diverse group of customers and kept her eyes open for likely properties coming up for rent in the same locale.

The problem was money of course. She had only started saving a year ago and it was certainly not enough to start a whole business.

Friends had told her there were government grants available for start-ups. Erin knew she should research these and begin the application process but somehow it never seemed like the right time.

Erin reflected on all of this, but it didn't prevent her love for her Great-Aunt and the accompanying guilt from pouring itself over her shoulders. "I let you down all this time Gams," Erin told herself. "I shouldn't have waited so long to return to Ireland."

Another wave of guilt washed over her. She would not let Gams down again. She had made up her mind to leave for Ireland the very next day.

# Chapter Two

At the car rental office in Dublin Airport, Erin collected a set of keys. It was only when she opened the driver's door of the vehicle, that she realized she was actually about to get into the passenger seat. She looked hastily around hoping no one had noticed the error that marked her immediately as a foreigner.

The parking lot was empty but just in case someone was watching through the rental office window, she ostentatiously waved her hand luggage in the air and deposited it on the passenger seat as if that had been her intention all along. She then walked around the car, kicking a tire gently and ran her hand over the paint work, giving it all a personal inspection.

She had chosen a manual car. Not only was it less expensive to rent than an automatic vehicle but it also offered the opportunity to drive stick shift in a less stressful environment than back home.

Pushing the gearshift into first, Erin practiced the balance between gas and clutch pedals before slowly allowing the car to roll forward.

There was a slight drawback when the car refused to move but that was soon resolved by releasing the handbrake.

"Right!" remarked Erin, "that old thing."

As she drove slowly out of the airport parking lot, Erin noted a signpost reminding visitors to 'Drive on the Left'. She braced herself for the stress of following that instruction. She'd had the forethought to enter the address on her phone and took comfort in the calm automated voice of the GPS instructing her to "Drive straight ahead."

"Straight ahead I can do," said Erin as she pushed the gearshift into second gear.

Just outside the airport, a junction led onto a busy highway, where a traffic circle was situated before her.

While Erin knew this was a way of slowing and controlling the flow of traffic around the circular island, her experience of negotiating such things was limited to having been a passenger in Gam's car, and a child at that.

"At the traffic circle, take the third exit on your left," advised the tinny voice.

Pausing at the entrance to the traffic circle, Erin noticed a sign on the left admonishing drivers to 'Keep Left' and another sign on the right of the road that read 'Yield to the Right.'

As if this wasn't confusing enough, a car came up from behind, swept into the right-hand lane beside Erin's car and paused. Her view obstructed, Erin was obliged to wait for that car to move before she could check if there was a car entering the roundabout from the right highway.

Cars continued to come up behind her and in the accommodating style of the Irish, they did not sound the horn impatiently but merely drove around beside her, paused a moment, and then plunged into the traffic circle without missing a beat.

They made it look so easy that Erin was fooled into believing this was the case for everyone.

Deciding the only way to get into the traffic circle was to go undercover of another car, she gathered her courage while readying her feet on the pedals like a race-car driver waiting for the starter signal.

When an opportunity presented itself, Erin roared into the traffic circle undercover of the car to her right.

All was fine until that car scooted ahead and turned off at one of the four exits, leaving Erin going around for the second time and still in the left lane with the GPS woman calmly telling her to "Turn around when ready!"

"I'm trying! I'm trying!" Erin yelled in a panic, for at each exit now, more cars joined the traffic circle, scooting in ahead of her and behind.

Erin's blood began to pump a little faster and sweat broke out on her upper lip as she considered she might be locked into this for all time, or at least until she ran out of gas.

After four or five turns on this deadly merry-go-round, and despite the unnatural calm of the GPS voice, Erin came off at the very next exit. She was just about to breathe a sigh of relief when she realized with dismay that she was on her way back to the airport.

Turning around in the middle of the road was not at all easy in a manual car. Her three-point turn became a nine-pointer as she shifted gears, pushed into first, pressed down gently on the gas and repeatedly hiccupped to a stop.

Traffic in both directions stopped a little way off to give her both the room to turn and, she thought wryly, to keep their own vehicles away from the danger of her erratic driving.

Eventually, Erin got the car turned around and managed to get into second gear without stalling it. This time as she came up to the traffic circle, she forced herself to take slow yoga breaths as if she was preparing to enter the wall of death at the carnival.

As she eased into the traffic circle the GPS again reminded her, "Take the third exit."

This time Erin counted carefully.

"One!" she said as two cars zoomed in from an access road.

"Two!" she said a little louder as a car to her right cut ahead of her. Hands sweating on the wheel, Erin breathed out in a series of little whooshes.

"Take the next exit."

"I'm taking it! I'm taking it!"

Finally, she was off the roundabout and onto the highway.

"Three," she squeaked, unable to breathe normally just yet.

Shaking and sweating, it was some minutes before Erin had the courage to increase her speed beyond twenty miles an hour.

Even after she sped up, she was still going so slow that cars were easily able to cut in ahead. However, they didn't honk their horns and for that she was grateful.

The toll booths were a bit tricky because she hadn't thought to sort coins ahead of time. With a line of cars forming behind her, Erin apologised profusely to the clerk in the toll booth.

"I'm so sorry. I didn't realise this was a toll road." Erin gave up looking for the correct coins and handed over a twenty Euro note.

"Ah, you're grand." The clerk gave Erin a broad smile as she counted the change out.

It was a three-hour run to Great-Aunt Maggie's cottage. Although the day was sunny, Erin knew from experience that rain was always imminent in that it would often rain for half an hour, clear up for two or three hours and then rain again. Erin had learned from her summers with Gams that the Irish simply accepted the rain as part of everyday life.

She recalled being caught in the rain while out walking with Gams as a child. An elderly woman also out for her daily walk greeted them with, "Sure and 'tis a fine day for a walk." Sensing there was no hidden humor in the comment, Erin immediately looked up at her Great-Aunt to see how she would react. Gams had merely nodded her head, rainwater dripping off the edge of her nose and replied, "It is indeed."

After they walked on Erin asked, "Why would she say such a thing Gams? It's not a fine day at all."

Gams smiled down at her and said, "Do we not have a roof over our heads, a warm fire and food in our bellies? Sure, it's a fine day Erin." She raised a gentle but admonishing finger, "And don't you forget it!"

For Erin as a child, it was when the sun came out after the rain that Ireland could be seen for its natural beauty.

Rain droplets would hang on every tree and blade of grass so that the world seemed to sparkle with enchantment. Erin would sometimes peer into the dark woods on the side of the road. There among the moss-covered rocks and fallen trees, a river of bluebells would call to her so that she would tug on Gam's arm and point, speechless in her childish appreciation of the beckoning woods.

On such occasions Gams would follow her gaze and smile as if far away in her thoughts. "Ah yes," she would murmur. "Bluebells."

Despite being pressed for details, Gams would refuse to say more on the subject, leaving Erin torn between the beauty of the scene and the mystery of Gams' fascination with such flowers.

*****

Erin saw with delight the daffodils that bordered the hedgerows of the highway all across the country. It reminded her it would not be long before the bluebells flowered.

She had been driving only an hour when she realized she had to pee. The pretty green fields were forgotten as the urgency increased.

The road had now taken her away from the N17 highway. This quickly developed into an interesting experience because although the Irish drive sedately on the main highways, they have in general, no fear of driving fast on the picturesque but frighteningly narrow side roads.

Every time another car came around a leafy corner, seemingly headed straight for her car, Erin took a deep breath. She was tempted to close her eyes tight, but in the end she mostly hugged the bushes and held her breath until the car stopped rocking in the wake of each passing vehicle.

Pulling off the road to accommodate an oncoming truck, Erin found herself at the gate of a field. It was then she decided this was the place.

She grabbed a handful of tissues from her purse and stepped out of the car. A line of cows gathered at the gate, seemingly very interested in the goings on by the unexpected visitor.

"I didn't expect an audience," Erin muttered, slightly amused by the strange scenario. A quick glance around reassured her there was no farmer accompanying the cows.

Another truck roared by, followed by a couple of cars. Desperate now, Erin opened both the driver's door and the back door of the car and relieved herself with a great sigh of satisfaction.

Sliding back into the driver's seat, she grabbed hand sanitizer from her purse and massaged her hands with it.

"Glad you could come out today," she told her audience through the window. "I hope it was worth it for you." One of the cows called a loud moo and turned away, obviously unimpressed.

As she drove on, Erin laughed about her audience of cows.

"Ah well," she said, "I'm sure it's not an unusual sight on such a long road." She was, however, a bit miffed when only ten miles on, she entered a small town with a gas station right at the entrance, in which there would no doubt be a restroom.

Traffic moved slowly through the colorful winding streets of the town. Erin did not mind the delay, delighted as she was to enjoy the sights.

She particularly loved the row houses, each one painted a bright, almost gaudy color and often quite different and not particularly complimentary to that of its neighbor.

Erin amused herself by guessing the difference between visitors and townspeople. Tourists carried backpacks, wore shorts and t-shirts with dark sunglasses and milled around on sidewalks or crossed the street almost without hindrance as cars waited patiently.

Local Irish people appeared to dress in casual clothing but with a polished style. They met in the middle of the sidewalk, occupied the space, leaned in and spoke earnestly with each other.

On every street there were at least two pubs with baskets of flowers hanging from their doorways to draw the eye and hint at the promise of a cool pint of Guinness within.

Traditional Irish music spilling out through the open doors had the desired effect. Tourists crowded in or stood about outside, enjoying drinks in the sun and some bouncing on their heels in time to the melody.

Erin considered breaking her journey to join the fun, but the chance of finding a parking versus the appeal of getting to Gam's cottage made the latter a stronger pull.

As she drove out of town, the houses became mostly detached and more spaced out, ranging from bungalows to double-storey homes that were painted in muted tones of cream with white trim or white with red trim.

Noting how small the fields were compared to North America, Erin supposed it helped give Ireland its pretty patchwork quilt effect. This was enhanced by a colorful variety of crops that varied from field to field through the ups and downs of the rolling hills.

At last, Erin saw the signpost for the village of Cuilrecool where Gams lived. 'Had lived,' she corrected herself mentally as her mouth automatically turned down.

Tears threatened immediately and she fought to control the lump in her throat, not wanting to become a danger to herself and others while driving if she were to start crying.

Slowing down, Erin watched for a huge ash tree which she knew from memory as a landmark where she would take a left turn. At that point the road narrowed with freshly cut hedges that meandered through fields of cows and sheep. At last, an opening in the hedge indicated the narrow lane that led over the old stone bridge to Great-Aunt Maggie's cottage.

Driving along this lane, Erin reflected it had been eleven years since she had been to Ireland. After her last visit, her parents went through a divorce that led to a struggle for custody in which compromise was difficult to reach. This caused her parents to split the future summers in half to each spend time with Erin, leaving little desire for them to fly Erin off to Ireland, not wanting to sacrifice their scheduled block with her.

Both Erin and her Great-Aunt were devastated. Sure, birthdays were remembered, and Christmas cards mailed but as time passed, summer jobs and then college claimed Erin's time and attention. Both Ireland and her magical time with Great-Aunt Maggie became a distant memory of her childhood.

Erin's heart leaped with a mixture of sadness and nostalgia as she recognized the long row of hawthorn and ash trees she now drove through. The trees met overhead, creating a passage of welcome on the final mile of her journey.

A small sign was set into the garden wall proclaiming the property as the Primrose Cottage.

True to its name, primroses tumbled around the base of every tree, even nestling into the mossy crevices of the garden wall.

Turning into the wide gravel driveway, Erin pushed the gear stick into neutral and turned off the engine, pausing in the bright tranquillity of the sunlit property.

Long and narrow, the cottage was constructed of white painted stone. Its walls were almost hidden by curling green ivy that crept along the entire front of the cottage and peeped into its windows, the frames of which were painted bright yellow to match the front door.

Pink roses around the doorway provided a charming contrast of color. These had been allowed to grow abundantly, almost without restriction except they had been tied back from wholly obstructing entry into the home.

About thirty years ago Gams had grown tired of the small windows that didn't let in much light. She hired a man to make the apertures larger and replace the windows with diamond lead because she liked the criss-cross effect of the metal against the glass.

As she told Erin about this, she tut-tutted in recalling the great mess and thundering noise of mallets and cursing of the workers as they cut through two feet of stone that Gams said, "The cottage hadn't received such a torment in all its two hundred years."

In her mind, Erin pictured great aunt Maggie coming out to greet her now with twinkling eyes and a wide smile that made her ancient, beloved face so pretty.

She could almost hear Gams lilting accent, "My darling girl. You're here at last and I am so happy to see you. Come in. Come away in."

Erin smiled at the memory of childhood summers when this cottage and great aunt Maggie had been her entire world.

With a sigh, she pushed open the yellow door which the solicitor had left unlocked for her. It had been a long journey and Erin was grateful she had taken up the offer to have the fridge stocked with fresh basics.

The air inside the cottage was still faintly perfumed with Gam's fragrance of lilac and lavender. Erin paused to appreciate the unexpected welcome as she looked around at the small queendom.

Cozy and inviting, the room was filled with rosewood furniture polished to perfection.

Beside the fireplace sat brass tongs and a shovel burnished with a cloth so that were she to pick it up, Erin knew she would see her face in the metal.

Cushions were plumped up on the chairs. Curtains looked freshly laundered. The attention to detail and pristine cleanliness had Erin recall that caring for the cottage had given Gams a great deal of satisfaction.

The room looked recently occupied. Erin half expected to see Gams come bustling in from the kitchen with a bacon buttie in one hand and a cup of tea in the other. At this time of day it would usually be a bacon buttie. Gams always called them butties rather than sandwiches.

Gams would settle into her favorite chair by the fire, nibble a little of the bacon buttie followed by a sip of the tea. She would always sit on the edge of her chair as if in readiness for the next of many little tasks she busied herself with each day.

Smiling to herself at this memory of Gams, Erin picked up a framed photograph from the dresser. It was taken on her last visit to Ireland during a day at the coast.

In the photograph, Erin sat in the shallows of the Atlantic Ocean looking back at the camera. Sun-streaked brown hair stuck wet-slicked to her shoulders as waves foamed up around her.

Erin's pale skin did not tan easily but there was a glow in her cheeks brought on by the warm wind.

She wore a pink t-shirt and shy smile that, as she crinkled her eyes against the sun, affirmed the uncertainty of her early teen years.

"Aw Gams," Erin said to the photograph. "I hope this wasn't your only comfort." With a sigh, Erin told herself that wallowing in guilt could not repair the past.

She placed the photograph back on the shelf and dragged her suitcase along the corridor, intent on taking a hot shower.

Her room was just as she remembered it, pale blue walls with white trim. The bed was freshly made with a soft blue comforter.

A vase of dried flowers sat on the bedside table. It was small, like a little potpourri, with a subtle fragrance of lilac and lavender. Erin gave a murmur of appreciation. 'Was that the perfume I smelled when I entered the cottage?'

She picked up the vase and held it close to her nose. 'Funny, it doesn't smell that strong.'

Tears ran down Erin's face at the fanciful notion that Gams might have placed the dried flowers there as a welcome. Sinking onto the bed, she allowed full rein to her grief until the sobs subsided into hiccups.

To calm herself, Erin took a long hot shower, then padded barefoot from the bathroom to the kitchen with a large towel wrapped around her body and another around her wet hair.

The little kitchen was light and airy with pale yellow walls, white trim and pretty curtains at the window, yellow with little sprigs of forget-me-nots.

On the wall above the window hung a series of dishes in colors that matched the curtains, three of them in a row, while on the window ledge a jug of the same color and pattern waited for flowers to grace it.

Filling the kettle under the tap, she had just set the kettle down on its heater pad and pressed the start button when she heard the latch lift on the kitchen door.

Erin turned to find a huge animal poking its nose around the door. Before she could speak, the animal hee-hawed loudly and pushed all the way into the kitchen. A dozen flies buzzed around its head.

She backed into the living room, a strangled sound at the back of her throat. The donkey quite brazenly followed her, giving another loud hee-haw which spurred Erin into action.

With escape in mind, Erin turned her back on the animal, pulled open the front door and ran out into the lane.

The towel around her head fell into her eyes, so that she didn't see the cows parading in stately fashion along the lane until she was in the middle of the herd with the donkey hot on her heels.

Pushing the towel back onto her head, Erin found her voice. She screamed as loud as she could and the donkey, as if equally surprised at finding itself in the middle of the cows, hee-hawed repeatedly and began to buck.

The approaching herd halted momentarily at the interruption. Their eyes opened wide and they took off in every direction. Some turned back the way they had come, while others ran into the ditch and up the bank that led into a field.

Erin's screams knew no end as she danced first one way and then the other, trying to avoid the stampeding cows and the bucking donkey.

As the towel around her body threatened to slip down to her waist, she secured it with one hand, just in time to hear the unmistakably angry voice of a man yelling.

"What the feck are you doing to my cows?"

Before the towel fell over her face again, Erin caught a glimpse of the man running along the lane towards her. His arms were outstretched as he yelled, "Whisht now!" to the cows running towards him, an action which turned the animals back toward Erin.

Expecting to be trampled by this second wave of cows, Erin squeezed her eyes shut and screamed again.

Faced with Erin's piercing shrieks and the donkey's hee-haws, the approaching cows turned as one and followed the others into the adjoining field.

Erin felt the breath of a face close to hers and took an unfortunate step backwards into a fresh cow turd.

Opening her mouth in a yell of disgust, she heard the hiss of an angry male voice close by, "Stop that feckin' noise!"

Erin closed her mouth and opened her eyes. The voice was attached to the man who moments before had been running down the lane, except now his face was extremely red. Whether it was from anger or merely weather-beaten she could not tell, but his face was way too close to hers and the tone of his voice was decidedly mean-spirited.

"It's my cows you have scattered to the four winds. It'll take me hours and a lot of coaxing to get them back."

Erin looked about with wild eyes as she searched for the culprit. She pointed at the donkey which was still cavorting about. "He … he c-c-came into the k-k-kitchen. I …"

The man turned his attention in the donkey's direction. He produced a stick from the ground and rapped the donkey hard on the rump. "Mykel!" he boomed with an air of authority. "You should not be out here boy."

To Erin's surprise, the donkey responded immediately and stopped his cavorting. The man grabbed the animal by the ear and spoke urgently.

Man and beast stared into each other's faces. Whatever was said, the donkey became docile, placidly following the man to a gate at the side of the cottage which led to the yard around the back.

Alone in the lane, Erin remembered she was wearing only a towel and had one foot buried in a cow turd. "Ugh!" she said and shook her foot in the air before stepping onto the relatively clean grass that ran along the middle of the gravelly lane.

Inside the cottage, Erin bolted the door and hopped on one foot to the shower where she returned for some time. As the water cascaded over her head, she wondered where the donkey had come from.

Mortified by events of the morning, she was determined not to show herself until she was sure both man and donkey were back in their place, which as far as she was concerned, would be far from this cottage.

## Chapter Three

*E*rin was enjoying her first cup of coffee the following morning when there was a knock at the door. She opened it to find a tall man with an expectant smile on his face and an official looking cap on his head.

Erin's eyes flicked from the man to the vehicle he had left in the middle of the narrow lane. The vehicle was green, displaying an 'An Post' sign. He had left the driver's door wide open.

The man smiled and held out his hand. "Padraic Monaghan, I'm the postman. You must be Maggie's niece. You've grown a bit since I last saw ye. What is it now? A good ten or so years I'm thinking."

Erin opened her mouth to speak but Padraic went on, "I dare say ye will have passed by our place on the way here, me and the wife that is, Nuala. Sure, you'll see Herself at the wake, so. It was her father left her the place when he passed on. We moved into it only a few years back."

Padraic didn't give her the opportunity to respond but continued on.

"Excuse me for knocking when I could have popped this through the letterbox." He waved a postcard. "Maggie told me ye were coming and so I thought I'd say hello."

"Oh! Yes, hello!" Erin held out a hand, expecting him to simply hand the card over. "That's kind of you."

"Now!" he said, holding onto the card. "It is from the electric people. They were here on the twelfth but they couldn't get in to read the meter. So, they'll be doing their own assessment this time around."

He handed the card to an astonished Erin. 'He'd read her mail and here he was telling her its contents. What a cheek!'

She opened her mouth to tell him exactly that but then closed it again. What did she know about the norms of this place? She was a child when she was last here and hadn't paid attention to such things.

Padraic who said, "Yes, Maggie often spoke of ye." He looked away a moment as if recalling a memory. "She liked to reminisce about the past so she did. I heard all about ye."

Erin wasn't sure whether she should be flattered or embarrassed. 'Probably the latter,' she surmised and waited to see what Padraic might reveal.

As it was, Padraic did not pursue this but paused as before and then changed the subject. "Ah sure, and didn't we all look out for her and help her where we could."

A car drew up behind Padraic's van and honked to be allowed past.

Erin glanced from Padraic to the car and back to Padraic. 'Was he really going to ignore the car?' Apparently so, because he merely continued his reverie.

"I wasn't the only one around here that helped Maggie when she needed it." He nodded his head in self-approval, "We look after our own."

He paused again and then nodded over his shoulder towards Erin's rental car. "Hired a car at the airport, did ye?"

"I did, yes." Erin said quickly, glad for the opportunity to speak at last.

The driver of the car honked again. Taking a longer look, she recognized him as the red-faced man with the cows from the day before. My, he was grumpy.

She looked away and fixed her eyes on Padraic who said placidly, "Good for ye now with the hired car, for ye won't be relying on taxis and the like to get about."

"Er... no," agreed Erin bemused at his seeming lack of interest in holding up traffic in the lane.

The driver honked yet again.

Finally roused to respond, Padraic turned his head to look. In recognition, he called out, "Is it you now Aiden? 'Tis an awful hurry you're in man."

Padraic nodded to Erin, walked calmly over to his van and with a last wave he drove away, followed by the grumpy cow man who gave Erin a parting glare.

"What?" she muttered. "It wasn't me who held you up, was it?" She closed the door firmly.

As she walked to the back of the cottage, the latch on the kitchen door lifted repeatedly. Erin ignored it, surmising it was the dreaded donkey trying to gain access again. Why he would want to do so was beyond Erin, but she was having none of it.

She had not only locked the kitchen door the night before but had also slid the bolt at the half-way point of the door which, if she allowed it, would permit the top half to be opened while the bottom half stayed closed.

The latch rattled again. "Go away," she yelled. "I don't know what you want but I'm here to tell you, you're not getting it. Not today, not ever." The latch rattled again. "I said… you're not coming in!"

The donkey's face appeared at the kitchen window. Clearly, he expected to be granted entry.

Erin made a face at the animal and then instantly regretted it, for at that moment, a lovely white pony with a shaggy mane appeared beside that of the donkey. "Awww!" Erin was at once all softness and empathy.

Leaning over the sink for a better view, she could see the pony had nicer manners than the donkey for she looked quietly into the window before being unceremoniously pushed out of the way by the donkey, who on seeing Erin still at the window, began to hee-haw loudly.

Erin was torn between a longing to pet the pony and abhorrence of the ill-mannered donkey. She wondered who the owner of the donkey might be and why it appeared to be living in Gam's yard. Perhaps it belonged to the angry cow man. What did Padraic call him? Aiden? He must live close by since she'd seen him twice in two days.

Putting the mystery of the animals to one side for the moment, she decided to go for a walk to clear her head.

Erin pushed her arms into a light rain jacket, because after all this was Ireland and if there was one thing you could rely on, it was the rain.

Pulling the front door of the cottage closed behind her, Erin stood in the lane deciding which way to go.

To the left the lane led into a dirt track that heralded the beginning of the bog. She recalled the area with its ever-changing array of wildflowers, gorse and heather.

Erin particularly loved the yellow myrtle shrubs and pink pimpernel flowers that grew in abundance this time of year. She looked forward to a stroll through the bog, but right then she had a hankering to see what had changed in the little village. Erin turned to the right and began walking.

She passed several cottages that were no longer inhabited. This did not surprise Erin for she had known the occupants who were already elderly when she was last here.

Abandoned gardens were overgrown with thorn bushes which never needed much encouragement. Sapling alder trees had seeded in yards and grown to almost twelve feet in places.

Green moss covered the windows of these cottages so that if Erin pressed her face close to the window, she knew she would not be able to see inside.

Ireland was like that, Erin mused. Due to regular rainfall and the fair temperatures, nature took back its own and quickly too if it was not kept in check.

Erin walked by four of these cottages before she reached the old stone bridge. The rushing water underneath was so enticing that Erin leaned on the top of the bridge wall to watch as the river bubbled over stones to create a little waterfall on one side of the bridge.

She noticed there was a large square stone poking half out of the water. She could see it was not naturally formed. A quick inspection of the bridge showed Erin that the top of one of the plinths was missing. This then, must be the stone she could see in the river that had somehow become loose and fallen off its column.

She reflected it probably would stay where it was for some time, as the local council would not often make repairs to a bridge which granted access to only three or four cottages that were currently occupied.

As she walked on, the sweet earthy smell of a turf fire lured Erin toward a double storey house.

It was painted white with red trim as were the barns and outbuildings that surrounded it. All of its windows were sparkling clean and bright in the morning sun.

A sheepdog barked as Erin approached the gate, causing her to pause. As she waited for the occupants to respond to the barking, Erin admired the green lawn edged with colorful flower beds, its pathway lined with white-painted rocks.

A woman looked out through the red-painted door of the farmhouse. She had a tea towel in her hand and a smile of welcome on her face. "Hello now!" she called but made no effort to move from the doorway.

"Hi!" began Erin raising her voice to be heard over the barking of the dog.

"Whisht Toby," the woman flicked the tea towel at the dog. "Enough of that now!"

The dog looked around at his owner, whimpered a bit then lay down with his paws out straight. He dipped his head momentarily and lifted it again, looking from his owner to Erin and back again as if to relay that he was ready for action when called upon.

The woman came down the path, wiping her hands on the tea towel. "Sorry now. I couldn't hear ye with Toby barking, so."

Erin smiled. "I'm Erin Egan. I'm staying at Maggie Egan's cottage and --"

"Ah sure ye are." The woman was all smiles. "I'm thinking ye won't remember me for it's been a while, so it has. No matter, for I remember ye Erin as a child. Had I known ye were here already, I'd have been down to welcome ye with a jug of Irish cream along with a bit of milk and cheese."

Erin was charmed by the woman's generosity and not a little embarrassed that she couldn't remember her name. "That's very kind of you, er…"

"Sure, I shouldn't be expecting ye to remember names after so long away. It's Nuala I am. But now you're home again, you'll settle in no time at all and soon be knowing your way around."

"I hope so," said Erin. 'Home? Did she just say I was home again?' Erin was about to correct Nuala by telling her she was staying only a week but then thought better of it. Nuala was so kind in offering to bring goodies that it seemed rude of Erin to make an unnecessary protest.

"Come away in," said Nuala as she opened the little wooden gate for Erin to pass through.

"I hope I didn't intrude." But it was no use protesting for Nuala held the gate with an expectant smile so that Erin had no option but to walk through.

"I was just about to make tea so you've come just in time." Nuala led the way up the path and into the house.

Toby the dog licked Erin's hand as she passed, possibly, Erin thought, in apology for having barked at her earlier.

Inside, the house was modern with an open concept living room and kitchen rolled into one.

Nuala led the way into the kitchen area that smelled of fresh baked cookies. She pulled out a chair at the center island which Erin took to be an invitation to sit down. As she did so, she was grateful that her shyness went unnoticed.

Nuala moved constantly and kept up a stream of chatter as she filled the kettle and set it to boil. She fetched cups from the cupboard, poured milk into a little jug and generously plated homemade cookies. All of these she pushed toward Erin.

"I was saying to Padraic the other day as he was leaving on his rounds," Nuala paused a moment and then continued, "Padraic's my husband. Ye may have met him. He delivers the post."

Her eyes opened wide as she waited for Erin to nod in confirmation that she had indeed met Padraic.

"Now!" she said. "I thought it would be a grand thing to bring ye a jug of Irish cream. You'll have been dying for a taste, it's been so long since you've had any at all."

Nuala beamed at Erin who smiled back, overwhelmed again by the charming generosity of the woman.

Erin made mention of the donkey and pony and wondered if Nuala knew who the owner might be.

Nuala laughed and said, "Ah yes, now that would be Maggie. Or at least they were Maggie's animals."

Erin's jaw dropped as her thoughts raced. 'No wonder the donkey kept trying to get inside the cottage. It must be hungry. How long had it been since either of them had been fed? She couldn't look after them, she was only here for a week. She would have to find someone to take them on. What was Nuala saying?'

"It's barley mash you'll be needing for the animals. Aiden will take care of it for ye."

Erin frowned. "Aiden?" She remembered Padraic calling a greeting to the angry red-faced man who had shouted at her yesterday and glared at her today. She quietly told herself that never would be too soon to see him again.

Nuala noticed Erin's confusion. "Ah, you're wondering who Aiden is, I can see. He has a small farm hereabouts. He took over the cottage just before the bridge there, not too far from yourself. Bought it from the Teresa Moloney Estate there when she passed away."

Erin spoke up. "I think I may have met Aiden already." She amended this. "Or seen him at least. So, is Aiden feeding the animals at present? He seemed to know the donkey and the donkey knew him."

"Sure, he'll be helping out, ye needn't worry about that."

Erin breathed a sigh of relief. 'Perhaps this Aiden guy could take over the animals. Maybe he could move them to his place, wherever that might be.'

Nuala pushed the cookies toward Erin again and took one herself, biting into it before adding, "Aiden came over from Galway so he did. Well, I shouldn't say it in such a way. It makes him sound like a blow-in and he's not that. His family are from around here, so it's come home Aiden is just like yourself. In fact, I believe ye know him from way back, for he was around during the summers when ye were a child." She smiled at Erin's surprise.

"Aiden?" Erin frowned, "You mean Aiden O'Sullivan?" Memories flooded Erin's mind. Aiden, the companion of her childhood summers and now here he was, a seeming constant thorn in her side since she arrived at the cottage.

"The very one. Did ye not recognise him?"

"I didn't." Conflicting memories of days where she had run across the fields with Aiden, laughing and running through the bog, while on other days they'd bicker non-stop til one or the other of them would stalk off, offended by some trifling remark. The very next day the two would be fast friends again.

"Aiden O'Sullivan." Erin shook her head. "I'd never have guessed."

Nuala smiled and seemed pleased that she had prompted Erin's memory. "Will I be letting Aiden know you're needing his help?"

"What?"

"To help ye with the donkey?"

"No, no. There must be some other way," Erin waved her arms. "I don't think so… What I mean is, I'm sure I can figure it out. I don't need to bother him."

Nuala smiled away Erin's protests. "Sure, and he won't mind at all. Hasn't he been down there looking after the animals since Maggie passed."

She nodded reassuringly at Erin. "He'll be showing ye where the feed is. Then you can get on with it by yourself."

Erin felt far from reassured, thinking she didn't know which was worse, facing the wild donkey on her own or having to see Aiden's angry red face again, although she had to admit to being somewhat intrigued that Aiden had turned out to be her childhood friend.

Nuala pushed a bag with the promised milk, cream and cheese into Erin's arms. "I'll see ye at Maggie's wake. Sure, half the county will be there for the craic and the day that's in it."

As she walked back along the lane to Gam's cottage with her arms full and Nuala's parting words in her ears, Erin felt a small uplifting welcome, as if she was not quite a stranger here.

## Chapter Four

When Erin arrived back at the cottage, a silver car was parked outside. She looked around but there was no sign of its owner.

"What the heck?" Erin opened the door of the cottage and walked inside. "Better not be Mr. grumpy-Aiden-cowboy back to complain. I'll give him a piece of my mind, childhood friend or not!"

In the kitchen, Erin slid the goody bag onto the counter. She could hear a voice in the backyard. Peering through the window she saw the owner of the silver car Mr. Grumpy himself, leaning over a large sack of something.

Curious, she watched without drawing attention to herself, trying to see Aiden, the boy she had known, in the face of the man before her.

His face was longer, more serious perhaps but there were laugh lines about his mouth that crinkled with his smile, even as she watched.

She noted the pony seemed to trust him for she nuzzled Aiden's hand. He in turn stroked the pony's long head and spoke in a calm voice so that her ears turned as if listening intently.

The donkey situated himself beside the man and was repeatedly trying to dip his head into the sack.

"Will you come up Mykel?" Aiden gave the donkey a friendly push. "You'll get your turn if you just wait a bit. Beauty will be wanting a feed too, you know." He turned back to the pony. "Won't you my beautiful girl?"

The pony snickered in agreement.

Mykel the donkey seemed uninterested at the idea of sharing and continued trying to access the feed. The pony stood quietly to one side, waiting patiently.

Still leaning over the sack, Aiden turned to look Mykel in the eye. "Let me get the feed into the bowls, now can't you?"

Mykel looked at him, intelligence gleaming in his eyes.

Aiden turned back to the sack. Mykel's nose followed him down as he scooped feed out, whereupon Mykel immediately turned his attention to the bowls, munching first from one and then the other.

"Not so fast there, boyo." Aiden quickly tied off the sack and whipped the two bowls away from Mykel. Standing up, he saw Erin's face at the window. "Ah good. You're back." He waved one of the bowls in a circular motion toward Erin, indicating that she should come out to the yard. Mykel's nose closely followed the progression of the bowl.

Erin shook her head. She had zero interest in going anywhere near the donkey.

"Come on now!" Aiden's tone was not exactly aggressive, but it wasn't gentle either. He waved the bowl around again. "You have to learn to do it. They're your animals now."

Erin backed away from the window. She folded her arms protectively and looked down at the floor while trying to think of an escape. 'My animals?' she thought. 'They're not my animals. I don't even have a cat.' She looked up. Aiden was still there waiting. There was nothing else for it but to go outside.

Opening the kitchen door, she poked her head around it and said reasonably, "I'm not sure what to do about the animals. I'm only here for a week, and--"

Beauty looked up at that moment and neighed softly. Erin smiled at the pony, "Sorry."

Erin tried again. "Look Aiden, you're welcome to the animals if you'd like them. I'm more than happy to hand over ownership if, er, if they're mine."

"Well of course they're your animals. Who else would they belong to, now that Maggie isn't here?" He frowned. "And I've no wish for more animals."

He elbowed Mykel's head away from the feed. "This is Mykel and that lovely animal there is Beauty. Now if you don't mind, they need to be fed. We can't wait all day so hurry up."

Sighing, Erin left the safety of the doorway but not before making sure to leave it ajar in case she had to make a run for it. As it happened, Mykel was too focused on the feed to pay any attention to Erin.

Gingerly, Erin approached Aiden who turned away saying, "This is the feed. It's a mixture of barley straw and oats. You can mix grated carrots and apples in with it if you've a mind."

Erin was dumbstruck. 'That sounded like a lot of work.'

"They each get a bowl mid-morning and again in the afternoon." He walked off toward the row of small barns to one side of the yard. Mykel and Beauty followed close behind. Erin trailed along at a distance, keeping a wary eye on Mykel. "Twice a day?"

"And toast first thing every morning," Aiden called over his shoulder.

"What?"

"Toast!" He gave Mykel a firm nudge with his elbow to stop him poking his nose into the bowl. "He likes a second breakfast so he does. Maggie gave them toast every morning."

Mykel hee-hawed and bucked about the yard, presumably in annoyance at the delay. Wide-eyed, Erin walked faster to catch up with Aiden who now led Beauty into one of the barns.

"So that's why the donkey came into the kitchen," Erin said half to herself as she scuttled through the door behind Aiden.

A cat appeared seemingly out of nowhere and followed them in. "I didn't know Gams had a cat." Erin bent to tickle behind the cat's ear.

Aiden gave Erin a strange look and frowned at her. "Not Maggie's. Lives at the farm next door. Anyway, wouldn't Maggie have told you if she had a cat?"

Erin opened her mouth to respond and then closed it again. She immediately felt the guilt rising. In an effort to push it down, she challenged him. "It's not something people talk about in expensive trans-Atlantic phone calls, so I wouldn't know if she had a cat, would I?"

"Hmm!" he replied.

Erin bit the side of her mouth but said nothing more. She didn't owe him an explanation anyway.

Aiden closed the barn door behind them and placed a bowl of feed on the floor of the barn. The cat walked over to investigate. Erin looked pointedly at the door and back to Aiden.

Seeing her expression, he said, "It keeps Mykel out of the way while Beauty here eats her food, otherwise she'd get nothing."

Aiden turned back to the pony and lovingly rubbed between her ears as she bent her head to the food. "Isn't that right, Beauty?" The pony lifted her head and snickered before addressing her food again.

"You agree with me, don't you girl?" He smiled as he turned back to Erin who couldn't seem to stop the sarcastic remark that fell from her lips.

"So ... toast? Is that with butter or ..."

From the expression on his face, he seemed about to say something derogatory then changed his mind. Instead, he stepped forward and held out a hand. "I don't know if you remember me. I'm Aiden."

Without thinking, she reached out and felt his hand close around hers. "Erin," she said. "I didn't remember you at first."

"The last time we met, you pelted me with apples."

"I did?" She frowned as she tried but failed to recall the episode.

"Sure, I probably deserved it."

They looked at each other.

"I'm sorry about yesterday," he said, "I shouldn't have reacted the way I did."

His hand felt warm around hers. He didn't seem quite so detestable as he had the previous day but still she frowned, suspicious of him still.

He said, "Mykel must have startled you. Isn't that why you ran outside? You said he came into the kitchen."

She pulled her hand back. "Yes, he did." She turned away, momentarily embarrassed as she remembered the scene in the lane.

Outside the door, Mykel 'hee-hawed' impatiently. Aiden picked up the other feed bowl and turned away. "Better not keep his lordship waiting." He pushed open the door and with Mykel close on his heels, strode to the middle of the yard before setting the bowl on the ground. Mykel paid immediate attention to it.

Aiden called over his shoulder, "Shut the door on the pony will you, or Mykel will be in there, as soon as he's done."

Erin closed the door leaving the pony inside the barn.

"D'you see that rock? Roll it in front of the door."

"Really?"

"Mykel's nothing if not persistent," Aiden said. "Determined too."

Erin did as she was asked and walked over to join him. Mykel had finished his food and was pushing the bowl around in his eagerness to lick every scrap.

"Maggie loved these animals," Aiden said, shaking his head. "They were neglected before she took them on. She came to their rescue and was prone to spoiling them as best she could. She'd tell me, 'It's time for a bit of spoiling when a body retires. My neighbors spoil me and so I'm passing it on to these animals now.'"

Aiden looked over at the cottage. "She was a sweet woman, your Maggie. I'd call in to see if she needed anything, but it was always her looking after me with tea and bacon sandwiches. Butties she'd call them. Bacon butties." He looked at her keenly. "She'd feed us bacon butties when we were kids, d'you remember?"

Erin smiled at the memory. "Bacon butties for elevenses and then jam butties with hot chocolate at night, along with stories by the fire."

"She was a bit of a storyteller, for sure."

Erin couldn't help responding, "She had an endless supply of them. So many tales of fairies and folklore… I remember one time asking her if she believed in fairies. She looked me right in the eye and said, 'Of course I don't believe in them.' But then as she turned away, I distinctly heard her mutter, 'But they're there just the same.'"

They both laughed and he looked at her inquisitively. He seemed about to say something more but at that moment Mykel trotted passed them on his way to the barn where he butted the door with his head.

The donkey took hold of the latch in his teeth and managed to lift it over the hook which opened the door slightly, until it hit the rock. Nosing into the small aperture, his tail swished in annoyance as he tried but failed to force his head through.

Determined to get at the pony's food, Mykel turned his attention to the rock.

"Shouldn't we stop him?" asked Erin.

"I'm sure Beauty will have finished her food by now."

They watched in silence as Mykel continued to paw at the rock until he succeeded in pulling it back by a foot. Nosing into the door again but still unable to obtain full access, the donkey paused as if considering the challenge. After a moment he continued scrabbling at the rock.

At this point Aiden headed over to the barn. Erin followed reluctantly, not wanting to be left alone as a focal point for Myke's attention should he turn her way. There was no sound from inside, which signalled that the pony had finished her food.

"Ah Mykel, you're an old scoundrel so you are," Aiden grumbled as he pulled the rock away from the barn door.

As soon as the door opened, the pony trotted out followed by the cat who leaped quickly onto the fence and disappeared into the undergrowth. Mykel pushed his way inside, obviously eager to see what was left of the food.

Beauty came up and nuzzled Aiden. "You're welcome!" he said and stroked her neck. Surprised to see this continued gentleness, Erin watched and said nothing.

As Beauty wandered off, Aiden picked up a shovel and walked about the yard. Scooping up animal droppings, he headed to the low-walled garden where Maggie grew vegetables.

"Tutty-hush," said Aiden indicating the dung. "That's what Maggie called it." He dropped the contents of the shovel into a bucket and placed it over the wall along with the shovel.

"She used it on her vegetables, said it made them grow better." He tossed her a wicked grin. "You'll have to learn to do this."

Erin grimaced. She was pretty sure she wouldn't be doing anything like it. Much as she had loved Gams, the vegetables would have to be harvested by someone else. She wouldn't be around that long.

"It's good soil here," Aiden said, his attention back to the garden. "Black and rich. Maggie always had a healthy crop of homegrown vegetables." He laughed. "She'd sing to the plants you know."

A pang of nostalgia gripped Erin as she recalled Gams telling her Ireland sang to her, so she liked to sing back to it. Erin swallowed hard, not wanting to become teary in front of Aiden. She looked away.

He followed her gaze across the field to the meadow beyond.

"She talked of turning the field into a meadow." Aiden rubbed a hand over his thick hair.

"She'd tell me the same thing when I was a kid. Too many hillocks and thorn bushes she'd say."

Aiden nodded. "It would have to be levelled first. I told her I'd help but we never got around to it. I feel bad about that now."

The pony came up beside Erin and she turned to pet the animal, grateful for the distraction.

"I've to get going," said Aiden. Casually he added, "Don't forget the toast in the morning, so."

She was about to give a caustic remark but remembered something. She said, "It's the wake tomorrow."

"So it is." Aiden shook his head. "It slipped my mind for a moment." He laughed and offered, "Try it yourself anyway, the toast." He winked, "You were more adventurous as a kid. You need to find that again."

He walked away whistling a tune. Erin watched him go. 'He probably deserved that pelting with apples,' she told herself and quite childishly put out her tongue at his retreating back.

## Chapter Five

The traditional custom of burying the dead within forty-eight hours had been held off for the sake of Erin having to fly in from North America.

Erin had said goodbye to her Great-Aunt at the funeral home. There, a staff member had shown her into a side room where Gam's coffin had been brought out ahead of Erin's arrival.

The top part of the coffin had been open. Gams lay on a white satin sheet, her curly hair a silver cloud against the soft pillow. Her face in repose was peaceful as if she had been content to leave this world behind.

Erin had almost been afraid to touch the cold marble skin but in that moment, she noticed the faintest wisp of the lovely fragrance Gams used to wear. It was so endearing that Erin was moved to reach out.

For a long moment she held a hand against her great aunt's cheek. "Goodbye Gams," was all she'd been able to whisper as the tears flowed unrestricted down her cheeks.

Blinking in the sunlight now as the mourners trailed behind the priest and into the graveyard, Erin thought there could not have been a finer day. The blue sky held only a smattering of clouds although she knew it would probably rain later on.

She had no clear idea of the meaning of an after-life, but she hoped with all her heart that Gams lived on, somewhere.

The funeral had been a formal affair, but the wake was another thing entirely. Wakes were often held in the home of the deceased but as Maggie lived alone and Erin barely arrived in time for the event, it was held instead at the little church hall right there on the church property.

It was close enough that people walked along the cinder path between the rhododendron bushes that had yet to flower.

A modicum of quiet decorum was held as mourners passed the house of the priest for the days were not long gone when such men held an unswayable power over their parishioners.

The hall itself was packed with people coming and going but mostly staying, for the food and the drink and the day that was in it.

Erin was surprised to find herself surrounded as soon as she walked in. It was as if she knew most of the people or at least they seemed to know her, for they greeted her by name.

There was craic to be had at funerals as at any other social event where the good people of Ireland were brought together.

One mourner told Erin with a wily expression, "Maggie would have loved to be here. Someone once said and I believe it to be true, that the terrible thing about dying in Ireland is, ye miss your own wake and the craic that's in it. Sure, it's the best day of your life. Haven't ye paid for all the food and drink and the sorrow of it is, ye can't join in."

He had winked at her then and Erin couldn't help but laugh. Perhaps it was this comment or her reaction, but it seemed to start an avalanche of stories that came with the seemingly endless handshaking of mourners waiting to greet her.

Folding tables had been set up along one side of the room and white cloths were carefully spread over these. The kitchen was abuzz. Women of the community worked around each other in such a way that made it obvious to the casual observer that they were all quite familiar with such events and at ease in each other's company.

People walked in with platters of food that Erin presumed were homemade and contributed from their own household budgets.

The food was handed over to the kitchen volunteers or taken directly to the tables where the women chattered with each other in subdued tones as they fussed about the food tables, turning dishes this way and that until they looked just right.

There were sandwiches of every description; cheese and lettuce, cheese and tomato, egg salad, egg with mayonnaise and cress, trays of pulled beef, and cakes of every kind including the expected wake cake which was a sponge baked with currants and with icing sugar drizzled over the top.

A great dish of Irish apple cake was placed in the center. Erin overheard the bearer of this cake say the sweetest apples she could find were sliced and folded into the cake mix and the top glazed with egg for a lovely golden finish.

Great urns of tea were set up on a corner table with jugs of fresh farm milk and bowls of sugar set to hand. Already a lineup had presented itself at the tea table where two volunteers vied with each other, pouring the hot brown liquid into cups as fast as they could.

Occasionally, these women would glance at the line as if trying to estimate whether or not the tea they had made would suffice or if more must be organized.

One of the urns was soon topped up with fresh water and tea bags to ensure the unthinkable could not happen, of the tea running out. Sure, didn't they all know it was imperative the tea remain in good supply for quenching the thirst that was in such a day.

Armed with their tea and a plate of food, the mourners quickly settled at tables with friends and neighbors and all tucking in.

A funeral brought on a terribly strong appetite for it was a reminder that this good life would and could end and that there was a finality to it that no one could escape.

Vases filled with flowers had been set among the plates of food so that it looked more like a festive event and Erin soon learned that an Irish wake was not particularly a time of sadness.

A fiddler and accordion player set themselves up on high stools in a corner near the stage.

After a brief and private conversation, they began to play appropriate music of which Maggie's favorite, 'The Mountains of Mourne,' was one.

As some in the room began to sing along with the music, the previously quiet buzz soon rose to a steady drone as if in competition with the music and the singing, and all interspersed with occasional laughter.

Gams had been well liked in the community so that there was no lack of storytellers eager to relate their memories of Maggie.

People spoke of her goodness, her love of animals, her cheery nature and how she had come to the village as a young woman and a pretty one at that.

"I wonder why she never married," Erin mused.

Padraic, who was there with Nuala said, "My father told me that when Maggie came here all those years ago, she was appreciated by the young men of the parish for her handsome looks and the fire in her eyes. Just the same, there was not a man she would consider."

Erin had sometimes wondered what kept Gams from returning to North America. Seeking an answer to this she asked, "So people made her feel welcome, even though they didn't know her?"

"Sure, and why wouldn't they? Weren't her people from hereabouts!" This wasn't a question but a statement, as if to testify of Maggie's heritage and therefore her place in Ireland. "Just like you're a part of that now Erin. Isn't it home here to Ireland you've come yourself!"

"I'm just here for the funeral, Padraic," Erin said. "I just wish I could stay longer in a way. But really I can't because, well I have a job to go back to."

"Is that so now?" asked Nuala, leaning forward and giving Erin a knowing look. "It's plain to see ye belong here."

"It is?" asked Erin bewildered.

"Wasn't it Maggie came home here herself and isn't that a fine example to ye?"

"Well ..." Erin began, unsure of how to answer. Nuala continued before she could formulate a suitable response.

"When Maggie came home sixty years ago, it was just after her parents died in America. She bought the place you're in now. Cottages back then were ridiculously inexpensive and so she still had a respectable amount to invest in the renovating of it. Without that, she wouldn't have been able to do as much as she did, for teacher's wages were small enough in those days. Did ye know it was a requirement back then, that teachers had to have a working knowledge of the Irish language, or Gaeilge?"

Erin shook her head, "No, I didn't know that."

"Maggie had been schooled in Gaeilge, enough to get herself a job teaching and I dare say it was soon added to. She'd to talk with the children in their native tongue every day for the hour or two that was required in the curriculum."

Nuala smiled encouragingly. "Ah, she loved it, so she did. And wasn't it Maggie talking about ye all these years Erin, and how she wanted ye to love the place as much as she did herself."

'Gams had taken lessons in Irish? I mean... Gaeilge', she asked herself. There was so much she didn't know about her great aunt.

She sat a little straighter and turned the ends of her mouth up in a polite smile and tried to concentrate on what Nuala was saying.

"It was Maggie that told Himself," Nuala indicated Padraic with a nod of her head. "She said you'd be coming here. We thought it was all arranged, didn't we Padraic?"

"We did." Padraic agreed.

Erin waited for Padraic to continue. Then, just as she thought he had abandoned his train of thought, he went on. "It was a day when I came to check on what groceries she might be needing, as I usually did. I'd often come in around that same time and find her sitting beside the fire with a cup of tea and a bit of bread."

Erin smiled at that. If it was morning it would be a bacon buttie.

"But this time Maggie was fussing about the cleaning and quite excited she was too, talking through a list of chores as we put the food away together there."

He paused, smiling at the memory. Then he indicated his wife with a nod of his head and a lift of his eyebrows. "I told ye this, didn't I Nuala?"

"You did Padraic. Go on with the story now. Can't ye see Erin is waiting to hear it?"

Padraic glanced at Erin who was leaning forward in her chair. "Right!" he said and cleared his throat as if he were about to impart great knowledge. "As I said, she was fussing about the cleaning." He frowned and muttered, "What was it she said now?"

Nuala cut in. "She said she had preparations to make, that the back bedroom would have to be aired, that she would open the windows and give the room a good dusting."

"That's right, she did." Padraic seemed a bit miffed that Nuala had intervened in his story.

He went on quickly as if to prevent another interruption. "Maggie insisted she wouldn't be needing groceries for the following week. She said she had enough for her needs. I was a bit taken aback for she always had a thing or two needed ordering. But then, before I'd time to argue the point, she had me pulling out the iron and the board, all the time chattering away about the blue comforter she would spread across the bed because Erin liked a pretty room."

Nuala and Padraic nodded at each other here as if agreeing that this was the correct version of events. "And then," prompted Nuala.

"And then did said the strangest thing," he paused again.

Nuala nodded encouragingly.

"Well, she said she would cut some lilac and lavender because Erin always loved the perfume."

Erin looked from one to the other, wondering what was so strange about Maggie's endearing intention.

Padraic held up a finger as if there was more to come. "She told me I'd need to do it, cut the flowers."

Erin waited, eager to hear of Gam's activities.

*51*

Padraic went on. "At the time, I thought she meant I was to cut the flowers right then and so I did and brought a bunch into the kitchen for her. But she laughed as she took it from me and I thought it was strange at the time. Now, I am near certain she meant I was to cut the flowers after she'd passed on."

"Oh!" said Erin. "There's a dried flower arrangement on my bedside table. It has a lovely fragrance."

"Ah!" Nuala nodded at her husband and took over the story. "When we knew you were coming, we decided to make sure the flowers were there as Maggie wanted. But then we weren't sure of the date you would arrive and if the flowers would still be fresh, so I went out and bought the dried flowers instead."

Erin was moved. "That is so kind of you."

"Well," said Nuala. "I think it was a bit of the sight Maggie had you know, that you were coming and that she wouldn't be here. I wanted to do my best for her."

"You think she knew she was going to … die?" Even though Gams had gone, saying the word just made it seem so final.

"Sure, that's what I think," said Padraic, "and I'll tell you why."

Nuala placed her hand on Erin's arm as if to steady her for the news Padraic was about to impart. Erin looked from one to the other.

Padraic lowered his face and leaned toward the two women. "Maggie never said it, but the fuss she was after making in the days before she passed! It was so unusual that I wondered if she'd lost her…" he paused and then re-phrased his sentence. "I wondered if she was a bit confused. She was talking of getting the chimney cleaned out and wanting to know if she could get it done immediately. What was it she said now?" He scratched his chin.

"The chimney?" Erin wondered what the chimney had to do with anything.

"The chimney, yes." Padraic seemed firm in his memory of the event. "She said Ireland can be devilish cold after the heat of a North American summer and did I think she needed to get it cleaned."

Padraic roused himself. "I reminded her she'd had the chimney cleaned only two years previously."

Nuala interjected, "Although they do say it should be done once a year."

"They do indeed, Nuala but I was after calming Maggie do ye see? I told her I didn't think she needed to go to such extremes and asked when it was that Erin would be coming home."

'There's that word again,' thought Erin, 'Home.'

"Not long now. That was what Maggie told me. Then she went off to the guest bedroom saying it hadn't been used and would need airing, so."

Erin said, "So you're saying she knew I was coming?" Tears of happiness formed in her eyes. Comfort surrounded her heart. 'Gams knew I would come.'

"Well now, over the next few days, the place was in a constant uproar whenever I dropped in to see Maggie on my rounds. Fires were lit in all the rooms to air them out whether they needed it or not. Maggie was not content until the whole house had a second spring-cleaning."

Erin sat up straight. She had a sudden desire to be comforted by someone she knew. As she looked around the room, Nuala noticed and asked, "Who are ye looking for Erin?"

"Aiden." Erin blurted out the name without thinking. "I - I thought he'd be here," she ended lamely, astonished at herself.

"Ah, the fiery one."

"Fiery one?" enquired Erin, still wondering why she had connected Aiden with the unexpected need for comfort.

"Aiden. The name means fiery one."

Erin smiled despite her inner turmoil. "That makes sense." She pulled herself together. "I was hoping to ask Aiden to come by and er," she searched her mind for a sensible answer to the sudden thought of him. "I mean, to help me with the donkey. I'm a bit anxious around it."

Padraic adopted a helpful expression. "Ah sure, the way to handle a donkey is to grab it by the ears and blow into its nose."

Erin managed a wan smile as laughter broke out around her.

Several of the mourners stopped at Erin's table to give their condolences. For a while Erin was distracted from the previous conversation until the three found themselves alone again and Padraic immediately took up the story where he had left off.

"Where was I now?" Padraic frowned a moment and then lifted a finger in an 'aha' moment before continuing. "Sure, Maggie even spruced up the outside of the house."

Nuala could not resist adding to the story. "The house was in perfect order when Maggie passed and Padraic here used the key to get in."

"It was under the rose trellis, where she likes to hide it," Padraic interjected.

"Under the rose trellis," Nuala agreed.

"Wait!" Erin made a time out sign with her hands. After a moment or two she asked, "So, how did you know she had died?"

"Ah!" exclaimed Nuala, "Well, she had left a note on the door. Padraic knocked anyway of course but Maggie didn't come to the door. So of course, Himself went into the house and found Maggie there dressed in her Sunday best and laying on the bed."

Erin was horrified. "She was … dead?"

"She was, so." Nuala sighed.

At this point, Padraic seemed to take offense that Nuala kept taking over his story. "Sure, ye were not there," he admonished her.

"No, but your good self has had the telling of it many times over, so that now I know it better than yerself!" Nuala quipped. They both laughed at this remark.

Erin interrupted the two. "And so ... was it you Padraic that called the authorities?"

"Eh, what for now?"

"Well you know, police, ambulance, emergency services, I don't know ..."

"Sure, it was plain to see she was already dead."

"Yes but," began Erin.

"And so, I finished my rounds delivering the mail. Of course, by the time I was done, everyone knew about it, so."

Nuala added agreeably, "How else would they have the knowing of it."

"Well, to be sure," Padraic was defensive. "The deaths are announced on the local radio three times a day."

"They are?" asked Erin, surprised.

"Why sure," said Nuala helpfully. "And if you're expecting notice of a funeral, there's a number ye can ring, in case you missed the announcement, so."

Erin suppressed a smile at this custom, but no-one seemed to notice.

"In any case," Padraic went on, "I stopped in at the priest's house and let him know. But as it happened, by the time the priest got there, the women of the community were already waking her."

Erin opened and closed her mouth. "What?" was all she could manage.

"Waking her," explained Padraic, then seeing her confusion he explained. "They'd already started the mourning so she'd not be left alone do ye see. There'd be someone with her throughout the day and night for the next while. Sure, they'd opened the window and covered the mirrors, although I believe they were uncovered again when Maggie was taken away to the funeral home. It's the custom," he explained to Erin. "We've done it for hundreds of years and it'll not change now, not in the West of Ireland anyway."

"At least Maggie went quickly." Nuala offered. "Now, when Eamon Dooley passed away, over at the hospital there, he dragged it out a good long while."

"And why wouldn't he?" Padraic interjected. "He had no reason to go, did he?"

Nuala bristled. "No, he did not, for he led that little wife of his in a good song and dance. She was clearly mithered by him the whole of their married life." She gave a sly smile. "But you know, Eamon had a great cure for the burn."

Padraic played along with the joke. "Did he pass it on, that cure for the burn?"

"Sure, and he did not," said Nuala triumphantly. "Isn't he going to need it where he's going?"

Padraic and Nuala laughed and turned to Erin for approval of their joke, but Erin was still puzzling over Gams, and what this all meant.

"But … to go to all that trouble just before she died. I mean, I love that she thought to prepare the guest room for me, but I still don't understand how she could know what was going to happen."

"I can tell you that." Erin turned to find Aiden standing behind her.

Erin touched her fingers to her throat as Aiden dragged a chair a little closer to the group and sat down. She felt surprisingly grateful of his presence.

Aiden began, "I had heard her make mention of the Bean Sídhe a few nights before she passed."

"The ban… shee?" Erin stumbled over the word.

"The Bean Sídhe," Aiden repeated. "If you hear the Bean Sídhe, it's a warning that either you or someone you know is going to die."

Erin's jaw dropped and her mouth with it. "Are you saying Gams may have heard this banshee? That she maybe knew she was going to die?"

"That's the way of it," Nuala interjected. "That is, most definitely the way of it." Nuala looked to Padraic for corroboration.

"'Tis only heard at night and as a warning of death," he confirmed.

Erin didn't know what to think.

Aiden went on, "The Bean Sídhe screams when there's a death in the family, and if she had heard it…"

Erin looked from one to the other as a small thought began to niggle at the back of her mind.

"Well now," continued Aiden, "Probably no one else would have heard the Bean Sídhe scream that night, if scream it did." He turned to Erin and explained, "Families, if we're keeping to the tradition of the folklore here, often have their own Bean Sídhe. So, if it was heard at all it would have been Maggie who would hear it and no one else, except you of course."

"Oh my gosh," Erin looked breathlessly from Aiden to Padraic, to Nuala and back again to Aiden. "I heard it. Well… I heard a scream in the night but when I got up to look, I couldn't see anything and… I thought it was a dream and went back to bed."

Nuala peered closely at Erin. "You heard it? All the way over there in America?"

Erin folded her arms protectively across her chest. "Well, I'm not sure if that's what it was."

Nuala nodded her head knowingly. "Ye truly are related to Maggie if ye heard the Bean Sídhe. No wonder she wanted ye here."

"Oh!" Erin wanted to believe it all, but her rational mind told her it could not be so, not really.

"Why else would she have left the cottage to you?" said Aiden.

"I don't know that she did, in fact," Erin began, "leave the cottage to me, I mean." She wondered how everyone could not only know Gam's business but also be certain of their information.

"Sure," said Padraic. "Wasn't she up there to Hanratty the solicitor only five or so years back, made sure of it she did."

Erin's nose crinkled at the remark. "I think you're making assumptions about the cottage. Anyway… I don't intend to stay."

"Slated for it, so ye are," said Nuala firmly.

"But…" Erin was lost for words. She looked from Padraic to Nuala who both raised their eyebrows knowingly.

Padraic put a hand on Erin's arm in a gesture of comfort and reassurance. "Now, Nuala here is fey. It's a gift do ye see. Myself I wouldn't know whether you would or you wouldn't be staying, but if Nuala says ye are and Maggie laid it out in her will, then you can be sure it's more likely than not, that it's going to be."

"Orla Hanratty…" Erin began. "I spoke to her on the phone. She did mention that there's a will."

"Oh sure, there's a will all right." Padraic nodded.

"Well," began Erin slowly. "I'll need to meet with the solicitor before anything can be decided."

"Sure," agreed Padraic. "Call her over Nuala, for I've not got the lungs of you."

Nuala obliged, hefting her ample chest as she raised her voice above the crowd "Orla! Would you step this way a minute?"

The room quieted slightly as Orla Hanratty made her way through the crowd nodding at this one and with a quick word to another until she was beside them.

A someone who believed in business first, Orla solemnly reached out a hand to shake Erin's. "Happy to finally meet you, Erin. Are you settled in?"

"As much as I can be for a short visit," replied Erin, beginning to feel rebellious. How could they all just presume she would stay? It was a bit of an imposition.

Padraic nodded towards Erin, "We were just telling Herself that the cottage has been willed to her. Now, she's not sure if she believes us. We need ye to confirm it, so."

"Well now," began Orla. The nearby parties were suddenly quiet as if everyone was straining to overhear. Erin looked about furtively and then up at Orla who had remained standing.

Orla coughed politely but then with an air of authority she said, "I cannot divulge the dying wishes of a client, in public."

An audible muttering of disappointment carried through the room.

"Sure, and that's the truth Orla. But we all know what Maggie wanted," urged Nuala. "And anyway, as I was saying earlier, we know Maggie visited you a few years back for this very reason."

"Be that as it may," insisted Orla. "I'll not discuss it in public, especially as I've not met with the family yet."

"The heir, don't you mean," said Nuala. "And isn't she here in front of you, so."

Orla admonished Nuala with a look. "I can see she's here, yes, but I mean to say, I haven't met with her officially yet."

The solicitor turned a benevolent smile toward Erin. "Why don't you come and see me tomorrow afternoon at my office. I'm right there on Wolfetone Square. Shall we say three 'o clock?"

A light groan echoed through the room from those listening in; cheated of knowing the results of Maggie's will and having to wait until the information reached them through the usual lines of gossip, the room shortly regained its former buzz of conversation.

Erin nodded her head at Orla, too bemused to argue or question the proceedings.

*****

Aiden left soon after, quickly followed by Padraic and Nuala. As the last of the mourners left, Erin stood at the door and saw them off into the rain that was just starting to fall.

In the background, several of the women had stayed behind to clear away the last of the dishes.

Their men set the hall to rights, folding the long tables and smaller square tables back into their place under the stage that stood to one end. The chairs were stacked one on top of each other in a corner of the room.

Erin had no inclination to chat with the women as they worked, it was enough to feel nurtured by the domesticity of the moment.

Dishes continued to clatter in the kitchen while the lilting voices of Irish women instructed each other on "where to stack the crockery," and "how well the day had gone," and "wasn't it grand that the weather had held off for the funeral itself?"

The rain was oddly comforting, Erin thought as she leaned against the door and gazed out at the steady downpour.

She knew it came with a promise as always: there would be a wash of golden sunlight to bring a sparkle to the end of the day.

## Chapter Six

"Breakfast for the animals," said Aiden when Erin opened the door to his knock. Erin pulled a face, but he was not put off. "You'll have to learn to feed 'em."

Erin spread her hands innocently, "I don't have bread."

Aiden produced a loaf of bread from a plastic bag. "Shall we?" he gestured toward the kitchen.

Defeated, Erin opened the door wider and he stepped in.

"Go ahead," she said grudgingly.

Aiden walked ahead and seemed well acquainted with the direction of the kitchen. 'Why not?' she asked herself. 'The whole village seems to know their way around Gam's cottage.'

Once there, they both looked toward the kitchen door as the latch lifted. The door didn't open because Erin had it securely bolted.

Aiden remarked, "He must have heard me drive in." He then called toward the door, "Wait your turn, you impatient animal!" The latch lifting stopped.

"Hmph!" said Erin. "Pity he doesn't respond to my voice like that."

"You just have to be firm with him."

Erin rolled her eyes behind Aiden's back and leaned on the kitchen counter to watch him work.

"Want some toast as well?" he asked as he reached down to the plate cupboard.

"Sure," she responded.

"Butter?"

"Yes... thanks," Erin took the butter from the fridge handing it to Aiden and busied herself with filling the kettle to boil water.

"Coffee?" she asked, as Aiden toasted four slices of bread.

"I'm a tea drinker."

"Right. The Irish are tea drinkers, of course. Okay, I'll make tea for both of us."

"Not all of us are tea drinkers. Anyway, I'm thinking Maggie would have a wee bit of the stuff hereabouts. He opened a cupboard and took out a box of Irish Breakfast Tea.

Erin pulled out a teapot and two mugs as Aiden opened the box. "Loose tea," she observed, looking over his shoulder. "I forgot Gams didn't use tea bags." Unsure of the proper amount, she dropped a spoonful of the loose tea into the teapot and put down the spoon.

Aiden interrupted, "Three heaped spoons should do it." He reached over and picked up the spoon, then looked up. "I like it strong," he said.

Two heaped spoons of tea went into the pot to add to Erin's contributions.

The latch lifted again. They both ignored it. The donkey could be heard hee-hawing its way across the yard.

"Although, I will drink coffee occasionally."

Erin forced a smile but didn't respond. He'd been pretty rude the first few days after they met so that she couldn't for the life of her, imagine how they had been friends as children.

She recalled that he had been difficult at times back then sure, but that's the way kids were. Nevertheless, she'd been prepared to dislike him based on that first impression since her return to Ireland. Although he had introduced himself in the yard and she'd seen a flash of the old Aiden she'd known as a kid. Perhaps he'd been having a bad couple of days. She decided at that moment to reserve judgement, and to try to not act cold toward him.

Erin poured the tea while Aiden buttered the toast. She noticed he made himself comfortable at the kitchen table whereas Erin shyly held back, choosing to sip her tea while leaning against the counter. When the latch began lifting in earnest, Erin put her mug down sighing "I suppose this is as good a time as any."

Taking a huge bite of toast, Aiden swallowed an equally large gulp of tea. He grabbed two slices of toast, strode over to the door, and flung it open. Mykel pushed his head in through the door immediately. The flies came with him, a buzzing coronet circling above his head.

Erin backed away in disgust, her confidence vanishing at the sight of the beast. "There is no way I am ever going to feed that animal!" Beyond the donkey, Beauty stood waiting a few feet back. "Now if it was just the pony..." Erin's tone changed as she gazed at the soft eyes and white mane, longing to pet her.

Aiden handed her a slice of toast. "Then that's where we'll start. I'll feed Mykel and keep him away while you make sure that Beauty here gets a piece of toast."

Aiden pushed Mykel out of the kitchen with one firm hand on his nose and the other waving the toast in the air so that Mykel had to back away in order to keep an eye on the treat.

Under cover of the distraction, Erin slipped out and headed for the pony. Stroking Beauty's nose, she whispered sweet nothings into her soft ear, delighted to have a moment with this lovely animal.

The pony snickered softly under her touch.

Soon enough, Mykel escaped Aiden's grasp and came over to get at the pony's leftovers. As there were none, the donkey followed Erin, trying to lick her buttery fingers.

Erin was appalled and ducked around the back of Aiden. The donkey followed her until she had done two laps in quick succession. Finally, she was able to make a beeline for the kitchen door where she ran through and slammed the bottom half shut.

"Go away, you persistent thing!" she told Mykel as he pushed his nose over the half door.

Aiden seemed to think it was extremely amusing and although he tried to pull Mykel back from the door, it was a half-hearted effort, keeled over as he was in howls of laughter.

Erin, unable to stand both the donkey's hee-hawing and Aiden's amusement, shut the top half of the door as well. "I'm glad you think it's funny!" she yelled.

It was several minutes before Aiden got himself under control. "Well," he finally called back to her. "I've to be getting on with the day. And it will be a good day with the memory of the craic we've had here. Sure, you'll get the hang of it by tomorrow …. or the next day."

She rolled her eyes again as she heard him walk away still chuckling at her discomfort with the donkey.

*****

That afternoon Erin presented herself at Orla Hanratty's office at the appointed time. She was shown right into the solicitor's office without having to wait.

Orla confirmed Nuala's words of the previous day but with an addendum.

"It was Maggie Egan's wish that you inherit the cottage, Erin. What you do with it is up to you but it was your Great-Aunt's hope that you would settle here in Ireland."

Erin's eyes opened wide in surprise.

Orla continued, "If you decide to stay, then I can help you do that. Maggie left a little something to get you started. Not much, mind ye, and I'm to give you an allowance as it were, to keep you going 'til you decide your way forward."

Erin opened her mouth, then closed it again when Orla held up a hand.

"There is a condition that goes along with the cottage and the money and that is to do with the diary."

"The diary?" began Erin slowly but Orla cut in.

"You've known about the diary, surely?"

Erin had a sudden visual of Gams pulling a shawl around her shoulders and telling her a story.

Before she could delve deeper into the memory, she became aware of Orla watching her closely. "Sorry," said Erin.

Orla continued, "Now I can only apologize for not knowing its whereabouts."

"There's a diary… but you don't know where it is?"

"That is correct, and the thing of it is –" Orla coughed politely as if slightly embarrassed by what she was about to reveal. "The thing of it is, unless it's found you cannot inherit the cottage."

"I don't understand."

"Ah … well … Maggie indicated you would know what to do when you have the diary."

Erin found herself echoing Orla's words out loud. "When I have the diary…"

"One moment." Orla was quiet for a while as she looked down at the will. Then, finding the correct part in writing she cleared her throat she read out Great-Aunt Maggie's words.

"It is my wish that Erin Egan follow the path which the diary leads, and that she use the gifts and talents she possesses to bring the past to life."

Here Orla looked over her spectacles at Erin and said with an apologetic smile. "I tried to talk Maggie out of that clause, but she was insistent I include it. I have no choice but to tell you again, that until you've pursued the aforementioned, you cannot inherit the cottage."

Erin gathered her thoughts. "The aforementioned what… condition?"

"Well now," said Orla, "Call it what you will." She gave a shrug of her shoulders. "The truth is she didn't make it clear what it was exactly. Except as I said that you would know when you read the diary."

"Oh," said Erin. Her response was an understatement of how she really felt, which was that a myriad of thoughts whirled around in her head.

What was she to do with the diary if, and when, she found it? And even if she did find it, did she really want a cottage in the West of Ireland... and what on earth would she do with the cottage anyway? It wasn't as if she made enough money to come for continual vacations to Ireland. It would sit here in her absence and fall into disrepair... Unless she could rent it out but what if no-one wanted to rent? Then she'd be paying for someone to maintain it.

Erin broke out of her own spell and back into the moment. "I have a job you see... and a plan to run my own business back home... eventually."

Even as she said this, a thought occurred to her that the job wasn't so important in comparison to the grand scheme of it all. But still, as much as she loved the idea of owning the cottage where Gams had lived, it was a headache she could not afford.

There was a silence in the room during which Erin waited for Orla to continue, all while Orla seemed to have no inclination to do.

Despite herself, Erin opened her mouth and said, "There must be more." She waited, hoping Orla would have additional information. "About the diary, I mean ... where I can find it, that sort of thing."

"Well, yes, I suppose there is more," Orla sighed, "Maggie called me several days before she passed. She said she would write you a note. I presumed she would let me have it or would leave it for you at the cottage."

Orla tapped a manicured fingernail on the wooden surface of the desk. "She didn't bring it to me but then, as it happens I did find it when I looked around the cottage before you arrived."

She spread her hands. "I cannot in all good conscience give the note to you until you've fulfilled the conditions of the will."

She adopted a soothing tone, but Erin could detect that underneath, there was a no-nonsense approach. "I'm afraid that's all I've got," Orla continued. "You've to make of it what you can."

There was more nail tapping while they regarded each other.

At last, Orla said, "Maggie spoke with great love for you and excitement that you would follow where the diary led."

Erin took a deep breath. She was beginning to feel exasperated, "But there must be more about the diary. Can't you tell me where it might be? A clue? Someone must know. Is it in the cottage somewhere?"

"I'm afraid I don't know that. She didn't give me the diary at the time of creating her Last Will and Testament, nor any time after. As I said, it's in a safe place … apparently. And now …" Orla's voice petered off.

Erin raised a hand in a chopping motion to emphasize her point. "If I'm to understand this correctly, I have a cottage here, but only if I find the diary?"

"And complete the er … requirements."

"And complete the requirements," echoed Erin.

"And there's the money," interjected Orla.

"Right, the money," agreed Erin. "But only if I follow what's laid out in this diary?"

Orla merely nodded.

Erin laughed lightly. "Which no one has seen."

"Well," began Orla.

"—Lately. No one has seen it lately. And no one, least of all you and I, know where the diary is now."

"That appears to be the case of it, yes."

There was another silence during which traffic could be heard passing by outside in the street.

"Look," said Erin. "I'm sorry to keep going over this but ... you're telling me that unless I find the diary and follow whatever is laid out in there, I won't inherit the cottage."

"Or the money."

"Or the money."

"Of which there's not much but it would be a start, so."

"Can you tell me how much money?" asked Erin.

Orla took a breath, "No, I'm sorry Erin but the whole thing hinges on you finding the diary. Follow the clues and wherever they lead, inherit the cottage and whatever money has been left to you."

Erin looked about the office as if a clue might at any moment leap out from behind a chair or perhaps in the pattern of the curtains.

"How long do I have?" Erin finally asked.

"How long?"

"Yes, how long do I have in which to find the diary and complete the task?"

"Ah! Yes!" Orla looked relieved to be giving a positive response this time. "You have three months, so."

"I can't stay here for three months! I have a job!"

"So you said," Orla nodded her head in agreement. "Be that as it may, once you have followed the clues in the diary to their natural conclusion, then you are to come back here to me and I will give you this check."

She picked up an envelope from her desk and held it between finger and thumb. It was small and flat and with no bulk to it.

Erin thought if she just reached out a hand, she might grab it and run.

"I'm sorry Erin," Orla said, as if anticipating Erin's wild intention. She slid the envelope into a drawer. "I really don't have more for you and even if I did…" She left the sentence hanging.

Erin supposed it wasn't Orla Hanratty's fault that she didn't have the diary or knew where it was.

"Now, in conclusion," Orla began. "If you are going to stay for the next three months, I am to ensure that you are provided with living expenses."

Erin stood up, "I have to think about this, okay?"

"As you wish. Let me know what you decide." Orla gave a half smile that Erin imagined it indicated that she was just as confused as Erin about Maggie's will and the diary and the requirements that went with it.

Erin left the solicitor's office and headed across the village square to a little tea shop. Tucked into a corner by the window was a table where flowers and shrubs grew from ornamental teapots and cups that were set out on a green and white polka dot tablecloth.

She settled herself at this table and looked briefly at the menu. Too distracted to make sense of it, she sat looking out of the painted window boxes to the bustling street beyond.

She mused, 'I never would have imagined… in a million years that I'd have the option of living in Ireland. Maybe if I find the diary, I could do whatever's required, out of respect for Gams, and then go home.' She thought a bit more. 'Maybe I could get a leave of absence for a couple of weeks…'

To her surprise, Erin felt an unexpected excitement, followed by a mental image of herself as Frodo in his first stirrings of interest at going on an adventure away from the Shire.

"Except, my adventure is *within* the Shire," she laughed, finding humor in the absurdity of her situation.

Unable to sit still any longer, Erin left the cafe and wandered about the little Irish village staring into shop windows. She found herself appreciating the village with a new, and less hurried attitude.

She told herself the place had grown and that it was surely a little town now, rather than a village.

Strolling along the street, she paused before a store that sold new and used books. The window display consisted of a pyramid of books with a base of thick, heavy tomes that gradually led book by book, to the smallest perched on the very top.

Tilting her head sideways, Erin peered at the title of one of the books that formed the base of the pyramid. "Tales of Mythical Ireland," she read aloud. "Hmm, what would happen if I went in and asked for that book. Would they refuse to sell it to me I wonder?"

"Sure, I think they'd sell it if ye were determined to have it, so."

Erin looked up. There, beside her reflection in the shop window was a woman about her own height and age with a flowing mane of red hair. Intrigued, she turned away from the window to look.

Four words came to mind: *smiling blue Irish eyes.* 'Did that make sense?' she wondered. 'Could eyes smile?'

"But sure, ye'd be obliged to help them find another book of a similar size."

Erin was charmed by the woman's wide smile and freckled face. "I wouldn't mind doing that. If I really wanted the book, that is. Although it would be a shame to destroy the display for the sake of one book."

"Ye'd have a fine time of it though, trying to get the book out and get another in its place without toppling the whole thing. Sure, the whole village would be watching through the window while you did it."

Erin laughed and looked around at the villagers who were paying no mind to their conversation. "They don't look that interested. Maybe we'd get away without anyone noticing."

"Is that what ye think now?" The woman was clearly amused. "It's naive ye are if ye think the Irish won't notice. Sure, aren't we the most curious people on the planet? They'd be out here taking bets as to whether or not it would topple."

"In that case I probably wouldn't have the audacity to ask for the book. I'd probably be nervous if it drew a crowd."

"It would be the best entertainment around here for weeks. You'd be a celebrity. Sure, I'd say you'd get free drinks in the pubs for ages after."

"Hmm... Maybe I will try it then!"

They both laughed and regarded each other. Erin liked the woman instantly. "I'm Erin," she said. "A celebrity? It would be more for notoriety I'd think."

"Probably true. And I'm Maeve." They shook hands. "So would ye like the book or not?" Maeve gestured toward the door of the bookstore.

"Do you work here?"

"I do, for my sins... so?"

"I think I'll pass this time." Erin paused a moment deep in thought. And then said shyly, "There is... this book I have. Well, I don't actually have it. And it's not a book. Well, it is a book," she corrected. "It's a diary."

"Ah!"

"Uh...I probably shouldn't have said anything. It sounds silly I know."

Maeve spread her hands expressively and waited, smiling.

"It's a diary left to me by a relative here in Ireland. She was from a little village near here, well more of a hamlet really."

"Ah! A gráigin."

"Excuse me?"

"Gráigin. A hamlet."

Erin stumbled over the word so that it came out as gragon, like dragon.

"Not quite." Maeve repeated the word, "Gráigin. Try it again."

Dipping her head in a more deliberate attempt, Erin said, "Grawg-in."

"That's right. Well done yourself!" Maeve rewarded the effort with an approving smile so that for a moment, Erin felt like a schoolgirl basking in the praise of a teacher.

"Anyone I know?" asked Maeve.

"Hmm?" said Erin, bringing her attention back to the moment.

"The diary you mentioned. Was it left to you by anyone I might know?"

"Maybe. Maggie Egan. She lived not far from here in a little..." Again she stumbled over the word, "grawn-in. D'you know of her?"

Maeve shook her head. "No. Sorry I don't. Were ye close?"

"Yes. I mean, we still are... *were*. But I haven't seen her since I was a child."

"A long time, so." Maeve leaned toward Erin. With a half-smile she asked in a conspiratorial tone. "What's in the diary? Secrets?"

"Funny you should ask," Erin pursed her lips, "There might well be."

"Old diaries are wonderful for the finding of family secrets. I wish ye joy of it."

"Thank you." Erin was suddenly shy again. "Well, I'm taking up your time."

"Ah, not at all. Come by any time. And bring the diary if ye want. I'll help ye divine it." With a last smile, Maeve turned and went through the door of the bookstore which caused a little old-fashioned bell to ring.

Erin turned away, thinking she might take Maeve up on the offer, if it came to it.

## Chapter Seven

The latch lifted on the kitchen door. Knowing it to be the insistent donkey, Erin ignored the sound. Instead, she cracked the window ever so slightly and threw two slices of toast out for the animals.

"Hey!" she yelled as Mykel immediately snaffled both slices leaving poor Beauty looking mournfully on.

Ten minutes later and armed with four slices of buttered toast, Erin opened the window again, this time wider than before. With as much of a throwing arm as she could muster, she threw two slices of toast in quick succession as far as she was able.

Mykel went after them immediately. Erin held out a slice for the pony who ambled over and took the slice from Erin's hand. "Lovely girl," she cooed. "No wonder they call you Beauty."

She reached out to stroke the long neck. However, she was unable to quite reach as the pony immediately dropped the toast and ate it from the ground.

In any case there was no time to dawdle as Mykel was already heading back with clear intent in his eyes. Afraid to call out a stern warning at Mykel for fear of disturbing the pony, Erin threw the last piece of toast toward the donkey which effectively headed him off.

By the time he raised his head again, the pony was done eating and had gotten herself out of the donkey's way.

Perhaps impressed that he had done so well out of the breakfast proceedings, Mykel hung around the window for some time, peering in and greedily waiting for more as Erin purposefully ignored him.

It was a cool morning, threatening rain. Erin decided it was a good day to begin looking for the diary. "But first I'll light a fire," she told the empty room.

She considered the wood burning stove. A little kindling had been left in a box on the stone hearth along with tiny firelighter cubes and matches.

To one side of the fireplace there was a stack of wood. On the other side was a mountain of turf. Erin picked up one of these. It was shaped like a brick, black and with pieces of old straw poking out on one side.

Erin held the turf to her nose. It had an earthy aroma. Gams used to say it was the smell of nostalgia, for many an Irish woman or man living abroad, had only to get a whiff to be instantly transported back to the Ireland of their childhood.

Opening the door of the wood-burner, Erin saw the ashes had been cleaned out and wondered, 'Had Gams had done this before laying herself down to wait for ... wait for ...' She paused, remembering what Padraic and Nuala had said about Gams found lying on the bed and wearing all of her best clothes.

"Aw, Gams." Unable to keep the tears at bay, Erin began to cry right there beside the fire. "I miss you so much. I wish you were here with me now."

After a moment, Erin thought she heard dishes clattering in the kitchen. "Oh no!" she yelled. "How did that darn donkey get inside?"

Wiping the tears from her cheeks she ran to investigate thinking for sure it was the dreaded donkey, only to find nothing out of the ordinary. All was quiet. Erin looked through the window for the cause of the noise but the donkey and pony were at the far side of the yard.

Slowly, she opened the cupboard where the dishes were kept, thinking perhaps it was a mouse, but there was nothing there. Shrugging her shoulders, she went back to lighting the fire.

The wood burned quickly with the help of a fire-lighting stick. Carefully adding a log of wood and a few turf bricks, she waited for it to catch and to inhale the wonderful earthy aroma that combined with a unique sweetness when the turf was lit.

"Ah!" she smiled. Sitting back on her haunches she watched the fire begin to roar as the straw of the turf brick curled into the ends of the birch wood. Erin sighed, a happy contentment seeping through her.

She leaned against the rocking chair. It was an action that recalled her childhood, when she would lean against Gams and listen for hour after hour and never tire of the stories or the lovely creamy lilt of her great aunt Maggie's voice.

Such happy thoughts had the effect of lulling her almost into a doze, when she became aware of the subtle perfume of lilac and lavender wafting in the air.

Erin sat up and looked around. "Gams?" she said sleepily.

Except for the ticking of the grandfather clock in the hallway, the room was silent, the perfume gone. Erin walked out of the room and into the kitchen.

Absentmindedly filling the kettle with water, she flicked the lever, setting it to boil. Out of nostalgia, she mixed chocolate powder into a mug with a little bit of Irish cream.

While she waited for the kettle, Erin thought, 'First the dishes and now the perfume. It was most definitely Gam's perfume. Could she be trying to tell me something?'

Pouring hot water into the cup, she stirred the mixture slowly while she considered all that had happened over the last few days.

Gams had left her the diary, yet without immediate access to it. Therefore, it would make sense that Gams might want her to search for it, which meant the search itself must be important. "Could that be so?" she said aloud.

It was in that moment as Erin thought of how much Gams loved her and had wanted the very best for her, that she decided she would find the diary and she would see it to its end, wherever it might lead.

With fresh eyes and attitude, Erin walked back into the living room and surveyed the terrain. "Where to start?" she murmured.

She began by searching the shelves of the dresser that was mounted onto the wall and filled with cups, saucers, glasses and numerous envelopes and leaflets that had been slid behind the assorted dishes.

Pulling out anything of interest, she opened envelopes and spread papers on the dining table, systematically creating two piles as she went through. An electricity bill showed a monthly charge of fifty Euro. "Hm, not bad I guess for a cottage of this size."

She looked inside an envelope and then another until she found an official looking letter which turned out to be from Orla. Scanning it, she realized it contained nothing she didn't already know. Placing the electricity bill and Orla's letter back onto the shelf, Erin threw the rest of the papers into the kitchen garbage.

Going from room to room in this way, Erin discarded outdated or unnecessary papers while keeping anything she thought might be relevant. It took most of the day and the light was beginning to fade before she had searched the entire cottage.

She even dragged the foldable steps from the kitchen into the living room. These she stood on so that she could reach the shelf that went all around the top of the wall. Since she had no idea how big or small this diary might be, she had thought there might be something in or behind one of the many jugs or teapots up there.

Finding nothing of interest, she topped up the fire with turf logs and took the steps back into the kitchen. From there she stepped into the utility room, wondering where she might search next that she hadn't already.

As she looked about the long narrow room, a little spider crawled up the wall and disappeared inside a panel that lay flat on the ceiling. If you hadn't seen the outline of it, you wouldn't know it was there at all. Erin admonished herself on forgetting about the attic, although to be fair she had never been allowed into it as a child.

"Now!" she said as she surveyed the panel, "How to get up there?"

There was a metal hook-ring at one end of it. "Hmm. Where there's a hook-ring there should be a..." Erin peered in the corner behind the small chest freezer. "There you are," she said triumphantly as she pulled out a rod with a hook at one end.

Hooking the rod into its sister loop, Erin pulled. The door of the attic swung down and with it came a set of wooden steps followed by a little cloud of dust. "Wow!" she muttered. "I'm thinking there'll be more of that dust up there... and more spiders where that one came from."

Behind her, was a drawer where Gams kept all her electrical bits and bobs. Erin took a long black flashlight from the drawer and clicked it on.

An immediate beam shone from the cylinder. "Well done, Gams!" Erin said approvingly.

Unfolding the steps, Erin climbed to the third rung and cautiously raised her head so that it was inside the attic. Slowly, she moved the beam of the flashlight around the dark space.

"Yikes!" was her first response at the shadowy lumps and mounds that appeared in the half light.

She searched the wall, careful of spiders. Finding a switch, she clicked it on. It wasn't a brilliant light but it did the job of making the darkness a little less unfriendly.

Items had been stored in a fairly organized way. There were suitcases and boxes, old dusty piles of books and what looked like an antique sewing machine next to an old bureau with one drawer left half open.

"Okay Gams. If that diary isn't up here, then I just don't know where to look."

Erin braced herself to step into the attic. "Spiders if you're around here, you'd better get out of my way." After a pause she added, "Please," and shivered.

Still clutching the flashlight, Erin climbed up further. Stepping onto the attic floor she made the mistake of looking back down into the kitchen and had a moment of vertigo.

Reaching out a hand she clutched the nearest object which turned out to be the knob of an old door that was leaning against the wall and wedged in place by boxes on either side. Holding onto this, Erin eyed the floor.

She didn't enjoy the thought of taking a step and falling through into the rooms below. However, a brief inspection reassured her of a solid wooden floor which she was still inclined to test by sliding her feet carefully toward the first stack of books.

Kneeling down for closer inspection, Erin discovered what turned out to be old encyclopedias. She picked up one after the other to assure herself the diary wasn't hidden among them.

Placing the books back where she found them, Erin went on to the sewing machine, shining her flashlight into the bobble drawer and under the treadle step before going onto the next item.

In this way, she slowly explored and examined everything in the attic from books to suitcases to the old bureau which yielded up nothing but a few ribbons.

Disappointed, she sat on her heels and looked back the way she had come. Something by the entrance to the attic caught her eye.

The dim overhead light bulb glinted on the knob of the old door she had grasped on her way in. She had thought it merely an old door left against the wall of the attic but now that she looked with more intent, it appeared to be part of the wall itself. "Could that be what I think it is?" Erin murmured.

Grabbing the flashlight, Erin made her way back to the entrance. She reached out a hand, grasped the doorknob and pulled. It was firm and didn't budge. 'Hmm... part of the wall itself?'

Taking a step back, she surveyed the wall. 'Maybe,' she thought, 'it was used as an extra bit of wood to complete the wall.' She looked again. 'But that wouldn't make sense.'

Placing the flashlight on the floor, Erin took hold of the doorknob. Using both hands, she turned it to the right with as much strength as she could muster.

There was a clicking sound as the knob turned and the door creaked slowly open.

Erin, gasping and laughing from surprise, pulled the door wide and grabbed up the flashlight to shine it fully into the space beyond the door.

It was a small room about four feet square, built into the side of the chimney breast. On the wall furthest away from the chimney was a short square table upon which sat a cardboard box about a foot in length and another foot in its width.

Erin uttered a small sigh. There was no doubt in her mind that this must be the diary. A long-forgotten memory of Gams flooded her mind.

*****

It was an evening long ago, beside a crackling fire, when a small Erin lay cosily wrapped up in Gam's embrace. Stroking Erin's hair, Gams told her of Irish history, about how many became what she called 'wild geese;' Irish people who had emigrated all over the world.

"Even in those far-away lands, they had never forgotten their homeland. They passed down to their children and their children's children, the memory of their lost Irish heritage, its folklore, music, language and identity."

Gams had told Erin how crucial it was to know not only Irish history but also the history of her own family. "Think of it as a tapestry," Gams had said. "Yes, the family is a tapestry."

She settled into telling the tale. "Each story is a single thread in a tapestry woven with lovely complex patterns, colors and designs. Like the tapestry, we are a combination of the culture, history and traditions we inherited from our own families and from the culture that was passed down to us over hundreds of years."

Gams waved a hand, "Sure, it was easy to pass it on because in those days, people didn't travel much out of their own area and couldn't get more than a few miles in a day just by walking alone."

Gams nodded her head sagely as if she carried the weight of all that history. "Our family stories are what give us a sense of belonging, a kind of identity. It's those very stories that help us to overcome the hardships we face in this life. If we know that one uncle died in the great war but that he died bravely leading his men into battle with the cry of, 'Onward lads, follow me!'" She sighed, "Well, such bravery would live on with us do you see?"

"Gams, is that real? Who was he? What was his name?"

"Well, no dear, it's just an example. But there now, it already inspires you to want to know more."

"I suppose it does, yes," agreed Erin. "If it were true."

"The point is my girl," said Gams with a slight note of impatience. "That we try to emulate the stories of bravery and determination. Now, why is that, do you think child? It is because we know those stories to be our own. It is because we come from that, we have those genes, so we do."

"So, what you're saying," ventured Erin, "is that knowing our history, makes us more... *us*?"

"Sure, and it does," asserted Gams with a satisfied expression. "Let's use the word 'authentic'. That means to be truly ourselves in this case. I believe the knowing of family stories makes us more *authentic*."

She paused a moment with pursed lips, clapped her hands and said "Now my darlin' girl, I have a story to tell you. In fact, it's yours, this story. I'm giving it to you."

At Erin's surprised face, Gams pulled a shawl around her shoulders and gazed into the glowing turf fire. When the room became quiet, Great-Aunt Maggie began the story of Erin's ancestor Bridget Egan.

"I grew up hearing story after story of Bridget Egan." Gams peered at Erin as if to make sure she was listening.

"Of course, she passed on long before I was born but here is the thing of it... her story was passed down from daughter to daughter, to my grandmother who passed it to me. And now here I am passing it on to you."

Erin had listened entranced, looking first into the sweet face of her dear Gams, then at the turf fire where visions of castles and mountains were busy forming themselves among the hot turf and wood logs.

"To be sure, or so I was told, the old lady was more alive and vivacious at eighty than I was myself at fifteen," she mused.

"For all that, they said she was sad at times. She'd get a far-away look in her eyes like she was seeing something beyond the laughter of the room. But such times were few and she'd shake herself out of it and be her laughing self again."

Erin's gaze began to wander, this time around the old fireplace at the glistening brass and glass ornaments that twinkled and sparkled in the light from the fire. Realizing she had missed what Gams was saying, she asked, "What was that Gams? I look like her?"

"Well now I never met her myself but, based on a photo of her in her older age, I should think so."

Erin gasped, "Can I see?"

Maggie smiled omnisciently. "In due time my child, but not yet."

Erin slumped in posture slightly, wishing to see the photo. She used her imagination to wonder what Bridget might look like. It was at this moment that Erin formed a closer appreciation for the ancestor she resembled. In truth, she couldn't help but admire and feel close to this woman who had so impressed generations of women and all within her own family.

'I look like this Bridget,' she thought. 'I wonder how that works?'

Gams interrupted Erin's thoughts again, "As I said, she was always laughing and singing or so I was told. She'd be waiting for the bread to bake in the big iron cooking range. She'd start humming a song and then she'd grab hold of one of the children with her two hands. The next thing they'd be dancing a wild Irish jig until they were both shrieking with laughter and gasping for breath, wisps of hair hanging down from the knot on her head that would never stay in place."

Gams was breathless just telling the story. She paused, smiling, and then sighed as she recalled childhood winter evenings, snuggled in the big wooden rocking chair with her own grandmother singing Irish ballads and telling the old tales of Bridget.

"Sure, it was the stories that brought me back to Ireland. Bridget and the stories," she sighed. "And I've never regretted coming home, no, not once."

*****

Erin placed the flashlight on the floor, reached out her hands and picked up the cardboard box in both hands. Carefully she negotiated her way out of the little secret room, or so she thought of it.

Placing the box on the floor, she felt with her feet for the steps leading down from the attic.

Tongue positioned carefully between her teeth Erin pulled the box carefully down, step by step until she reached the kitchen floor.

Pushing the attic door closed with the rod, she dropped it back into its place against the wall behind the freezer. The palms of her hands were sweating with anticipation as she carried the box into the living room and placed it on the dining table.

Erin pulled out a chair and sat down. She looked at the box and wondered how she could have forgotten Gams telling her about Bridget. And why hadn't Gams mentioned a diary when she'd told her that story?

Pulse racing, excitement took hold of Erin as she opened the flaps. Inside surrounded by tissue, lay a leather-bound book.

Erin lifted the book and set it on her lap, letting the tissue paper fall rustling to the floor.

A Celtic triquetra adorned the front and back covers of the book that pressed against her skin. Erin gently stroked the cover as she savored the expectation of what might lie within, a story, a whole life, a priceless jewel. At last, Erin opened the old book. She sighed at the faint wisp of dust that scented the air.

The cream-colored pages were brown with age at the edges, falling away easily from their cotton binding. She gazed at the old-fashioned handwriting, wasteful in its fancy curls and twirls, long looping necks poised to sweep down through elegant bends.

The writing was vibrant, penned with beauty and care. The letters danced as Erin wiped tears of emotion on her sleeve, blinking as she read the first words.

*Bridget Egan, her book*

*May 1846*

'How sweet,' thought Erin. She turned the page.

*Today is my thirteenth birthday.*

The beginning of the next letter faded on a long downward descent as the quill ran out of ink.

Erin ran her finger lightly over the words and felt with a shock the presence of another person in the room.

Erin sat up and looked around. The diary almost fell off her lap. She kept very still for a moment, heart beating rapidly, the only sound came from the logs falling against each other in the grate.

She almost got up to switch on the overhead light but after a moment, she pulled the diary towards her once more and placed a finger on the page. She didn't believe in ghosts but that there was a presence was unmistakable.

After a moment, she decided the energy was powerful but not hostile. Erin concentrated on her breathing and realized she felt the presence only when reading the diary and tracing the words. She gathered her courage and forced her finger to trace the letters once more.

A youthful hand darted over towards a stubby bottle of ink. The hand dipped quick and steady, careful not to drip, returned to the letter, reviving it into a full word and another, careful and precise.

In a swirl of emotions that ran from shock to excitement, Erin realized she was not only reading the words, she was actually reliving how young Bridget felt at the moment she received the diary.

Enchanted, energized and fully awake, Erin gave herself up to the experience.

*****

"This is for me?" Bridget's eyes were shining when she looked up at the Missus.

"Struth child!" The Missus shook her wrist so the fan in her hand opened fully. She fanned her face energetically to hide her pleasure at the girl's surprise and urged, "Open it, girl! Open it!"

Bridget did as she was bid, gasping in delight at the beautiful leather book that lay inside.

"But…" Bridget looked up and whispered, "what is it Ma'am?'

"Why, 'tis a diary child." The Missus rocked back and forth and flicked her fan closed with a snap. "You are to write in it often."

Bridget looked down at the soft leather and stroked it carefully. "I am sure I would not know what to write."

At this, the Missus reached over and rapped Bridget on the knuckles with her fan.

Bridget quickly withdrew her hand with a grimace before remembering the Missus was doing her a kindness and would expect gratitude for the instruction.

"You must write about your life." The Missus waved her fan about as if Bridget's life stretched beyond the very walls of the house. "You must tell of things that happen to people you love, to your family."

She looked at Bridget sharply. "You may not write about me, of course." She looked over her spectacles, "Unless of course it is something admirable." She waved the fan again. "In which case you may most certainly write about me."

Resting her hands in her lap at last, the Missus said something that Bridget thought most interesting. "When you are old, you must pass the diary to your children and ensure a promise that they will pass it on to their own."

Bridget could not help but interrupt, "I am sure my life would not be so interesting, Ma'am."

Bridget received another sharp rap on the knuckles, a reminder that the Missus did not take kindly to interruption. This time, Bridget managed not to flinch or to grimace quite so much.

"I have a diary written by my grandmother," continued the Missus. "'Tis exceedingly precious to me and I have read it many times. Your own children will no doubt value your words as much as I have my grandmother's."

The Missus' face softened. She looked off into the distance as if remembering the diary of which she spoke.

After a moment the Missus looked up and seemed surprised to find Bridget beside her. She gathered herself and continued on. "I purchased a diary with the happy thought that I would write in it for my grandchildren." Here she choked a little and cleared her throat before continuing. "'Tis my misfortune that I never had any grandchildren." She sighed, "Or children for that matter."

She sat up straighter. "Now off with you and put the diary away, safe in your hope chest." She peered at Bridget over her spectacles again. "You do have a hope chest?"

"Oh yes Ma'am, indeed I do. Although it is very small to be sure."

The Missus nodded approvingly. "As befits your station my girl."

Bridget was overcome with gratitude and without thinking, leaned forward and placed a kiss upon the Missus' powdered cheek.

"Enough child. Be off with you now." The Missus flicked open her fan and began to use it vigorously before her face.

Hugging the diary to her chest, Bridget stammered her thanks yet again. In a flurry of excitement, she all but ran up to the little room in the attic where she lay her head each night.

The candle stub gave barely enough light in the windowless room, but she was too excited to care. She dipped her quill into the inkpot with a shaking hand.

Chewing the corner of her mouth, Bridget paused with her quill above the page thinking of what she might write. At last, and with resolve she touched the quill to the page and began the testament of her life.

*****

In her mind's eye, Erin felt and saw Bridget push her long auburn hair back from her face and sigh with satisfaction. Erin paused with Bridget as she tucked the end of the pen in her mouth and considered what to write next.

Pen dipped into ink and paused above the paper before at last, touching the page.

*First, I should write with gratitude that the Missus has been very kind to me. She is an old lady now but still grand, with white hair and little round spectacles that perch on the end of her nose. Her eyesight is not as sharp as it was. This is why I am here in her employment.*

*When I was but 12 years, Mr. Finlan passed away. His widow, the Missus, asked Mr. O'Grady at the National school if he could find a girl to read to her after school. She had a fancy to help a girl of poor means.*

*I was proud to be singled out as the best reader as well as being very tidy. Mr. O'Grady advised me in private that he had chosen me because I had previously attended a pay school near my village, where parents paid what they could afford and gladly.*

*Such schools were of course hidden away, often under cover of hedges where the all-pervasive eyes of the English could not easily find them.*

*Parents encouraged their children to attend so they might have the education of their fathers. Sadly, these schools are fast becoming a thing of the past. Education, especially in the Irish language is forbidden, enforced by the most drastic measures.*

*National schools have been established so that a rudimentary education might be had, yet this is mostly achieved by repeating lessons in rote. But in truth, the national school education is nowhere near the standard that was before reached under the simple tutelage of the travelling teacher.*

*My own dear parents were most determined that I should have an education so that when the tutor no longer came to our village, I was among the few who were encouraged to attend the national school.*

*As my arithmetic was found to be of good quality, I was already well ahead of the children who had not the benefit of the pay school but had attended only the national school.*

*Mr. O'Grady quietly informed me that he heartily approved of pay schools and was saddened by their passing.*

He added that I was never to forget the good learning I had received there, nor the dedicated men and women who had selflessly travelled the countryside to provide it, even it was under a hedge.

Naturally, I assured him I would endeavor to always remember his words and his kindness in recommending me.

After being taken on by the Missus, I read to her every day for a year.

At the end of that time, the Missus said she was pleased with my work and asked me to work full time.

I was so excited at the prospect of living in town and having a place in a big house, that I did not mind at all when Cook tutted at me or the housekeeper frowned if I forgot to use the back stairs.

Since then I have become a sort of companion. I spend my time running errands about the house and fetching trays of tea from Cook who tells me to be careful and not to let the tray rattle so that the tea spills.

*I write correspondence for the Missus, although she says I tend to hold my tongue between my teeth as I form the letters just so. I try not to do it but then I forget and my tongue creeps out again.*

*The Missus admires my writing. She says I have a good hand. I must confess that her words made me feel proud ...*

# Chapter Eight

Erin woke with a start to see the fire had gone out; the logs burned to ashes hours ago.

A lilac bush waved gently in the early morning breeze and the sun streamed in, adding a golden glow to the bright colors in the comfortable room.

The quiet of the morning was undisturbed except for the grandfather clock ticking solidly in the hallway.

She rescued the diary from where it had slipped in the night down the side of the comfortable chair.

Gazing at the diary on her lap, she thought about the strange experience she'd had the night before. She wondered if it had been a dream.

Fitting the diary carefully back into its box, she brushed her hand across it like a caress, before placing it on the rosewood side table.

'Gams felt you couldn't know who you were until you knew where your roots lay.'

"Is that what I believe?" Erin mused aloud as she went to brew a pot of tea. She wondered if she was becoming more Irish in her preference for tea this morning instead of the usual coffee.

Mug of tea in hand, she gazed through the kitchen window into the yard. In her mind, she could almost hear Gams singing as she tended her little vegetable garden just beyond the yard.

The thought gave her comfort, surrounded as she was by the spiritual presence of her great aunt. It was like being wrapped in a favorite cozy comforter. "I love you Gams," Erin said softly.

It was a lovely morning. Erin watched as Beauty dozed on her feet in the center of the yard. The pony's back legs were held tight together at the knees. Erin wondered if positioning her legs like that, created the tripod effect of holding her up.

A black bird with a white breast sat on Beauty's back searching for ticks and pecking them off. Erin decided Beauty must enjoy this because she didn't snicker or flick her long white mane to sweep the bird off its perch.

The neighbor's cat crossed the yard which caused the bird to fly away. At this, Beauty opened her eyes briefly, swishing her tail once before closing them again.

The cat flopped against the cool flag stones by the barn and rolled onto his back clawing at a butterfly who happened by but managed to stay out of reach.

Clearly disappointed, the cat rolled to his feet, swished his tail sharply and stalked off into the barn. Beauty opened her eyes and peered out through her long white mane but seeing nothing of interest, resumed her dozing.

The white-breasted bird swooped in again to land on the ground between the pony and the barn door. Without hesitation, the bird walked into the barn. Erin could see it walking about in there on its little feet and wondered if it was about to become lunch for the cat.

She began to open the window to shout a warning, but the bird was quicker. It suddenly flew out of the barn, twittering in alarm.

The pony opened her eyes at the flurry of activity. The cat appeared in the doorway; head turned upward as he followed the bird's flight over the rooftop.

The pony blinked at the scene and turned around to face the sun. After a shake or two of her head, she proceeded to crop the grass in the yard.

Erin sighed in appreciation of the idyllic scene. She pressed her face against the kitchen window, wondering if she might slip out to pet the pony without Mykel seeing her. He was nowhere in sight, but Erin hesitated, not quite brave enough to take the chance.

Disappointed in herself but vowing to try again the next day, she decided to make the diary her priority.

Thinking she might ask Orla for more information now that she'd found the diary Erin called in at the solicitor's office later that morning. Fortunately, Orla was available and showed her right in.

Erin fidgeted with her earring as soon as she sat down.

Orla observed her for a moment and then asked, "Now! You've found the diary I take it."

"How did you know?"

"Sure, you wouldn't be back here if you hadn't, now would you?" Orla smiled at Erin. "How can I help you?"

"Well … I'm playing with the idea of maybe taking a little bit of time off from my job. If I can swing it, that is. The thing is I really don't know where to start or what it is exactly that I'm supposed to do. Can you … well could you point me in the right direction?"

"Ah!" Orla seemed pleased with Erin's question. "I can help you with that a little." She adopted a brisk air. "Now! It just so happens there is an Egan Clan Gathering coming up this weekend and I think you should go."

"A what?" Erin was surprised. "Did you say there *happens* to be a clan gathering this weekend?"

"Interesting, isn't it?" Orla's eyebrows went up as another smile lit her face. "That Maggie Egan now, she certainly had impeccable timing."

Erin was speechless. Questions ran through her head one after the other. 'Impeccable timing? Is that what it was? But how could Gams have known?'

Orla nodded her head. "I can see your head is whirling and to be sure I have no answers for you."

She paused here and seemed to consider. "I'm a solicitor. I deal in facts alone. All I can say is Maggie gave me instructions to steer you towards the gathering. More than that I cannot tell you, not at this stage, so."

Erin found her voice. "You mean … there's more? You have clues that you haven't shared with me?" She tried to adopt an appealing smile, hoping the solicitor would reveal everything she knew but to no avail.

Orla was implacable and merely spread her hands in a gesture of professional helplessness.

Pinching her lips together, Erin considered how she could extract the information she needed. While she gathered her thoughts, she allowed her gaze to wander about the room. A framed photograph sat on the desk, of Orla and a young woman in cap and gown. "Oh!" began Erin. "Is that your daughter?"

Orla picked up the frame. "Yes. It was taken last year at her graduation." She smiled at the photograph. "She lives in Dublin. It's where I lived too, before I set up my little law firm here."

"Very pretty. What's her name?"

"Kath ... short for Kathleen but I never call her that." Orla laughed. "Unless she's in trouble."

Erin laughed too. "I can see she wasn't in trouble there."

"That's for sure."

"I remember precious moments like that with Gams, I mean, Great-Aunt Maggie when I was here. They're so meaningful now…"

They smiled at each other and then without a blink Orla said, "But I still can't reveal any more than I already have."

The smile drooped from Erin's face. "But…"

"I'm sorry Erin. It's Maggie's wish that must be respected and upheld here. Otherwise what's the point of writing a will, so?"

Erin sighed and gave up. "You're right. I know you're right." She sighed. "Fine. Give me the details of the gathering."

"Good girl yourself. You won't regret it. Ah sure, you'll have a fine time."

Orla drew out a card on which the details of the gathering were already written and handed it to Erin. "You'll need to book yourself in at a B&B. If you'd like, I'll call the organizer to let them know you'll be joining them for the event."

"Will I get with such short notice?"

"They'll be glad to have you. The more the merrier."

With the card in her purse, Erin found herself back out on the street with no plan to speak of except to turn up at the clan gathering and hope the next step would reveal itself.

"There ye are again," said a voice. Erin turned to find a smiling Maeve, her freckled face bright and welcoming. She nodded her head toward the solicitor's office. "In to see Orla were ye?"

"I was. You know Orla?"

"Sure, she's the only solicitor around. Doesn't she have the ear of everyone in the village so."

"Oh, right." Erin changed the subject. "Out for a walk?"

"I was just off to do a bit of shopping. Have ye had time to look in at the store?"

"Er no, not yet. I should though. I'm running low on a few things."

"Come along with me. I'll show ye around."

Erin smiled, happy for the distraction, and glad for the opportunity of a companion.

They strolled along the main street together, pausing to admire a banner advertising the upcoming summer festival billed as The Old Town Fair. "It's next weekend," said Erin.

"Sure, and there'll be grand craic to be had."

"I remember going to this event with my Great-Aunt. It was fun. There were so many children playing musical instruments. I couldn't get over it. Irish kids are talented. I wonder why that is?"

"I'd like to say we're just naturally talented and we are of course, but I think it's more that we keep the old traditions alive. We send our kids to learn Irish dancing and music. It's a cultural thing."

"There was dancing in the village hall when I was a kid, but I was too shy at the time to join in."

"A Ceili was it? Ah, there's a Ceili every night of the festival. It's plenty of talent we have with a different band each night."

"I can't do Irish dancing, so I'm not sure…"

"Ah don't you worry at all. There are classes for it. You'll be here still?"

"I'm seriously playing with the idea of staying, for a couple of months anyway." Erin looked at Maeve shyly. "Oh and… I found the diary."

"You did?"

"I searched the whole cottage! It was in the attic of all places and hidden away."

"The old lady must have valued it well."

"I think she did, yes."

"Have you started reading it?"

"I have …" Erin paused and then smiled. "One thing I remember was Gams. Well, she said something one time about the importance of knowing where you come from. Gams was a great believer in family history."

"We're like that here in Ireland. Well, most of us at any rate. A while ago there was a march to remember the Irish who were lost in the great war. It was the hundred-year anniversary."

"Gams told me a story about the great war. She'd have liked the idea of a remembrance march."

"Well now. She'd have been in grand company for all the volunteers were dressed in clothes from the era. Sure, it was busy there at the old theater. They raided the costumes and handed them out. We all wore hats. It was good craic for a while, trying things on.

"But then we formed up into a column. Five thousand of us from Sligo alone. That's when it got serious.

"We marched in step through the town. It was eerie you know. I don't remember anyone saying we shouldn't talk. But we didn't, not one of us. There was just the marching."

"It must have been a dramatic sight."

"It was a strange event. Back then in the war the Irish were in two minds. While those men and women were away fighting, there was a revolution going on here at home."

"Wow! And when those soldiers came home…"

"They were not welcomed. No, they were not. And I think this was reflected in the spectators during the march I'm telling ye about.

"The town was full of people shopping and going to church and the like. So, to have complete silence in all the streets, it was a sight all right. It was like the actual homecoming of all those soldiers was being re-lived right there before our very eyes."

"So, you're saying," Erin sought appropriate words, "that holding a march such as that, can sort of rekindle the emotional reaction of the event itself."

"They can and they do," agreed Maeve. "And more so because every one of those marchers was given a card with the name and birthplace of the person they were marching on behalf of. Sometimes the card would have the name of someone from the actual village where the marcher was born."

"It must have been pretty emotional?"

"Well now, certainly for those who took the march seriously and why wouldn't they, for there they were, marching in the drama of the moment."

The two women were silent for a long moment, Maeve recalling the event and Erin imagining it all.

Erin spoke first. "I think Gams would say we recognize parts of ourselves in events like that especially when they're experienced by the whole country."

Maeve nodded. "That's it exactly, the marchers and the spectators. We're great ones for the history."

Maeve stopped outside the grocery store. "Here we are now. Will I give ye the tour or d'you prefer to explore on your own?"

"I think I'll explore if you don't mind."

"Right then," Maeve smiled. "I'm just in and out so maybe I'll see you soon. Drop in at the bookstore anyway, next time you're in town." And away she went, long hair flaming, her sandaled feet slapping the floor as she walked.

Erin explored the market from one end to the other. She was fascinated by the lovely lilting accents all around her.

Not being in a rush, she dawdled and fancied herself part of it all. For as long as she was able to keep her mouth closed, no one would know she wasn't Irish herself.

It was a lovely feeling. Even at the checkout, Erin tried to blend in, waiting quietly.

"Now! Is this what ye have for yourself today?"

Erin nodded and pushed her items along the counter.

"That will be eleven euro." The clerk sat patiently while Erin went through her coins, a fine perspiration breaking out on her forehead as she laboriously sorted through the coins and told herself she really must learn the different coins as quickly as possible. A little breathless with effort, she handed over the money.

"Ah, there's grand ye are with the right change."

Erin smiled again and turned away from the checkout, pleased and imagining she had pulled off being Irish all the way through and out of the store.

Once outside she told herself 'They probably saw through me right away, but it was fun being Irish, if only for a little while.'

That afternoon Erin made herself comfortable in Gam's old rocking chair with a cup of tea. She had smiled as she brewed the tea, thinking it wouldn't be long before she was nibbling on a bacon buttie just like Gams used to do.

She reached out to touch the diary, enjoying the feel of the leather binding and wondering that its contents were so quickly having an effect on her life.

Lifting the book onto her lap, she opened it at a random page. The writing was more carefully formed now, indicating a maturity not seen in the pages she had previously read.

## Chapter Nine

*I am fifteen. Imagine that. These years I have worked full time for the Missus. It has been a good arrangement I think, for I have learned much and most certainly I am happy in my work. Yet I cannot deny tis my afternoon off that I look forward to each week, for it is then that I see Mam and Da ~ and Terry ...*

As she walked along the leafy lane, Bridget skipped in sheer joy. It was her half-day and she would spend it, as she always did, with her family. It was a two hour walk but she could shorten it by half an hour if she kept up a brisk pace.

The Missus allowed Bridget the distinction of staying over at her parent's cottage on her afternoon off. Cook reminded Bridget not to let the Missus down by returning late as this leniency was dependent on Bridget returning before six the following morning.

Winter or summer, she was up before dawn for the start of her walk back to town with her mother's kiss still warm on her brow.

As she trudged on towards her village, Bridget carried a basket prepared by Cook. Inside it sat a good-sized slice of Irish cheese wrapped in a muslin cloth.

There was also a generous piece of apple cake and a pot of preserve. Bridget was always provided with such a basket on her visits home, for the Missus was mindful of her duty to the poor.

With youthful exuberance, Bridget sang a lively tune. As she reached the last line of the song, she kicked up her skirts, twirled about and ended with a little jump.

She had never needed much encouragement to sing and was blessed with a good strong voice that others told her was pleasant to hear.

Splashing through a puddle left by rain earlier that day, Bridget's heart gave a little flutter. She stopped for a moment and hugged herself in delight.

"Terry," she breathed. The very thought of him caused her to twirl on the spot. The smile on his lips and in his eyes when he looked at her, sent ripples up and down her stomach like butterflies taking flight and then settling down on a field of yellow daffodils.

'Sweet Terry mo ghrá.' Bridget mused. 'He is not so handsome as some might describe it, yet he is strong and reliable and has a peace about him.' Pressing her lips together, she nodded her head in agreement with her inner thoughts.

Just last week as he walked her back into town, Terry had asked Bridget to marry him. Laughing in delight at the memory she said aloud, "He makes my heart flutter!" and ran along the lane until she was quite red in the face and breathless.

Today she would speak with her Mam and Da but was not sure how to bring up the subject, because they were so used to receiving the quarterly purse she earned from the Missus.

Once she and Terry were married and if she were allowed to remain in service to the Missus, they would need the money to help make their new home together.

With these delightful thoughts, Bridget hardly noticed the ten-mile walk although as always, the sun was well above the horizon when she arrived at her village.

It was the hazel trees she saw first, growing as they were alongside the road and on the hill behind the cottages.

As she rounded the final bend in between the hazel trees, she bent to pick wood-sorrel as she always did when they were plentiful. Pushing a leaf into her mouth, she smiled as the sweet-sour taste combined with the welcome fragrance of turf fires. She breathed in the smoky turf that was like perfume to her. The smell of home and sweet it was.

How she loved coming home to her village. There she knew every occupant of the stone walled dwellings and thatched roofs and each of them knew her in turn and had done since birth.

Outwardly, one cottage was like the next, although some of the homes had an extra room that served as a place to sleep, separate from the main living area.

The cottages formed a ragged line along each side of an open common area of grass where sheep that belonged to the villagers kept it trimmed.

An oak tree provided shade to an old man who sat on a wooden bench and looked out on the life he had once been an active part of. Now he was content to observe, a pipe between his teeth.

His hands clasped a stick that he kept between his knees. This was firmly planted on the ground 'til he should need it to help him hobble home again, to the welcome of a turf fire beneath the thatch of his own cozy cottage.

People in this village were fortunate as Bridget was well-aware, for every week on her way to and from Castlebar, she passed the less privileged who lived in single room mud cabins.

The men of her village were all away working the fields. As tenants of His Lordship, they were obliged to work three full days a week on the lands belonging to the great house. Bridget's Da was a valued member of that workforce because of the strength of arm he brought to his labors.

At this time of the day, the village was lively with women toiling alone or with children, on their small plot of land or tending to the chores. Old Roisin sat at her door; carding sheep's wool ready for weaving.

Erin could hear Niamh calling her boys, wild rascals every one of them, gone up the hill and playing when they should be minding their Mammy's call.

Baby Aisling sat on a grassy spot outside Niamh's cottage, her chubby little hand holding a potato and rubbing it in the dirt, presumably to improve the flavor.

Chickens waddled at will in and out of the cottages, as welcome as any of the children. Several pecked about where Aisling sat, as interested in the potato as herself and just as willing to share it.

The villagers called their greetings and Erin called back, glad to see them and they her.

Bridget's cottage lay at the end of the village across a stream that sometimes ran too high to cross. Today the water was low, so that she could step easily from stone to stone.

Mam was glad to see the basket of gifts from the Missus for she took it as a personal show of respect, both for the good work that Bridget did at the house as well as the way in which she and Da had brought up their child.

Mam said they were all things she could make herself in the big iron bastille that hung from a hook over the open fire. She would say this but would then add with an approving nod, "'Tis the thought that counts, so."

Erin was quick to say, "In truth, my favorite meal in the world is your colcannon."

Pleased to see Mam's answering smile, Bridget hugged her mother. "'Tis a pleasure to taste your colcannon Mam. With a knob of your clover-flavored butter on the top, it cannot help but melt in."

They both laughed, for it was well known the only clover in the mix was whatever the cow foraged and ate on the hillside, that in turn flavored the milk in the end result.

Sometimes in the kitchen at the Missus' house, Bridget yearned for her Mam's colcannon. She told her mother this while she helped spread laundered clothing on the bushes outside their cottage.

After working side by side for a while, Mam asked, "Now my pet, what is wrong with ye today? You're full of fidgets."

Bridget paused to smoothed out the skirt she had just spread to dry. She didn't look up for a moment, unwilling to speak outright of her plans with Terry. "I'm parched Mam. I'm sure ye are too. Will we take a cup of bainne tiubh together?"

Mam nodded. "Please."

Bridget noticed Mam reach one hand around to rub her back and paused to help her to the bench beside the door.

From a covered pail inside the cottage, Bridget poured two cups of old milk. She also added a little more turf to the open fire that sat to one side of the room, keeping it ready to cook their evening meal.

As Bridget came outside, she took a sip of the mixture. "Mmm! I love the bainne tiubh best when sour." She handed a mug to her mother. "Ye know how to mix it just right."

"Thank you mo stór," Mam smiled up at Bridget. "'Tis glad I am to see your sweet face, home again." She sighed then and settled back.

Sipping at the cool drink, she flexed her shoulders. "Where does all the energy of youth go, I wonder."

Bridget had no answer and told herself she had not the experience to know of such things just yet.

Mam leaned back against the wall of the cottage, closed her eyes and lifted her face to the sun.

Bridget left her there and went inside, tidying and humming to herself, then peeped out in time to see Mam stretch out her arms with a contented sigh that spread through her body like summer sunshine.

"Just hearing you about the place makes me feel glad," said Mam. "And with a good man coming home from the fields soon enough, it makes me feel this day could last forever."

Bridget sat beside Mam and chose her words carefully.

"'Tis a long time you have been married to Da."

"We have indeed," Mam agreed. "A long time, so."

"How old were ye when ye married?"

"Oh," said her unsuspecting Mam. "About your age as I recollect." But then she turned to look at Bridget, her blue eyes piercing.

"Are ye thinking of marrying already?"

"Well…" Bridget allowed the sentence to trail off a moment while her mother continued to scrutinize. She began again. "Terry and I are walking out a great many times of late as ye well know."

It was as if a shadow had crossed the sky. The contentment seemed to fall from Mam like a cloak in the wind.

"What Mam?" Bridget tried to control her shaking voice. "What can ye see?" Bridget caught Mam's hands as her eyes became unfocused and a solitary tear ran down her face.

"Mam!" Bridget shook her gently then sighed with relief when her mother's eyes focused again.

Mam blinked and looked directly at Bridget. "Ah mo stór," She gripped Bridget's hand. "Terry is a good man, a fine young man."

Bridget's face broadened in a grin which died as her mother whispered, "Do not speak of marriage yet awhile."

"Why Mam? What did you see?"

"I dreamed last night of fields dark with rot."

Bridget looked at the green crop of potatoes in full flower. "See Mam. All is well. Do not fuss so about dreams." And yet Bridget knew Mam's dreams were often of great import.

Heeding the alarm in her daughter's voice, Mam roused herself. "Surely it was merely a bad dream."

Bridget could swear a chill seemed to grip her like a knot in her chest. But before she could press further on the subject, Da's voice could clearly be heard as he came along the lane singing and misquoting an old folk song.

*"Eileen fair beyond compare
Asleep upon a bank I spied…"*

"Wisht now," she said. "Say nothing to Da of marrying." Mam's voice was firm in a way that would brook no argument.

Bridget's mouth dropped into a pout and her brow furrowed with impatience. Immediately, she was ashamed of herself and lifted her head, ready to greet her father with a smile.

> *"Upon tiptoe I sought her side*
> *And kissed her down in the daisies."*

Da came into view as he rounded the bend. The athletic height of him cut a romantic figure with his black hair and blue eyes. He ended the verse by drawing out the last word, hugging himself as if to emphasize the ardour of such a kiss.

From the welcome that spread across Mam's face it was evident she thought him handsome indeed.

As Da came striding towards the cottage, he called out. "Is this what awaits a man after a hard day's work? The two women in my life sitting around drinking goodness knows what, for all the world as if they had nothing better to do. Is it ladies of leisure ye are today?"

Mam laughed, "'Tis bainne tiubh is all it is, so."

Bridget restrained herself from running to greet him like the little girl she used to be.

Da called out to Ma, "Are ye bringing Bridget up to be a fine lady with all the book learning and writing in diaries and now companion to a rich woman."

Mam laughed again, smoothing her apron as she stood to greet Da for she had heard it all before. She walked into his open arms.

Her voice was muffled against his chest as she reminded him, "'Tis just a diary. Our Bridget is writing the history of her life."

Bridget corrected Mam. "I am writing the history of our lives. Yours and Da's as well as my own."

"The history of our lives." There was wonder in Da's voice as he repeated Bridget's words. "Now who would be interested in reading about our family. Sure, aren't we poor tenant farmers nowadays?"

He kissed the top of Mam's head and tucked his arm about her before continuing, "Ye should write the history of the Egan's as it was five hundred years ago, when we owned all the land from Tipperary right down to the River Shannon."

Mam laughed and tugged at Da's ear to pull him out of it before he got a bee in his hat as he often did about such things. "Don't be filling Bridget's head with all that nonsense. Landowners indeed. Whatever will ye be telling the girl next?"

But Ma need not have worried for Da winked at her then said, "Bridget me girl, will ye cut me a slice of bannock with butter?"

"I will Da."

"And spread thick mind, the butter."

"Will ye take a cup of bainne tiubh, Da?"

Da raised his eyebrows and opened his eyes wide to make bulge with feigned shock. "No, I will not for 'tis a raw thirst I have on me now."

He laughed then and said, "A jug o' léann ábhair would go down well enough." He cocked a questioning eye toward his wife.

Mam laughed. "Sure, and ye can have a jug of barley ale if ye want it, so." Grinning, he sat down on the bench and pulled Mam down beside him. "'Tis a good woman ye are."

He nuzzled Mam's neck which had her giggling like a girl. "Did I ever tell ye how pretty ye are? Sure, you're more lovely than the sun, up there in the sky."

He reached out as if to grab hold of the sun and made to pull it down in his fist.

"Arra, stop now Joe!" said Mam but half-heartedly for it was easy to see she was loving the attention.

Da held out his closed fist to Mam. "Eileen Egan, if I could give ye the world I would, so." He opened his fist. "But here is the sun in the meantime for all it does not come near the beauty of yourself."

Bridget shook her head and left them gazing into each other's eyes. As she prepared a bite and a drink for Da, she caught snatches of their conversation though their voices were low.

"Had we still been landowners Eileen, I would give ye anything ye want. What would ye want if ye could have it?"

"I have you Joe and I have Bridget. What else would I need?"

"Sure, I wish I could give ye more. Did I not hear it from my father and he from his, that we were landowners right enough before the English came."

Bridget came to the door in time to see Mam nestled into the crook of Da's arm from where she murmured, "That's as may be, but it does not do to remember those times. Anyway, what difference can it make to us now?"

Da relinquished his hold on Mam and accepted the jug of ale and bannock from Bridget. "It could make the difference to us now alright."

He took a long thirsty draft and smacked his lips noisily. "It could help us remember who we are and what we came from. 'Tis our heritage and it belongs to each of us just as Ireland belongs to us and not to the English, for all they own the land here now."

Bridget was well aware of the history for Da never tired of telling it, but she had a question. "Da, if they own the land, why do they not live on it? Why does His Lordship live in England and not here in Ireland?"

Da laughed shortly and explained. "Those are good questions. Maybe His Lordship has so much to do in England that he cannot find the time to see to his Irish lands and tenants."

Da paused a moment before adding. "The truth of it is that I do not understand their ways." He sighed then and looked across the fields before continuing, "But I do know that we Irish once owned the land and that we were cheated out of it."

"Stop it now," said Mam and pinched his cheek. "Ye will have us in tears if ye go on much longer." She patted his knee. "Drink your ale and don't be bringing the melancholy down on such a fine day. Ye will bring a storm with that long face."

Mam kissed Da's cheek coaxingly until he smiled again and took a bite of his bannock.

It was the evenings Bridget loved best at Mam and Da's. It was when Ma finally stopped fussing around and sat down, Mam and Da in their chairs and Bridget at Mam's feet. It was then as they gazed into the slow flame of the peat fire, that they told each other stories.

Bridget's Da had lots of stories although none so fine as the travelling storytellers.

No one could better the O'Maolains for the telling of a tale. The husband and wife duo loved to regale an audience with stories of Ireland as old as time itself. Da on the other hand, would tell about things that happened while he was at work in the fields with the other men.

In Bridget's opinion, the O'Maolains had stories that lifted her out of herself and made her feel grand like she was part of some great heroic warrior people.

Da might have visions of former grandeur, yet it was the stories he told beside the fire at night that made her laugh, for he had a way of imitating people that seemed to bring them right into the kitchen. He could even imitate the voices and sometimes he would rise from his chair and walk around like the person in his story. He would have Bridget and Mam falling over with laughter.

Tonight though, he stroked Mam's hair and called it her crowning glory. Looking up, he saw Bridget watching and said, "Your hair is just like your mother's, bright and plentiful." He looked from one to the other of them. "Brown it is and with streaks all through it like polished chestnuts."

Bridget smiled at this. "My hair is shining for the many brushings it receives at the Missus' house. I've to brush her hair with one hundred strokes every night before bed. She insists I do the same for my own hair although to be sure I almost fall asleep as I do it, for I am so very tired by the end of the day."

But Da was looking at Mam again. "Sometimes Eileen, when your hair catches the light," he told her, "It reminds me of sunset spreading through an orchard, so it does."

Bridget watched them a moment longer, basking in the love they so obviously held for each other. Knowing she was forgotten in that moment, she quietly rose.

Ignoring the beckoning bed in the alcove by the flickering fire, Bridget headed instead to other room where she rolled herself in a blanket, curled up on the bed and quickly fell asleep.

## Chapter Ten

Erin rescued the diary from where it had slipped down the side of the comfortable chair.

She stretched and relaxed again, trying to decide if she would go to her bed, her body made the decision to stay where it was. She slumped in obedience to the demands of her body and allowed her mind to wander where it would.

She thought about the love Bridget's parents had for each other. They seemed to be such good friends as well as lovers. She thought she would like such a relationship for herself too.

She puzzled over why it was that Bridget's mother didn't want her to marry Terry. What could she have against him?

Erin considered reading on to find out what happened next but then she found herself wanting to appreciate each aspect of the story before moving on to the next entry.

Eventually, she hauled herself out of the chair and placing the diary on the little rosewood table, took herself off to bed.

The sheets were cool so that she pulled her knees up to her chest and shivered a little until her body warmed the sheets enough for her to relax and fade into sleep.

*****

Erin became aware of the morning sounds outside the cottage. A cow lowed in the near distance. A tractor cranked into life. She stretched catlike and full out on the bed, twisting her body first one way and then the other until relaxing, she sighed contentedly.

Mykel hee-hawed outside her window and her smile faded. "Himself is looking for breakfast I suppose."

Smiling at the ease in which the colloquialism came to her lips, Erin swung her legs out of bed. Pushing her feet into slippers, she padded through the cottage and into the kitchen.

Raising the blind on the kitchen window ever so slightly, she peeped out onto the yard.

Aiden had agreed to come over and feed the animals while she was away. Erin had decided that prior to leaving for the Egan clan gathering, she would gather her courage and feed the dreaded donkey.

Today therefore, if the animals were not to starve, it was up to her to get the job done.

Hoping for a better view of the yard, Erin pressed her nose up against the glass, and looked first one way and then the other. Convinced the coast was clear at least for the moment, she made her decision.

She quickly pulled on Gam's wellies as it had been raining and the yard was muddy. Teeth gripping her bottom lip in concentration, she quietly turned the key in the door. Pulling it open an inch or two, she poked her head out.

There was no sign of Mykel. Picking up the two feed dishes she had prepared, she stepped out, closed the door quietly behind her and made ready to dash across the yard.

Two steps out and still the yard was clear of animals. She decided the donkey and pony must be around the side of the cottage. They seemed to enjoy hanging out there for entertainment purposes, as there was a good view of the lane and occasional passing traffic.

Careful to avoid the muddy puddles, Erin tip-toed at a fast rate across the yard to the barn which was mercifully open.

Placing one bowl on the floor of the barn she turned around, just in time to see Mykel trotting around the corner followed by Beauty who as usual, maintained a discreet distance.

"Damn!" muttered Erin as the donkey's head went up and he began a beeline straight for the barn. "I should have left Mykel's feed in the yard before heading to the barn."

Hopping in panic from one muddy wellie to the other, Erin almost decided to lock herself into the barn but then reasoned she'd be stuck in there all day with two bowls of animal feed and no way of escape.

She gritted her teeth. She'd have to make a run for it.

Adopting a sprinter stance and still clutching Mykel's bowl, Erin shot out of the barn. She took a circular route in the hope she would lead Mykel away from Beauty's food.

Her plan worked very well except that she forgot to put Mykel's bowl down. This created an entertaining diversion for Mykel who wanted his food but at the same time, apparently couldn't resist the opportunity for a game.

Mykel began to buck and heehaw, his teeth showing alarmingly as he pursued his prey. Erin finally realized she was still clutching the bowl of feed. In a moment of panic, she flung it into the air which resulted in a cascade of mushed oats and barley grass falling like globs of thick rain into the mud of the yard.

The donkey paused to sniff at his feed bowl which was now divested of most of its contents. He raised his head as Erin, mud flying from her wellies, raced across the yard, goal in sight, hoping to make it to the kitchen door. Mykel gave pursuit.

Breath wheezing, arms pumping, hair streaming, Erin reached the door with only seconds to spare.

So close was Mykel behind her, that Erin could almost feel his breath on her neck. She flung open the door in the nick of time and went slip-sliding into the kitchen as the mud from her wellies met with the tiled floor.

Slithering around, she managed to shut the door on Mykel and slapped the bolt at the top before turning the key, which was already lifting up and down, up and down as Mykel tried to gain entry.

Panting, Erin staggered to the kitchen window. Putting her thumb to her nose she waggled her fingers at the donkey and yelled, "You've the divil in ye so ye have!"

She laughed at herself. "Have I developed an Irish accent and I've only been here a few days?"

Mykel soon returned to the feed Erin had spilled. He licked it up with apparent relish and disregard for the mud that accompanied it.

Beauty trotted out from the barn, having finished her feed in peace for once. "Well at least I gained you a bit of time, hey Beauty!"

Mykel looked in Erin's direction. The animal pulled its lips back in what looked to Erin like a victory grin.

She frowned. "If any one thing were to put me off staying here in Ireland, it would be you, my friend!" Fed up, she stomped off to pack a weekend bag.

Raincoat, boots, and freshly washed wellies. With the necessities taking up most of the space, there was barely room for a change of clothing. Pushing the bag closed, she noticed the diary on the bedside table.

After a moment of deliberation, she placed it carefully between two layers of clothing and sat on the bag until it flattened enough to allow the zip to finish the job.

Soon Erin was in her car. It was a two-hour trip, so she looked for a gas station as she drove through Clonakilty. With the gas tank filled, Erin entered the store to pay at the cashier's desk.

She was immediately dazzled by the array of chocolate and candy that was not available back home. She dallied for several minutes before a choice of purple and gold or red and yellow wrappers before picking out one of each.

Standing in the line to pay, Erin wondered aloud, "I wonder which is better, the flake or the twirl?"

Quick as a whip, a male voice replied, "I'm not sure about the flake but I'd be happy to give ye a twirl if you'd like."

Erin's mouth opened in an unspoken "What?" Turning, she beheld a tall young Irishman with a cheeky grin that reached all the way to his green eyes. Erin's face flushed with embarrassment that quickly turned to smothered laughter, for who could take offense at such wit?

"Just passing through are ye?"

Keeping her mouth firmly closed so the words couldn't spill out, Erin thought 'Oh my gosh, cute Irish guy alert! The place is full of them.'

A giggle spluttered through her closed mouth which now opened despite her efforts to the contrary. "I'm here for a few weeks. In the village I mean."

Immediately, she reprimanded herself. 'Are you flirting with him?' She looked up. 'What's that he's saying now?'

"Well then," he smirked. "It's my good luck that ye couldn't decide between a flake and a twirl now, isn't it?"

"Er - ha ha," was all she managed. 'Get a grip woman,' she told herself sternly.

"Finn," he said and extended his hand.

"Finn? Is that a name?"

"It is so." He scratched behind his ear. "Finn, like Finn McCool. My mother had aspirations for me, I think. Or it could be the hair."

He rubbed a hand through his russet-colored hair that seemed to have a mind of its own, sticking out as it was in every direction.

Erin blinked, confused. "Sorry?"

"Y'now, Finn McCool."

Erin searched her mind for the name. A movie star perhaps, possibly with crazy red hair. She drew a blank.

He tried to help her out. "Irish mythology, so it is."

"Ah!" said Erin, her brain clicking in. "Mythology."

She recalled the many stories Gams had told her as a child. Finn McCool came through the mists of her memories. "Yes. Leader of the Fianna Warriors, right?"

"That's it," said Finn.

Erin looked behind him. "So, where are your warriors today?" she asked with a saucy smile. "Did you give them the day off?"

"Ouu!" he said, "Touché! Ye can give as good as you get."

Erin laughed, pleased with herself.

The checkout clerk called "Next please!" Erin stepped forward to pay for her gas and chocolate.

She was back at her car when a voice called out, "Hey, I don't know your name."

Pausing, she smiled before turning around, "Erin. It's Erin."

"There's a festival next weekend." He walked backwards a few steps before turning to open the door of a white van emblazoned with signage that read 'O'Brian's Electrics.'

"The Old Fair Day," said Erin remembering the event from her childhood.

"That's the one." He sprang lightly into the cab and slid the window down. "Come to Connolly's pub this weekend."

"This weekend?"

"Sure. Have ye something better to do now?"

"Oh!" She couldn't keep the disappointment out of her voice. "I'm busy actually with..." she considered her pursuit with the dairy, "uh... things."

"Well now, that's too bad, so it is." A smile lifted one side of his mouth. "No twirl then!"

"Ah!" she said. "Ah Ha ha!" Erin clamped her mouth shut. 'Sheesh! Make a sentence.'

"Sure, if it's just the weekend you're away, the fair goes on 'til Monday at midnight. If you're back, come on into Connolly's." He winked. "I'll look out for ye."

"I might do that," She managed to say. His smile was irresistible.

As she drove out of the gas station, Erin was still grinning. "Finn O'Brian is it? Well! Well!" She turned on the radio and sang along with the music.

*"Ain't no mountain hiiiiigh enough*
*And ain't no valley looooow enough*

*The fair to see a boy maybeeeee
La la la la la la la la laaaaa ..."*

As she drove to County Clare, Erin felt a great deal more confident driving on the left and handled the traffic circles with comparative ease.

About two hours later, Erin turned off the highway onto a country lane. She soon caught a glimpse of the castle as the road veered up and down between tall hedgerows and overhanging trees.

Parking her car at the side of the lane a little way before the great iron gates, she stepped out into bright sunshine and birdsong.

Roses, pink and sparkling from the recent spattering of rain, nestled in a thick green hedge that ran the length and breadth of the property. Pushing her face into the cluster of velvet loveliness, Erin closed her eyes to inhale the sweet perfume.

A faint buzz, as of bees, caught her attention. Opening her eyes, she looked about to locate the sound. It seemed to come from the castle itself and Erin stepped back for a better view.

It was a square fortress, with a few small windows on several floors but it was not as wide as castles she had seen in Dublin and England. Admittedly, she had not seen very many apart from those featured in tourism brochures.

Erin could probably walk around this entire edifice in less than two minutes. "I guess they built for smaller groups back in the day," she murmured.

Despite its lack of size, there were battlements at the top and a projecting apex. "I'll bet the views are great from up there."

Approaching the castle wall, she reached out a hand to touch the rough exterior, expecting to find it cold and unwelcoming. Surprisingly it was warm, perhaps from the sun, for it was a hot day despite the intermittent showers.

The buzzing caught her attention again. She followed the noise around the corner where she found huge doors of thick wood, strengthened with steel running sideways across the surface.

Along with the buzzing, a deep shadow spilled out from within, promising a cool retreat from the heat of the day.

Erin stepped inside and was immediately enveloped, not by the insistent buzzing of bees but instead by a cacophony of voices all vying with each other. The sound came from an opening near the back of the small foyer.

On closer inspection, steep stone steps were revealed, carved into thick walls that led up, around and out of sight.

Climbing the stairs took concentration as the light came from one small aperture part way up, while the only security was a thick rope looped by metal hooks into the castle wall itself.

At the top of the stairwell Erin came out into a great room filled with people. Clustered into small groups, they all seemed engaged in earnest conversation.

Swallowing a sudden nervous anxiety, Erin clung to the periphery of the room.

A group of young women much like herself in age opened their ranks to her. When she stepped forward, they closed about her, their faces smiling a welcome she had not expected and was most grateful to accept.

An older woman with a friendly but proprietary air made her way through the crowded room, quietly inviting everyone to "Come sit down as we're about to start."

In the general movement towards the seating area, Erin was separated from the group of young women. She sat between an older man with an Australian accent who said, "G'day, how are you?" while on her other side a young man with a Canadian accent said, "Hi. I'm Ryan. Good to be here, hey?"

Erin was too excited to do more than mumble her name. She looked about, wondering what she might learn here today.

The woman who had called the meeting to order, was off to the side talking to an elderly man with gray hair that fell in soft waves down to his collar. He now stepped front and center and smiled around at the group before speaking.

"So many," he paused as he nodded his head and looked about at his audience. "So very many Egans, and all of you come together here from right across the world. I hope you enjoy each other's company with as much joy as it gives me to welcome you all."

There was a murmur of appreciation from the group, for which he waited a moment or two before continuing on. "My name is Colm MacEgan and I've been elected your Taoiseach or Clan Chief for my sins."

A polite smattering of laughter greeted his attempt at humility but was quickly interrupted as he said, "Now we have a full weekend. It's off we'll be going to various sites around that are peculiar to the Egans.

Before that now, we'll meet here each morning for presentations on the various aspects. Today, it's a brief history we have on the Egan Clan, beginning with the Annals of The Four Masters going forward and back from there."

At this point, his female companion began distributing programs at the end of each line of chairs so that every person took one and passed the pile onto the next.

In the buzz of conversation that now rose, Erin thought excitedly, "Forward and back from the Annals of The Four Masters. It sounds pretty spectacular whatever it is. This is going to be interesting."

With the program in her hand giving her something to read so that she didn't feel quite so alone, Erin decided this was not so very different from a college class. Beginning to feel at home now, she relaxed and prepared to enjoy the experience.

The day went by quickly with historical chart presentations and genealogy that stretched back to 800 A.D. with strange names that seemed to revolve around the word fire.

There was 'Little Fire', 'Bright Fire' and 'Daughter of Fire'. Erin quite liked that one and wondered if she could adopt it as her personal avatar but then recalled that Aiden's name meant Fiery One in old Gaelic Irish. 'Hmm!' she thought. 'Two fiery people.' No wonder they locked horns.

Erin soaked in the information, suddenly feeling very intrigued by her Irish roots and more importantly, how they might connect to Bridget.

*****

Erin was booked into the Oisin Lodge Bed & Breakfast, a pretty two-storey home painted white with red trim as were many of the older style Irish homes.

The proprietor was a cheerful woman who showed Erin to her room where a tea tray was already set out. There was a kettle of water along with scones, jam, and a little jar of thick Irish cream.

Tired after such an exciting day, Erin showered and changed into pyjamas. She settled into bed with her tray of tea and scones and picked up the remote.

Flipping through the six available channels, she couldn't find anything that appealed to her. "Just like home," she said aloud. "Only there it's hundreds of channels and most of them not worth watching."

With a sigh, she pressed the button to turn off the television and pulled the diary onto her lap.

## Chapter Eleven

Yesterday, I arrived home to find that the O'Maolains had arrived at the village only hours before myself. The O'Maolains were said to be the very best of all the travelling storytellers. There was an air of expectation in the village for all of us looked forward to the evening's entertainment.

"Mam, hurry!" Bridget called to her mother and performed a little jig in her excitement.

"I am ready," said Ma as she came out of the cottage wearing a clean apron. She looked her daughter over. "Put on a clean apron Bridget and come over as soon as ye can."

Bridget looked down at her own apron which had become soiled while she had busied herself with chores about the place. "Go ahead Mam. I'll catch up."

As Mam walked along the lane, Bridget lifted the water bucket and ran into the cottage, untying the ribbons of her apron with her free hand.

She left the bucket in its place near the door and threw the soiled apron into a basket where the laundry was kept.

Pulling a clean apron from the dresser she ran out, tying it behind her as she went. Although Erin was not one for worrying over her looks, as she smoothed her hair back from her face, she hoped she looked pretty.

There was no mirror in the cottage to make sure of this and she expected to see Terry that evening with others from nearby villages.

Niamh came from a nearby cottage. "We missed ye last week Bridget," she said by way of greeting.

"The Missus was ill. I am not allowed home when that happens for, she needs me beside her to read the news."

"Sure, and is there not another who could read in your place for one afternoon a week?"

"If the Missus needs our Bridget, that is what she will have." Mam looked over at her daughter. "Ye do not mind Bridget?"

"No but sure, I would rather be home here with ye here," said Bridget.

Mam beamed at her. "Of course, ye would my pet and we would rather have the seeing of ye. But duty is duty and glad we are that ye can offer it."

"Sure, and the coin comes in handy too," laughed Niamh.

Mam shrugged as the point could not be argued. They walked on, between the two lines of cottages.

Their clean white aprons made a pretty picture against long dark skirts, below which showed an occasional inch of red petticoat. The three O'Brien sisters joined them as they walked.

The topic of conversation were the Seanchaí, or storytellers. Always popular for the stories they freely imparted, they would spend several nights in the village before continuing on their way.

"I never tire of the old stories," said Diedre O'Brien. "Sure, tis like hearing tell of good friends."

"Truth be known, I am ready for the tellin' of a new story or two," countered Theresa.

"Do ye tire of the stories ye already heard?" enquired Diedre.

"I like them fine. 'Tis a good thing to have them fresh too. It gives me something new to think about in the weeks that follow their leaving."

"True it is indeed," agreed Diedre.

Not to be left out, Molly added, "I wish they could live among us for then we could hear the stories every night."

"Ye would soon tire of them so," said the ever-practical Theresa. "Sure, they would have no stories to tell if they stayed in one place. Is it not how they gets their tall tales, from hearing them as they travel."

"I am sure you are right but still, t'would be pleasant to have the telling of tales in my own cottage of an evening."

Bridget and Mam looked sideways at each other and winked, knowing they had the joy of listening to their own resident storyteller in Da.

Niamh said, "The men will have been at the poitín while they're waiting for the storytelling to begin."

"Well now," said Theresa. "I do not mind a drop of uisce beatha myself, on a night like this."

"Ah 'tis the water of life or so my husband calls it," said Molly.

Mam laughed. "Men have their fancy names for it. But sure, 'tis whisky or poitín just the same."

Theresa ended the conversation with, "'Tis the morning after, they will be feeling the póit and holding their heads with the ache of it, the whole lot of them."

The women laughed in good-natured banter for the bright evening ahead of them.

At the cottage where the O'Maolains were to stay for a night or two, the men of the village were gathered outside to enjoy a pipe and a bit of the hard stuff under the stars.

Most of them wore shirts and jackets with knee breeches and clogs below that. One or two wore a stovepipe hat.

Bridget searched the faces until she saw Terry's. She waited until his eyes met her own in answering welcome. It would not do for them to sit together openly until Bridget's parents had agreed to the match. For the present, they had to content themselves with shy smiles and glances.

Pipes were stuffed with tobacco so that the air was redolent with it. There was snuff to hand as well for those who wanted a pinch.

Anecdotes were passed back and forth, mostly about the work and the day that had been. There was laughter but it was controlled and decorous since the evening was still young.

Liam Reilly leaned against the wall of the cottage. With his precious uilleann pipes. Sometimes he travelled with the O'Maolains and was just as welcome as the O'Maolains themselves for the music he provided on such occasions.

This evening, Reilly was barely able to get a mouthful of the plate of food that had been pushed into his hands before he was being urged to start the music.

An easy-going man and quick to please, he positioned the pipe bellows under his arm and began pumping rhythmically with his elbow, followed by a squeal from the pipes as life was breathed into them.

He passed his fingers playfully over the chanter and launched into a reel. The toes of his audience began tapping and bodies moved in place until one man was urged to, "Give us a bit of a step now would ye?"

Obliging, the man stepped his way forward, feet clicking rhythmically in time to the music while the small crowd encouraged him with cries of "Hip! Hip!" and others clapped.

Adding further substance to the entertainment, the women swayed with the rhythm of the music so that an inch or two of their red petticoats showed beneath their skirts. The men gave yelps of encouragement to the man who danced in the center of the circle for them all.

O'Reilly played reel after reel until finally, as if by common consent between him and his pipes, they sighed to a close.

Da called for Bridget to, "Give us a song now."

Bridget protested but she was gently urged into the center of the group. Resigned to her happy task, she waited as her father produced his fiddle and began to play a sentimental air.

Bridget's face took on a wistful expression as she sang about young love. Her voice was pretty, but it was the depth of emotion she had, that could move people to tears.

As the song came to an end with the lovers dying in each other's arms, a collective sigh circled the group.

Bridget allowed her downcast eyes to flutter in Terry's direction. This action quickly found its reward in the smile of delight that lit the face of the young man she loved.

As if called by an unseen voice, people began to collect inside the cottage. Those that couldn't squeeze into the small space, stood at the doorway or as close as they could get.

Catherine O'Maolain the storyteller, was referred to as Kate by her adoring husband. Together they were called Seanchaí as a mark of respect.

The O'Maolains were by the nature of their calling a walking library, a repository of folk wisdom, fairy lore and mythology.

Their stories were often wickedly entertaining and subversive of authority. Whether it was against priests or lords it was all the same to them, although to be sure they were ever careful when they spoke of the fairy kind, referring to them always as 'the good folk'.

With her hair grown long and gray down her back and his coat which had seen better days, their combined bearing was nevertheless that of a benign elder and learned gentlewoman.

Yet for all of it, they had a well-tuned and earthy sense of humor. The crowd expected much hilarity and good craic for the night that was in it.

As usual, the Seanchaí did not disappoint. With a fine sense of rhythm, they waited 'til there was quiet, in which only a glowing turf log falling in upon another, could be heard.

Leaning back on her stool, Kate began by pushing away her half empty cup. She cast her eyes slowly around the room until every man, woman and child felt drawn into the excitement, the drama of the moment.

With one hand on her hip and the other resting on her knee, Kate took her cue and began. "C'mere till I tell ye."

In the flickering shadows of the little cabin, the entire audience leaned towards her as one.

"In Ireland long ago, a king's son shot a raven." The company sighed and settled back a little. They knew the story well, as if it were a much beloved bedtime story and they, the contented children hearing it.

"Now this prince, he looked at the raven and told himself never saw anything whiter than the snow, or blacker than the raven's skull, or redder than its share of blood, that was a'pouring out."

"Ah!" The audience shifted in their chairs or on their feet as they settled into the comforting rhythm of the tale.

"Sure, Himself was after looking for a bride at that very moment in time, and impressed he was by the signs he was seeing."

Heads nodded for they were not averse to looking for signs themselves.

"Now!" said Kate, luring her audience. "What do ye think, but he puts himself under the geas."

The company sighed for they knew this particular geas or obligation.

"Now the prince could not eat two meals at one table or sleep two nights in one house, until he should find a woman whose hair was black as the raven's head, and her skin white as the snow, and her two cheeks red as blood."

Every person in the room knew the result of this vow was sure to mean a long journey, for as they were all well aware, a woman with such definitive coloring could not be easily found.

"Sure," Kate rocked slightly on her stool to produce a good rhythm for her words. "Was it not the truth that there was no woman in the world like it but one woman only, and she away there in the eastern world."

Bridget and Terry took advantage of the distraction to sneak a glance across the room at each other.

Around them, villagers shook their heads at each other in muted wonder at the very idea of a journey that might take them so far. For not a man or a woman in that small space had been much beyond their own village and the next.

"There was nothing for it, but the youth must journey toward the eastern world." Here, Kate paused for dramatic effect.

O'Maolian, her partner storyteller, leaned toward his audience and asked, "Now what do ye think happened not long after he started off?"

Most shook their heads but for one who called out, "He met a short green man." Laughter greeted the comment, yet they all looked toward the storytellers for confirmation of something they already knew to be true.

"He did indeed meet a short green man." O'Maolain picked up a pipe which he now sucked on while he waited for responses.

"He needed the company, so." said one.

"Sure, 'tis better to travel with a fellow rather than without." said another.

O'Maolain nodded, teeth firmly clamped around the stem of the pipe. It was not long before his dalliance was rewarded.

A boy in the crowd called out, "Tell of the funeral!"

There was much nodding and urging in favor of the funeral.

At last, the storyteller took the pipe from his mouth but kept it near to his face as if about to place it back between his teeth.

He continued, "Now, the prince started his journey with twenty English pounds in his purse."

There was a quick outburst of comments among the listeners for such a sum was princely indeed.

All the men and women, girls and boys in the room dreamed for a long moment of how they might spend such a princely sum.

O'Maolain was in no hurry and again sucked on the pipe until the room quieted somewhat. Thereupon, he continued the tale in a low, slow voice so that each was shushing the other and straining to hear.

"Himself had hardly begun the long walk to the east. In fact, he had not three steps walked, when he came upon a funeral."

"Ah there 'tis, the funeral," said one of the listeners and was immediately shushed roundly by his neighbors.

O'Maolain raised his voice a notch. "Now the custom was at the time, that a man could not be buried if he owed money."

"Tch! Tch!" commented Bridget's Da.

"Sure, 'tis a terrible thing is debt," said another.

Again, there were several admonishing shushes heard in the little space.

The storyteller continued, "Well of course, the prince was Irish and not above helping his fellow man and that is exactly what he did.

"And so it was that each time he placed a five-pound note upon the coffin in payment of the man's debt so he could be buried, wouldn't you know it, but another man came along and lay another writ down upon the very same coffin.

"Sure, it was not long before he was fully divested of all the English pounds he had in his pocket."

The Seanchaí puffed on his pipe again.

His listeners took full advantage of the pause to discuss the generosity of such a man. The merits of the deed were fully and openly discussed until the noise inside the cottage proved deafening as each strove to be heard over the other.

At last, they remembered they had storytellers in their midst and after many more 'Sushes!' and 'Quiet Now!' admonishments, they finally settled down to hear the rest of the tale.

O'Maolain continued, "Now, it was not long after this that a short green man appeared. That man offered his services as such, in return for the kissing of the prince's wife before the prince himself should have the kissing of her."

The storyteller shifted a little on his stool. Objections ran from mouth to mouth around the room as all discussed whether such a boon could or should be asked in return for companionship, even if it was to a far-away place as the eastern world.

Again, the teller of tales waited while pipe-smoking men adjusted the now empty pipes between their teeth and either nodded in agreement or shook their heads like men who had done a great deal of travelling themselves.

And so between them, the Senchaí led their willing audience to follow the tale as it wound its way across the island of Ireland.

The prince collected a variety of followers who would in time prove their worth. They ranged in usefulness from a man who could break stones with the side of one thigh to a man who must walk with one foot on his shoulder, lest his innate swiftness spirit him away too quickly.

As each of these compatriots were collected, the storytellers provided a variety of voice from strident to soft. They did this so the change in tone would indicate to the company, which of the travelers was speaking.

As the prince pitted his wits against the many challenges placed in his way and each of his companions added their unique strengths and talents to aid his quest, the senchaí added their own subversive slant of authority, to the delight of the audience, against the interference of a parish priest and a lord who each tried in vain to stop the prince from reaching his goal.

There was laughter and tension as the story took a modern slant at the world in which they lived.

"Now here's the thing," began Kate as she took over the story and readied her voice for a booming increase of tempo and tone. "When they reached the eastern world, Herself was found to be under an enchantment!"

Bridget, along with other young women in the hut, sighed to hear of it. This was as much in pity for the state of the girl in question as it was for her not knowing that her true love was come.

She looked at Terry under her lashes. He with the others, like moths gathered about a candle, gazed steadfastly at Kate, who continued the tale.

"It was discovered that the woman the prince was pining for, did not particularly want to be anybody's wife. To be sure, she would much prefer to decorate the spikes which adorned her castle with the prince's head."

Kate paused here and allowed a wry smile to play about her mouth.

There was much guffawing among the men in the room at the rebellious notion of the woman the prince desired. Their women merely smiled and looked to Kate, nodding quietly as if in feminine conspiracy.

"Now!" exclaimed Kate in a loud voice. "To this end she set the King of Poison on the prince."

The room gasped at this turn of events that was completely expected yet which always surprised them.

They gasped yet again as the short green man solved the dilemma by striking the head off the king of poison as he was sleeping.

All knew the story was a long way from over and settled themselves more comfortably as the jug of poitín was passed about the room for each to take a sip. Pipes were lit anew and soon they could hardly see each other for the smoke that was in the room.

"Now the short green man stepped forward for his prize and sure, he ignored the expression on the face of the prince as he took the bride into a dark cave for the first kiss as he had been promised."

Bridget and the young women turned their heads squeamishly as Kate, the Senchaí told of the short green man setting upon the woman to remove snakes from her, that had all the time prevented her from responding as she should to the young prince.

With a show relief, the women old and young sighed as the two Senchaí between them reached the close of the story.

O'Maolain took over for the finale. "So it was that the woman was brought before the prince. Rid now of the only impediment to their happiness, they spent a happy life one with another."

Everyone blinked and clapped at the expected ending. O'Maolain paused now for three reasons.

The first was to allow the story to settle, the second was to allow the crowd to absorb the happiness of the pair. The third was that the story was not yet quite over. He knew it and they knew it.

He picked up his fresh topped up drink and took a good swig, wiping his whiskers as before and gazing into the fire as if there was nothing more to be said.

The room was quiet for a long moment and then, "But what of the short green man?" asked one.

A murmur ran through the gathering which O'Maolain allowed for another little while before he stirred himself.

Clearing his throat for effect he sighed as if he were doing everyone a favor by continuing the story.

"Well now, the short green man drew himself up to his full height, which in fact was not so very much."

Some laughed briefly but most waited with bated breath for the beginning of the end of the story.

Some of them even mouthed it silently as O'Maolain spoke the words, for hadn't they known the story all their lives.

"The man said to the prince, 'you can be with your wife now for I am the man who was in the coffin that day and these companions were sent to ye to be your loyal servants on this long and arduous journey.'"

O'Maolain looked about. He held the gaze of every man, woman and child before saying the words of the grand finish.

"And with that, the short green man took all the companions away with him and they were not seen again from that day to this. Now as for the prince and his lady, didn't they live a good and happy life together."

He sat back, his story done. Kate and O'Maolain nodded at each other for a job well executed.

A sigh swept through the company like a wave from the sea, along with claps of joy and smiles of contentment.

Bursting into excited discussion on the merits of the story and the many talents of the O'Maolains for the telling of it, they called for another story and then another after that.

The O'Maolains to their credit, gave them all they had and for as long as the drink kept coming.

Bridget stepped outside into the clear and starry night. Terry quickly stepped out to join her.

Under cover of the shadows, hands entwined one with the others. Their faces smiled innocently at the moon until a moment when people seemed engrossed in the goodnights of leaving.

Taking advantage of the cover of darkness and not being noticed, Terry's hand lifted to Bridget's face. Cupping her chin, he gently pressed his lips to hers so that Bridget tingled all the way down to her toes.

"Bridget," her mother called, peering into the shadows. "Where is the girl?"

Bridget pulled reluctantly away from Terry's kiss. As she did, she saw the glint in his eyes as he looked down into hers with a proprietary air that claimed her as his own.

Reeling from the kiss and dizzy with happiness, Bridget joined her parents near the light that emanated still from the door of the cottage.

"There ye are Bridget," said her mother. Bridget could tell by the way the breath settled in her mother's chest that she was not innocent of the exchange between the two young people.

Contented and cozy with the hearing of tales and the drinking of poitín, the company dispersed to their own cottages until all of the laughter and chatter disappeared bit by bit under the cover of their little thatched homes.

As Bridget walked home arm in arm with her parents, she hoped with all her heart that she and Terry might also find happiness like the maiden in the story.

*****

Erin sighed. Bridget's life seemed idyllic. She could not imagine a more perfect family and wished she could find a love like Bridget had for Terry or indeed as she had already acknowledged, the love that Bridget's Mam and Da had for each other.

She thought of her busy life back home and wondered what it would be like to live in a small village such as Bridget's where storytellers came to stay, and the villagers knew each other so well.

If the village where Gams had spent her life were half as nice as Bridget's, then it was no wonder she had stayed in Ireland for all of her eighty years and a bit.

'If only Mykel weren't in residence,' she thought. 'I might be persuaded to stay myself.' But then she pulled herself together because after all, she had a job to go back to, didn't she?

With a stern expression on her face, she firmly placed the diary on the bedside table and settled down to sleep.

## Chapter Twelve

The following morning, Erin descended the narrow, thick-carpeted staircase of the B&B and followed the aroma of coffee.

A little shy about eating breakfast on her own, she peered through the stained-glass window of the dining room door. Seeing no-one inside the room, she pushed open the door and went in.

Two large group tables dominated the center of the room with evidence of diners come and gone. Smaller tables dotted the outskirts of the room.

Erin seated herself at the table situated in the bay window and admired the room while she waited for service.

The walls were papered in cream-colored regency stripes and covered with framed prints of what appeared to be a mixture of family portraits and local scenery.

Sanderson linen drapes hung at the windows, gracefully pulled to the sides with cream-colored cords. The tables were beautifully set with snowy white cloths and blue patterned dishes.

Erin ordered sausage and egg with toast and coffee. 'I need the protein anyway,' she told herself.

After breakfast, Erin's day was busy from the moment she set foot in the castle. Indeed, the entire weekend was filled with lectures and discussion.

She met so many interesting people that she became a social butterfly, never settling on a group but flitting from one to the next, trying to glean as much information about Egans and their shared heritage as she could.

*****

It was on the last afternoon when she finally understood the history of the Egan Clan, when the group drove to a site on the banks of the River Shannon.

Those who arrived first waited by a farm gate. Some tapped impatient feet as car doors slammed, with stragglers hurrying to gather before the group proceeded across the fields.

The freshness of the afternoon air after a late downpour reminded Erin of walking as a child, with Gams along the shores of the Wild Atlantic Coast.

"Breathe in," Gams had instructed. "In through your nose."

Erin had taken an exaggerated breath. "And out through your mouth," continued Gams.

Expelling the air like a dragon trying to set the beach on fire, Erin had made a game of it.

*152*

Gams had been a great believer in daily exercise and fresh air, with a good helping of cod liver oil every Friday night. Erin's mouth puckered at the memory of the foul-tasting stuff.

Looking up from her thoughts, she hurried to catch up with the others who were already close to the destination.

Erin joined the large crowd of Egans gathered in the center of a tall structure. She felt small inside the huge space.

Plants and trees had grown throughout the eight-hundred-year-old edifice. With only three walls now and no roof, it was easy to see all the way up. She realized from the placement of the window-like apertures that there must have been several floors.

As Colm MacEgan began to speak, Erin listened with an eagerness that as she learned more about her Egan heritage, became more than mere curiosity.

"This was a place of learning founded in the 6th century, a university if you will. The Egans held a kind of school in this building that was probably based on the Bardic system of learning. Here in this building, they taught law and history."

Colm paused for a moment to allow his words to hold the moment.

Egans looked about from the stone walls to the open sky to the trees and bushes growing in the space. They imagined the droning of teachers with the sun shining through the high apertures onto the heads of attentive students at their learning.

Colm waited until eyes focused back on him, indicating they were ready to hear more.

"Later, as Christianity spread to Ireland those who taught the old ways either became travelling teachers known as druids or they stayed on here as monks. It is possible that some spent their days copying already ancient manuscripts onto scrolls made from vellum."

"Vellum?" asked one member of the party. "Is that made from animal skin?"

"It is indeed," agreed Colm. "And lovingly decorated with the most beautiful artwork, similar to what you may have seen in the ancient manuscripts kept in Dublin, the Book of Kells and the like."

Their guide allowed the silence again, for it was in such moments that impressions might be made, and the memory of the place have a chance to settle into their hearts.

After a while Colm continued, "This is where the Egans were ousted during the time of Cromwell."

"To hell or Connaught," said one in the crowd.

"That's correct. Cromwell was determined to force the Irish landowners out. He said he'd drive them to hell or Connaught."

"Why Connaught?" asked another.

"It's rocky ground. Not as rich and fertile as here in County Offaly."

"That's to the west of Ireland?"

"It is, yes."

"Still, I've heard it's lovely there, good soil and green too."

"Sure, but when you get onto the moors on the way to Ballina, you'll see the difference and how the stones dot the whole landscape."

"I'll be sure to go that way." Several in the group agreed and nodded their heads. It was on their agendas now to follow the migration of their ancestors to Connaught.

"There were villages and hamlets all around this castle," said Colm, "And all filled with Egans. Those that survived the terror of those days, took to the roads, many of them indeed heading to Connaught."

Erin was quiet as she reflected on the stories Gams had told her. It must surely mean her own ancestors were driven out of this place by Cromwell.

She imagined the Egans running, driven out by the roundheads as Cromwell and his army were called, a name derived from the round helmets they wore. She could almost hear the screams of the Egans and the clash of bloody swords in this very room where she now stood.

Squinting in the sunlight as she looked up, she had a feeling as if she were being gifted with a connection to the distant past, a weight of knowledge that she could not deny.

The group were quiet as they trailed back to their cars.

Colm passed by just as Erin was about to step into her car. On a whim she asked him, "Connaught? Is that where Castlebar is?"

"Yes, that's right," he said. "D'you have relatives there?"

"Maybe," she said and climbed into her car.

## Chapter Thirteen

Much too early on Monday morning, Erin woke in the guest room of Gam's cottage to the sound of a hammer being applied determinedly and very close by.

She had become accustomed to the rural setting of the cottage where the nights were silent and early morning traffic noise was now replaced by cocks crowing, and sheep baaing in the distance, as well as the odd cows lowing as they were driven to pasture along the lane that ran beside the cottage.

All of these rural sounds she had embraced and enjoyed. However, the relentless hammering caused her to cover her head with a pillow and shuck the duvet up around her ears in a futile attempt to shut out the noise.

It was no use. Erin opened one eye and gazed sleepily at a sunbeam that stretched across her bedroom through a gap in the curtains.

The hammering stopped as suddenly as it started. After wavering a moment, her eyelid closed and gentle snoring resumed.

Moments later the same eye popped open again at the sound of a loud cracking noise. It sounded like something big being forced apart from something even bigger.

"What the heck?" she mumbled, rolling over.

"Get out of it!" A voice deep and growly came from somewhere above her.

"Aiden?' She flopped onto her back.

The sound of wrenching and then, "Ah! Got you!" A muffled thud as something hit the ground. She raised her head off the pillow with the unkind thought, 'If that was Aiden falling off the roof, I could probably get back to sleep.'

Aiden began to whistle a tuneless melody to accompany the hammering which now began in earnest.

Erin's head dropped back onto the pillow as she groaned in defeat. With a sigh, she sat up and swung her legs over the side of the bed.

Pulling on jeans and a lavender colored t-shirt, she tied her hair into a loose topknot. "I have to give that man a piece of my mind." She mumbled, staggering a little as she stepped away from the bed, still tired after arriving home late from the clan gathering. "Tea first I think."

Stumbling into the kitchen, she sagged against the counter as she waited for the kettle to boil.

Sipping from her mug, Erin pushed open the front door and stomped around the side of the cottage.

"Hey!" She yelled not so politely from the foot of the ladder.

Aiden stopped whistling. He looked down and nodded at the tea. "Is that for me?"

"What?" She held the tea against her chest protectively.

"I'll come down." He placed his hammer carefully on top of the wall and climbed down the ladder, giving Erin a close-up view of his rear end and muscular back.

Despite herself, Erin's face began to color. 'Where did that thought come from?' She frowned a little to compensate.

Aiden turned to face her. "This is very nice of you."

His lips were full and firm. 'Stop it,' she reprimanded herself.

Tearing her eyes away, she glanced down. 'Big hands.' Now she really did blush. 'Pull yourself together!' she told herself sternly.

In her distraction, she was unresistant as Aiden took the mug of tea from her and said, "Is this what you do to all your neighbors?"

"Eh?"

"Ply them with tea?"

Erin coughed and recovered herself. "Only those who wake me up by hammering just after dawn".

It was Aiden's turn to blush "I'm sorry. I just presumed you'd be awake. Actually, to be truthful I never gave it a thought."

'Why am I not surprised!' she told herself.

"Maggie asked me ages ago to fix the slates on the roof."

"Oh!"

"We keep early hours here in the country."

"Of course you do," Her voice was steady again.

Aiden took a gulp of the tea and grimaced. "Needs stirring." He broke a twig off a nearby alder and stirred the tea.

A truck could be heard negotiating its way in low gear along the lane. They both looked toward the sound.

"Here come my supplies," explained Aiden. "I'm building an extension on the back of my place."

"You build things? I didn't know that."

He laughed then, "Most farmers around here do their own building. I enjoy it." He drained his mug and handed it back to her, "Thanks for the tea."

Aiden strode off to meet the truck, on which the back-up beep could be heard as it reversed slowly in the near distance.

Erin watched him go, guilt tugging at her earlier annoyance of him waking her and the unexpected information that he was following the wishes of a deceased woman by fixing her roof.

And then there was her startling reaction to his physical presence. 'Anyway,' she told herself. 'It wouldn't do to get too close to Aiden.' If their childhood friendship was anything to go by, they'd never stop arguing.

Erin sipped at the mug before realizing it was empty.

The pony neighed. Curious, Erin walked back to the front of the cottage and on around the side to find Beauty looking over the gate. She snorted when she saw Erin.

"You're so beautiful," Erin fondled the pony's neck. It's nice to see you without his lordship around. At that moment, his lordship trotted around the corner. Beauty vacated her position at the gate and moved off to the side, giving Mykel pride of place.

"Tch! Tch!" muttered Erin shaking her head in a gesture of solidarity with Beauty. "You have to learn to handle this guy." Mykel jerked his head up and down with a loud hee-haw. Erin took a step back. "Me too, I guess."

*****

That afternoon, Erin parked her car in town and headed into the street festival.

Colorful flags hung all throughout the small town and across the square. Competing musicians strolled about with instruments under their arm or across their backs.

Children so small, their violin cases were almost as big as themselves, trotted proudly after older siblings. Their wide eyes and bright smiles clearly showed how glad they were to be included in the musical events taking place outside pubs and stores around the center of the town.

The aroma of curried fries and burgers competed with that of candyfloss and fried donuts.

Erin paused for a moment to inhale deeply. "Mmm!" She wanted to try all of it. 'I'll wait for Maeve,' she told herself.

As she approached Maeve's store, Erin could see women trying to gather a straggling mix of children in and around the doorway, while from the pub next door men briefly abandoned their beer to bring out stools for the players.

The young musicians bent their ears to the individual instruments which they self-consciously tuned as they prepared to play.

Parents stepped back and began chatting with their neighbors, trying to look relaxed and pretend they weren't proud of their offspring.

A small group of official looking people stood to one side, clipboards in hand. 'Probably the competition judges,' thought Erin.

A young woman unfolded a stand and pinned her music onto it with the aid of a clothes peg. Picking up her baton, she rapped on the stand three times. Harp, accordion, flutes and bodhran stalled.

The caterwauling scraping of violins came to a raggedy halt. Earnest young faces turned towards their conductor who spoke to them quietly and then raised her arms, eyes wide as if to encompass the entire group.

Then one, two, three and with a downward sweep of the hand, she led them in a lovely Irish melody, sweet and soothing and in direct contrast with the various jigs and fiddle music pouring out from other venues.

A smiling Maeve looked on from the edge of the group. As Erin approached, she waved and walked over to join her.

"Aren't they precious?" said Maeve. "I just love this festival. I've candy for them all when they're done."

"That's nice of you, Maeve."

"Ah sure, it's the least I can do for them bringing all these people to my shop." Maeve winked and could not disguise a mischievous smile. "They'll all stream inside after the kids, and most will stay and buy a little something. It will be fast and furious but it all helps pay the bills, so it does."

As the children finished, they waited with sunshine faces as the judges made notes on their performance.

"Wait for me, will ye?" Maeve urged as she left Erin's side to disappear briefly inside her store. Moments later she returned to the doorway with a tray of candy which the children eyed with full and undisguised avarice.

As soon as the judges moved on down the street toward the next group of young hopeful musicians, the children streamed around Maeve who backed strategically into her store.

The children attached themselves to her like magnets, hands reaching ready to dip into the tray to acquire the promised candy.

Parents and onlookers followed the children into the store. After several moments, the children emerged clutching sticky sweets, their excited chatter filling the air and merging with the lively jig coming from the next group of children along the way.

Unwilling to leave the festive atmosphere for the confines of Maeve's store, Erin waited on the pavement. She watched through the window as Maeve efficiently handled sales and enquiries before she turned to enjoy the crowded street scene.

A small line waited outside a cafe offering fries with curry gravy. Now that she had located the source of the scrumptious aroma, Erin's stomach grumbled that it was time to eat.

Fortunately, it wasn't long before Maeve came out of the store after the last of the customers. "Smells good doesn't it?" she said, following Erin's line of sight.

Locking the door of her shop, she linked arms with Erin and they strolled down the street to join the lineup at Raphael's.

They sat on a bench in the square with containers of curried chips hot and fragrant.

Erin admired the statue of a woman and her child and wondered if it had been erected to commemorate the Irish famine as were many such statues around the country.

Maeve laughed when Erin voiced this. "No indeed. It's to slow the traffic. Can't you see her hand outstretched as if to say, 'slow down you lot you're going too feckin' fast round here."

Just as they finished the last of their food, a gaggle of teenage girls walked by. One of them asked in the cheeky way of teenagers. "So, how are ye today?"

Maeve was quick to answer, "Just great and thank you for asking. How are ye yourself?"

The girls answered in a chorus of responses then sailed on like a collection of colorful flotillas until they came up in a clump outside the music shop. There they chattered and giggled together, pointing at the posters on display in the window.

The car park near the square was full of caravans. Traveler folk stood about or sold their wares behind brightly decorated tables set up along the middle of the street.

The bikers were out in force too. In such a tiny town square with hardly any room for parking cars, twenty or so motorcycles roared down the road in a seemingly unending line.

"You'll always find bikers at the fairs, a favorite destination for them," explained Maeve raising her voice to be heard above the noise. "Especially when the sun is shining and there's good craic to be had."

They watched as the bikers parked their machines, many of them waiting in line for hot curried chips where they chatted good-naturedly and slapped each other on the back.

Maeve pointed to a store on the corner. "Cassidy's has the most delicious ice-cream. Homemade. D'you want to try it?"

"Yum!" agreed Erin, "Let's do it!"

As they waited for ice-cream, they found themselves behind another group of motorcyclists. Erin wondered at the hardy bikers waiting so calmly in the lineup, before realising she was stereotyping.

Two bikers walked by with soft-whip cones. Maeve leaned in and whispered "Sure, we're all softies when it comes to ice-cream."

Erin laughed and pointed across the square where one of the bikers was showing off, performing a wheelie in the middle of the road while his partner raised her ice cream cone to cheer him on.

At the counter, Erin was mesmerized by the myriad flavors on offer. She finally decided on a scoop of chocolate chip vanilla with a Cadbury's flake bar pushed into the center.

Licking ice-cream as they walked along the street, they were obliged to pause a moment to fasten their jackets against a sudden downpour of rain. No one bothered to take cover from the rain or the sudden cool air that came with it.

Erin reflected that the big advantage of eating ice-cream in Ireland was there wasn't much chance of it dripping in the sweltering heat. For the most part it was never too hot, and most people carried jackets or windbreakers to be on the safe side in case there was weather, which there invariably was.

Unafraid of the rain or the bikers and their noisy machines, volunteers walked up and down threading through the crowd, holding out large buckets into which people dropped money that was collected for local charities.

For such a small town, there was a lot going on. A group of teenagers in a car, wound their windows down and drove slowly through the bikers yelling happy insults to which the bikers jeered good-naturedly, raising their own double-topped ice-creams in response.

Maeve walked the feet off Erin, up and down the hills of the town where every street boasted at least three pubs, several bakeries and gorgeous stores filled with fashion items along with traditional Irish wear and jewelry.

Erin stopped to admire a fashionable torc necklace based on the ancient Celtic style. She couldn't bring herself to move from the shop window.

"Come on. Let's try it on or you'll never be satisfied." Maeve dragged her into the store where she prevailed on the assistant to let Erin try it on for size.

"It's lighter than I thought it would be." Erin commented.

"Well sure, the stones are not real. If they were, they'd not be letting us try it so easily, now would they?" Maeve said reasonably.

Erin turned this way and that, imagining herself as an ancient Celt. She admired the raised silver threads that looked like vines with tiny aquamarine stones positioned as flowers to catch the light. "Such an unusual design."

"Sure, torcs have been found in bogs all over the country." Maeve adjusted the torc to sit around Erin's neck with the opening at the front instead of at the back where Erin had positioned it.

"The original torcs were made from gold or sometimes tin studded with coral and silver. Most that you see in stores now are more often made of silver like this one."

Maeve paused and eyed her new friend. "Well, are you going to do without it or leave it on?"

Impulsively, Erin said, "I'm leaving it on." She turned to the store assistant. "How much is it?"

When she was told the price, Erin's eyes widened. She chewed her lips for a moment but then she looked back in the mirror and knew there was no going back. She pulled out her wallet and handed over a credit card.

Maeve laughed. "I could see ye were going to buy it no matter the price, for ye were in love the moment ye saw it in the window there."

"I think you're right."

"I know I am."

Erin couldn't resist another look in the mirror. She colored suddenly in embarrassment as a thought occurred to her.

"What?" demanded Maeve.

"Well ... I almost forgot ..." Erin paused.

"You're blushing." Maeve cocked her head to one side as she considered Erin. "Ah! There's a man in the picture! Is it that Aiden you were telling me about, the one with the temper?"

"No," Erin giggled nervously, "er ... it's another one."

"Sure, and here ye are, only a couple of weeks and grabbing all the available men for yourself! Greedy thing you are!" Maeve laughed. "So, come on. Who is this 'other one' and when will I meet him?"

"Tonight, I guess. He said he'd be at Connolly's pub. Will you come with me Maeve?"

"Probably. I can't let you go wandering about the town picking up all the men without supervision, now can I?"

"I'm not picking up men!" Erin was taken aback by her friend's words but Maeve waved her protests away.

"I'm just playing with ye. Who is it anyway? I probably know him."

"Finn O'Brian."

Maeve paused and then nodded her head slowly. "Well, he's a good looking one all right with a mouth to match and I'm not referring to the shape of it."

Erin frowned as she tried to grasp the meaning of Maeve's words.

"Quick with the words he is and not afraid to use them on unsuspecting females."

"Ah ... you mean he's too flirty and plays the field?"

"He went through a breakup a while back and hasn't shown real interest in anyone since then. I was thinking he was just not ready, so." Maeve peered at Erin. "Or maybe he just hasn't met the right girl yet."

Erin quickly parried, "It's just nice to be invited out. At least I think I was invited out ... to the pub at any rate. So, you'll come with me?"

"Didn't I say already? Come on then. Now's as good a time as any."

Inside Connolly's pub a lively Irish jig streamed out to meet Erin and Maeve as they entered.

A group of itinerant musicians were gathered in one corner of the pub. In a jovial mood, they made merry conversation through the medium of music, smiling or laughing quietly together as one or another led off in a new and melodically tricky direction.

The pub was crowded but Erin quickly spotted Finn's bright hair in the midst of those gathered about the bar.

In that moment, Finn turned. His eyes lit up when he saw Erin which caused her to react in a similar way.

Maeve, who was commenting on the musicians, turned toward Erin just in time to see the color rise in her face.

Following her line of sight, Maeve sighed in apparent resignation. "Come on then," she said. Grabbing Erin's arm, Maeve led her through the crowd of determined revellers until they reached the bar.

"I'm glad ye found us," said Finn acknowledging the friends behind him with an airy wave of his hand.

Erin, not wanting to appear too eager, said, "Maeve wanted to stop in for a drink so, here we are."

Finn looked from one to the other. "Maeve," he acknowledged with a hearty smile.

"Finn," returned Maeve. "I'll get drinks shall I?" and pushed her way through to the crowd around the bar.

Finn turned and signalled the barman, pointed to Maeve and then to himself. The barman nodded his head. Satisfied that the drinks Maeve ordered would be paid for by himself, Finn turned back to Erin.

"I'm glad ye came." His cheeky grin combined with the sparkling green eyes were more than Erin could handle.

"Me too," Erin said. 'Keep your cool!' she told herself.

"Nice torc."

"Thank you."

"The stones match your eyes."

"I've been told that," she smiled shyly.

"Sadhbh wore a torc."

"Sigh?"

He spelled it out. "S-a-d-h-b-h. You say it like Five but with an S at the beginning ... Sive."

Trying to make the spelling jive with the pronunciation was difficult. Erin stumbled over the name and then asked, "Who was she? Is it a she?"

"Sadhbh was the lover of Finn McCool."

"Oh! Is that so," Erin touched the torc as her eyelids fluttered. 'He's such a flirt,' she told herself.

"Of course, when the Celts went into battle that was all they wore - a torc." He winked at her.

"Oh! Did they?" Erin dropped her hand from the necklace. 'Sheesh! Was he being matter of fact or was he implying something?'

"Well, that and blue paint designs. Y'know, to scare off the invaders."

Maeve returned with two drinks, one of which she handed to Erin. "Thanks for the drinks," she told Finn.

"My pleasure," he said.

Maeve raised her glass at Erin with a sly wink and then addressed Finn. "What invaders?"

"Any invaders. All of them," Finn waved his hand dismissively, presumably at the invaders.

Maeve looked to Erin for an answer.

"Finn was just saying, when the Celts went into battle, a torc was all they wore."

"And blue paint," added Finn.

"And blue paint," agreed Erin.

"Come meet my friends, Erin." He nodded at Maeve as well. "Ye probably know most of them I'd think."

"Probably but sure, introduce me anyway why don't ye!"

The three pushed into the crowd who turned to welcome them. Finn was right, Maeve did know several of the company and she was soon deep in local politics which as any Irish man or woman knows, is a fine form of socializing and not to be turned down when an opportunity presents itself.

Erin and Finn talked on until finally Maeve pushed her face between the two. "Will ye come on with your messing!" She looked from one to the other. "It's time to dance!"

She downed her drink and passed the empty glass to Finn. "Listen!" she told Erin. "They're setting up for the dancing."

Erin cocked an ear and sure enough beyond the noisy conversation in the pub, a band could be heard outside.

"I'll be out there," Maeve said. She turned her back on the couple and pushed her way through to the door.

"Is it that time already?" Finn checked his phone screen for the time.

"Yes, I think it is." Erin tipped her head back to swallow her drink. "Thanks for this." She handed the glass to Finn then turned and went after her friend.

"Hey!" called Finn. "Will I see ye again?"

"Maybe." Erin was non-committal. "We're going dancing," she called over her shoulder and disappeared through the door after Maeve.

Erin found Maeve over at the bandstand in the middle of the town square. A group of musicians were fronted by a singer who belted out the lyrics in a full contralto voice.

A crowd had quickly formed around them and some were dancing an old-style quickstep, while others jived or simply moved from side to side. Maeve clicked her fingers and bounced lightly on her feet to the rhythm.

"You're in the mood to dance!" said Erin.

"I am!"

"Hey, what d'you think of Finn? I wasn't expecting him to be so …" she wasn't sure how to put it.

"Forward?"

"Yes!"

"Ah sure, he's a flirt all right!" Maeve's eyes flickered over to the pub they had just left.

"My Great-Aunt Maggie said, 'Irishmen make wonderful lovers but terrible husbands.' I wouldn't mind exploring the 'wonderful lovers' part of that quote though."

"Well," said Maeve with a serious expression, "Was she speaking from her own experience, otherwise how would she know?"

Erin shrugged. "Maybe that's why she never married. Poor Gams."

"We should toast to lost loves." Maeve looked around as if expecting to find a drinks bar in the square.

"Never mind drinks," said Erin as she pulled her friend into the crowd. "Let's dance!"

And they did, to everything the musicians played for the next two hours until they collapsed exhausted onto the steps at the side of the pavilion.

*****

That night as Erin pulled the diary onto her lap, she thought of her evening and the fun she had enjoyed with her new friends.

The whole weekend was like being love-bombed by Ireland with the Egan clan experience and the fair and being in Gam's cottage.

It was with a strong feeling of connection that she read the first words of Bridget's next entry.

*Ah the day I have had. Mmm the kisses that Terry brings to my lips.*

"Ouuu!" said Erin. "You go girl!" She peered at the page for there was a sentence written very small with the letters cramped together as if to avoid detection. Erin held the diary up to the light to see it more clearly.

*And there is more besides…*

"Well! Well!" Erin smiled. "Good for you, Bridget" She turned the page and read on.

# Chapter Fourteen

Pebbles knocked against pebbles as the tough bare feet of the villagers trudged along the track that led into the bog. Voices were subdued as befitted the eerie, still moments that hovered just before dawn.

Bridget was among the walkers. She had arrived the previous afternoon with special permission from the Missus to take part in the full day's event. She was not expected back in town until the end of the day.

Nor would any of the children attend school this day. It was understood that an entire family was expected to help with the cutting and gathering of turf if there was to be any warmth in each of the humble cottages throughout the long winter months.

A few of the young men shyly looked on at Bridget as they walked. Her frame had soft curves to it, as she had seemingly become a young woman since the last season. Bridget carried on, unaware of the affectionate lads as she was more focused on the thought of seeing Terry today during the craic.

As the villagers neared the bog, a chorus of chaffinches rose in sudden crescendo to greet the coming day. Somewhere, a cock crowed and as they passed the last of the grazing fields, a cow lowed in greeting.

Although they faced a gruelling day of near back-breaking work, it was in good spirits that they walked, for warm weather and the good company of their fellows promised high expectation of the craic expected for the day that was in it.

Nor were they fearful of the Aos sídhe, for weren't the villagers all walking together in a clump and hadn't they left the obligatory offering of milk and bacstaí outside their doors the previous night.

Bridget reflected on the old rhyme associated with this dish ...

*Bacstaí in the griddle*
*Bacstaí in the pan*
*If you can't make bacstaí*
*You'll never get a man.*

While she was not sure the getting of a man could be attributed to cooking alone, she was certainly thankful she could make a good pan of bacstaí for hadn't her Mam taught her right way to go about such a dish.

In addition to the leaving of food and drink outside for the other folk, Bridget was in no doubt that in each cottage, the villagers had this very morning uttered the age-old prayer to the fair folk before venturing out...

*"Circle us o saints*
*Keep hope within*
*Despair without."*

So it was, as the sun stirred from pink to gold on the horizon, with faith in the saints and the good folk on their side, the villagers scattered about the springy surface of the bog.

Biding their time until they could see clearly enough to begin, the chatter grew in volume.

Women settled their children while men sharpened tools and urged each other on with good natured banter, to see who might foot the turf faster or show more for his efforts before day's end.

The turf was created by naturally compressed peat moss, sedge, and shrub. Cutting into the bog to create lines of turf sods had been completed a month previously, for it was well known a man was not worth his salt if he were not about on the bog by mid-April.

These banks were mostly rented from a local farmer who owned moss-land. They were carefully measured for the purpose of turf cutting, the length of which was determined by family size.

Turf cutting was a man's job and required strength combined with a certain style and rhythm that created an aura of pride among the men and certainly among the women who watched them work.

It was so for Bridget when she made sure to walk over the bog on the day that Terry and the families from his village worked their turf banks.

Remembering the sweat as it glistened on the muscles of Terry's arms, she smiled to herself now as she inserted several good-sized jugs of water into moss holes.

These had been dug specially for the water that trickled in to keep the jugs cool throughout the long hot days of working with the turf.

Stripping of the turf sods to divest them of the top layer had been completed several weeks after the cutting. Left to dry in the sun, a thick skin had developed.

Now they were sufficiently solid to be handled without quite as much risk of falling apart due to the muddy wet of being freshly cut.

The work of this day was to stack or foot the sods. This would enable drying in the warm winds that swept gently through the boglands under the May sunshine.

Sods were lifted and footed together in a pyramid style to allow air to circulate around them. Bridget was happy to work alongside her parents in this task although her favorite was rickling, which would begin about a week after footing and could only take place when the sods were sufficiently solid.

Bridget always enjoyed rickling because it was like building a wall. She liked the precision of placing three rows of eight sods in a horizontal row east to west with approximately one sod space between them topped with a further three placed north to south with another two or three placed east to west on top of that.

As the first squishy sod was laid sideways on the surface of the bog, the general chatter subsided, and work began in earnest.

Men dragged the sods that had been cut into brick sized wedges over to the women. Stacking the bricks into teepee-like shapes of five or six, the women worked with their backs bent to the task. Occasionally, they would stand and stretch, looking about to ensure their work had created straight lines of teepees.

Small boys mimicked their mothers and played at stacking the squelchy sods. The boys would then stand up straight with a hand to their back as if feeling the strain of the labor before tumbling and jostling one another in pursuit of new adventures that took them over and around the turf.

Sleepy-eyed toddlers explored the bog, climbing over the bricks of wet sod until they were scolded by their mothers.

Mostly, they were left to wander at will. The only danger was the large pools of water which had collected at the side of the banks where the turf was last harvested.

Younger girls were assigned to ensure none of the toddlers fell into these. Some of these girls sat together and with one eye on the toddlers, they passed the time making daisy chains to set in each other's hair or gazed about the bog as if in wonder that it could stretch so far in each direction.

Late in the morning, the workers took a well-deserved break to stretch their bodies out among the fragrant banks of wildflowers. There they waited for the women and girls to bring bowls of colcannon, all the more delicious for being eaten among friends in the good fresh air.

Despite their sore backs and aching shoulders, all were ready to enjoy the craic with their neighbors.

Pushing back loose strands of hair from their sweating hair-knots, women gathered babies and toddlers and sat under the sun with their men.

One or two of the women picked wood sorrel to cool their skin. Lips pursed as they pushed a floret into their mouths which immediately brought the welcome tang of berries bursting over the taste buds.

As always when Bridget came from the Missus' house, she had a small basket of food gifts provided by the cook. Now she pulled out several small meat pies that ran with delicious gravy when their thick buttery pastry was bitten into.

As her parents ate their picnic and chattered with their neighbors, Bridget stood with hands on hips looking about at the bog.

She inhaled the fragrance of wet golden gorse and thick purple heather that ran from one end of the bog to the far distance where bluebells nestled in the shade of whitethorn hedges.

The day seemed full of goodness and with a hope for the future that was bright as the sun that warmed her upturned face.

Bridget was not surprised when Terry joined them during their break, for they had spoken of such a ploy in their hope of obtaining Da's permission for their marriage.

Terry nodded hello to Bridget, but he made a beeline for Mam and Da who exchanged a quick glance between them. Mam's face showed concern but Da stood up quickly and held out a hand to take Terry's in his own.

"Welcome young man," he said.

Terry looked relieved. He looked over at Mam who mustered a smile although it seemed to Bridget that it was half-hearted at best.

Da was soon in close conversation with Terry, serious expressions on both their faces.

Bridget felt sad that Mam gazed steadily off across the lines of turf as if she would have no part in it.

Subduing a bubbling resentment, Bridget treasured the knowledge that at the end of this day, Terry would walk her back to Castlebar all the way to the square. There he would watch her walk beneath the oil lamps and safely into the house of the Missus.

Bridget sighed at this happy expectation and then became aware of the discussion among the workers as they ate their food.

"I heard tell of the potato blight coming back across from the east." said one.

"They say nothing good comes from over east," said another.

"'Tis a sad day if it comes this way again." said the first.

There was silence at this for none of them had sufficient grasp of the rumors to have the full reporting of it. However, such a lack of knowledge did not mean they could not hazard a guess and one of them voiced it now.

"T'was in some parts a year or two back. Rots the potatoes, right where they lie in the fields."

"Surely not? I could not imagine such a thing."

"'Tis truth and a hard thing to think on, for we depend on potatoes."

"Sure, we will eat oat bread as we always do between potato harvests."

"Aye, that is true. Still, we would have to be quick about planting for the next harvest if we were looking to have potatoes for the winter at all."

All were quiet at this, for it would mean many long hours working in the fields to keep ahead of the food requirements they would need to sustain them through the winter.

One brave soul whispered, "Sure, t'would be the other folk bringin' such a blight."

The company shifted on their haunches, unsure if this reference to the Sídhe ought to be continued. Most pursed their lips against the words that might tumble from their mouths unbidden and which if this happened, would surely call the disfavor of the faeries upon their own heads.

The same brave soul added, "I heard tell it was a faerie battle in the sky with the good folk playing a hurley match between them."

One or two nodded for it was well accepted in the region that faerie battles took place in the night sky during this particular time of year, when thunder and lightning storms abounded.

Another man spoke up then. "If 'twas such a thing, the lands of the vanquished army would be cursed so the potato wouldn't thrive at all."

The O'Brien sisters were sat close together with their skirts spread wide and folded over their knees.

Molly O'Brien looked about furtively as if an appearance of the other folk could be expected at any moment. Almost whispering, she said, "'Tis said they are beautiful beyond imagining but sure, they can be twice as wicked."

Theresa O'Brien answered, "Sure, but they can be plain as old bread with faces more ugly than you would want to see."

Not to be outdone, Diedre O'Brien added, "But they have a strange look in their eye that would give them away although to be sure, I would not want to meet any one of them on a dark night."

"Away with the lot of ye," said their mother. "Will ye look at the fields filled with ripe green potato plants and all of them in the way of flowering soon enough." As if by way of appeasement toward the faeries she added, "The good folk are gentle enough and mean us no harm."

Despite her words, she gathered her youngest child close to her breast and covered his head with the end of her apron as if to hide him from the prying eyes of the good folk.

At her words, the group took comfort and continued to munch on apples and drink their cooled water. Yet some looked about as if to ensure that blight was not at that very moment hovering in shadowy menace.

It was difficult to imagine, as butterflies fluttered among the wildflowers and bees buzzed about in the sunshine, that any such thing could happen. For what could possibly mar the very evidence of plenty that was there before them for anyone to see.

The very idea was impossible, that their small children would not always have their stomachs filled. It was difficult to imagine such things as they gazed at the children lying in the sun, their legs splayed out in happy sleep among the dregs of the picnic.

Lulled by the very evidence of plenty that was before them, laborers, refreshed by their meal and urging each other on as before, returned to their work.

Terry got up with Da and went to join the other men. Both Da and Terry winked at Bridget as they passed her. She pressed her lips together in secret delight for this could only mean that Da had approved of Terry as a suitor.

A competition began among some of the men to see who could drag the most turf sods to the footing area within a certain time.

Terry worked hard and fast beside Da, seeming eager to please the older man and prove his strength and value.

Women rolled their eyes in good-natured affection as they were urged by their men to "Foot faster, woman! Foot faster!"

It appeared that Mam could not ignore the combined efforts of the two men without bringing the notice of the other women as she also called out, "I am working as fast as I am able."

The sun smiled down as it moved across the sky in glorious benevolence. Toddlers woke and cried for a drink at which small girls ran at their mother's bidding as they were admonished to watch out for their siblings.

Soon enough, the villagers began to trail away from the bog. Lilting Irish voices drifted soft across the late afternoon.

Eyes looked with satisfaction over the footed turf to which they would return in a week or two for rickling and then clamping, a process of turning the bricks to ensure they were dried on all sides before they could be considered ready for stacking against the east wall of the cottages ready for winter fires.

Terry walked with them all the way to the cottage and sat outside with Da, as Mom brought them both a jug of ale.

Bridget busied herself in preparation for returning to town. She scooped out the floating bodies of insects that had collected in the rain barrel.

Splashing water over her face and head, she washed in the cool water until she felt refreshed.

Dressed in what she considered her town clothes, she hugged her parents goodbye. Mam was stiff with her but Da held her close and said, "'Tis a fine young man he is. I like him."

Comforted, Bridget and Terry headed for the road to Castlebar. At the turn of the road, she had the inclination to turn and look back at the village where she had grown up and which she felt great love for.

As Bridget drank in the sweet smell of burning turf that curled in a blue haze from each of the cottages, memories flooded her mind.

Visions of helping her father set traps for the hunting of rabbits and the times when they fished the river together and splashed about in the shallow water and watched the spray catch in colorful rainbows against the sun.

She thought of her mother and the times when they baked oat bread together and sighed with love for her place in their family and the joy she felt when they were together. She suddenly regretted leaving her mother with unresolved feelings between them.

Sighing, for there was nothing she could do about it at the present moment, Bridget turned again toward the path between trees which formed an overhead arch on the road that led away from her village.

For appearances sake, Bridget and Terry marched along side by side until a mile down the road, they rounded a bend and slowed.

Terry reached out and held her hand in his. They dawdled where the line of hazel trees ended. Bridget looked up to meet the brightness of Terry's admiring grin with her own answering shy smile.

Something in the way he looked at her, held Bridget still as a sapling.

"'Tis lovely as a spring day ye look to me Bridget."

Her lips opened in a delighted smile as he continued, "Ye are beautiful mo ghrá, filled with sunshine as ye are." Bridget blushed as they walked on, for she knew her skin had a glow to it from their day in the fresh air of the wetlands.

Their path led between grassy banks where bluebells nodded in the lazy breeze of the early evening. There they slowed again as if by mutual consent.

In a moment that seemed suspended in time, Terry's eyes roved over Bridget's hair and face, until at last, his gaze rested on her lips.

She could smell the perfume of his sweat mingled as it was with hay and loam and something else that came to her as the sweetness of desire.

She felt the strength of his arm as it tightened about her waist and pulled her close to his body.

The blue of his eyes merged with the blue of her own as his face bowed toward hers until the firm of his lips touched the softness of hers.

The world spun about as butterflies rushed down from her belly to a place that sparkled with a delight she had not before experienced, and which seemed to hold the entire world in pause.

With his eyes on hers, Terry led her from the road. Gently he lowered himself onto the soft carpet of wildflowers and gently pulled her down beside him.

Surrounded and secluded within a sanctified chapel of lavender colored bluebells, Bridget melted into his arms.

Held together by the dew that formed on their lips, it was as if they were between the worlds in a time that was not a time.

Bridget's eyes fluttered closed onto an eternity of slow-moving moments that led through silent avenues and undulating fields of wheat that rippled softly in hazy welcome.

An enchantment of light and dark brushed like gossamer wings across her body in wave upon wave that took her breath away.

Her mouth fell open and her body rose up to meet his.

An explosion of sensation shattered through the very center of her being, so that her body was lit in a fire that had no beginning and no end.

A sigh fell between them as he breathed the words, "Is breá liom tú."

"I love ye also," she whispered.

They gazed deep, each at the other. In wonder they mentally and visually traced the enchantment of the experience.

It was as if they had breathed a prayer, had worshiped together in sacred harmony. Neither could move or wanted to ever move again from this sanctified and hallowed place.

Only the lateness of the hour and the need for Bridget to return to the house before the housekeeper retired, drew them to their feet.

They dressed in shy appreciation of their nearness, glances brief but always coming back one to the other.

Terry took her hand as they softly tread back to the road. As twilight closed about them, they made their way toward Castlebar.

Bridget walked as if on the softest of clouds, bathed as she was in the warmth of his nearness and the promise of his masculine strength.

At the edge of the square, they dallied a moment, hands loosely touching now they were in so public a place. This, despite the fact it was night and lit only by the gentle glow of oil lamps dotting the way across to the imposing houses that lined the square and led off down the side streets to the house where Bridget worked.

Bridget left Terry's side, her fingers still tingling from their last touch with his. She sighed in happiness as she crossed alone beneath the lamps.

At the center-point, she began to turn to wave at Terry.

To her surprise and before she could fully turn, she felt a shoulder brush her own.

She had a sudden awareness of a young woman, very like herself with chestnut hair that tumbled down her back.

The woman had a look in her blue eyes as if she were searching for something ... for someone. A feeling of love emanated from her that enveloped Bridget as if this were a person that she knew and cared for.

Bridget was transfixed and could not move. She had thought nothing could displace the experience she'd had with Terry only an hour or so before but now, this vision held her in a golden warmth that dropped over her head like a veil. It transcended anything she had ever felt in her young life.

For an eternity, she was held in the moment until at last, the apparition and its accompanying warmth washed away, leaving her blinking in the sudden dim of the oil lamps.

Erin looked about but no one was near, the vision had gone, yet the feeling remained lingering.

Overwhelmed by the unexpected event, she thought to run back and share the experience with Terry but as she hesitated, she realized that if she tarried any longer, the door of the house would be locked against her.

Waving only briefly at Terry, she had no recourse but to turn and hurry into the house through the kitchen door.

Cook was seated in her little room off the kitchen with the housekeeper Mrs. Murphy. As usual at this hour, they had their heads together over a glass of porter. So busy were they with whatever tidbit of conversation they had overhead from upstairs, that they did not notice Bridget as she entered.

To Bridget, it was as if she all but floated through the kitchen and up the stairs to her room on the servant's floor of the attics. That she was uplifted by her experience with Terry could not be doubted but combined with the encounter in the square, the two vied for attention in her mind, leaving her in a state of both belief and disbelief. She was at a loss to explain what had happened yet could not deny it for the encounter was strong upon her still.

Yet the feeling of love that came with the vision, for she told herself it must have been a vision, stayed with her throughout the night. It wove in and out of her dreams, intertwined with tender thoughts of sacred, secret love among dancing bluebells.

## Chapter Fifteen

*E*rin trudged around the side of the cottage wearing an old pair of bright pink wellies which had belonged to Gams. She carried a large pail of wildflower seeds she had purchased in town.

As she passed the gate that led into the yard, she paused as she considered for the umpteenth time that morning, whether she was brave enough to cross the yard to gain access to the back field.

Beauty was standing alone in the center of the yard, sunning herself in the early morning rays. How Erin longed to pet and stroke the pony's silky ears and how she wished she could get over her fear of the donkey.

The pony looked up and seeing Erin, snickered gently. Erin made a move toward the gate but then paused as Mykel trotted into the picture. He stopped beside Beauty and nuzzled her gently for a moment.

Pleasantly surprised, Erin kept perfectly still so as not to disturb the lovely scene.

Inevitably, Mykel looked up and when he saw Erin, gave a loud heehaw and began to buck with high energy. Beauty ignored him and bent her head to nibble at something on the ground.

Erin sighed. It was no good. She was still unable to face the donkey and resigned herself to walking all the way around the area, to approach her destination from an adjacent farm.

Tearing her gaze away from Beauty, she continued on past the gate and out into the lane. 'One day soon,' she thought. 'Surely I'll be able to pet the pony without Mykel being around.'

Wondering if she could prevail on Aiden to lock the donkey in the barn for half an hour while she had a little time with the pony, she followed the grassy track that ran along the center of the lane.

A profusion of tiny blue and lavender wildflowers had appeared almost overnight among the tall buttercups lining the hedgerows, which in themselves presented such a variety in shades of green that it was quite astonishing to behold.

Adding to the sparkle of the morning, the sun was still low in the sky so that as it filtered through the leafy hedgerows, it cast shadows which added further layers of green upon the green.

'It really is quite beautiful,' Erin thought and wondered why she had not noticed all this radiance before.

Turning right by the old and long abandoned Christie cottage, Erin stepped around the rusted metal gate that hung on one hinge and walked into the field that ran parallel with that of Gam's property.

Picking her way carefully along the edge of the Christie field, Erin was careful not to slide on the muddy ground which seemed to become even more wet and treacherous with each step she took.

Reaching the corner where Gam's field began, she found to her surprise that Mykel had preceded her. With Beauty beside him, they stood looking over the fence with apparent interest at her progress.

Erin frowned at the wily donkey and wondered how he could possibly have known her destination. Was he so interested that he had actually followed her progress? Certainly, she had been noisy enough as she had slipped, groaned and gasped her way along. She decided to take the animals into her confidence.

"It's time," she said, motioning with her chin at the field. "I'm going to turn that field into a meadow. It's what Gams wanted." Mykel responded by biffing Beauty gently in the shoulder which pushed her toward Erin.

"Right!" agreed Erin. "It's up to us to make it happen."

Her mouth set in a determined line, Erin worked her way through the wires of the fence, twisting her body first one way and then the other until she was through into the field. She pulled the carton of wildflowers after her and straightened up.

Mykel feigned disinterest and nibbled at Beauty's ear who snickered in response.

Turning her back on Mykel, Erin prised open the carton and inspected the seeds. There seemed an abundance of variety and she hoped the seeds would grow and flourish under the summer sun. She was saddened that she would not be around to see them flower but took comfort that the field in her absence would produce a glorious display in memory of Gams.

She popped the lid back on and clutching the carton under her arm, proceeded into the field and headed for the center.

The field, while muddy around the edges, was essentially wetlands, possibly because it was so close to the nearby bog.

Realizing quickly the need for care, Erin entered the large muddy expanse one step at a time.

Barely four meters in, her wellied foot sank into the progressively wet, almost boggy ground.

With hands flailing in an interesting parody of a windmill, the top flew off the carton, releasing the seeds which flew out and landed in a clump. Erin fell flat on her back directly on top of the seeds, narrowly missing a wide thorn-filled bush.

The donkey who was still watching from the fence with the pony, hee-hawed as if amused. Erin responded by yelling an insult back at him.

At that moment she heard Aiden's voice. "Erin! Are you back there?"

Erin turned her head toward the sound of his voice but lay still. Perhaps he wouldn't notice her behind the thorn bush and would go away. She kept very quiet.

Mykel and Beauty had no such reservations. They both turned their heads at the sound of Aiden's voice but neither of them moved from their position at the fence.

The donkey hee-hawed and the pony snickered, but both were reluctant to avert their attention from the field where the spectacle that had just taken place beyond the thorn bush was obviously far more interesting.

Erin waved at the animals and hissed, "Go away." Unfortunately, neither of them understood Erin-speak and merely stretched their necks further over the fence, as if unwilling to miss the entertainment.

Aiden, drawn by the focused attention of the animals, strode over to see what was going on. "Erin! Is that you? What happened?" His attention was drawn to the solitary pink wellie sticking up out of the mud. "Ah!" he said. "I see!"

Erin raised her head and peered through the thorn bush. She could see Aiden preparing to climb over the fence into the field.

"Sheesh!" she muttered then called out, "I'm okay." She sat up. Placing one hand on the mud beside her, she leaned her weight and watched the arm sink halfway up the forearm in mud.

The wires of the fence made a springing sound.

Determined to manage without help and aghast that Aiden should see her in yet another embarrassing situation, Erin quickly rolled over, shifted up onto her knees and began to rise.

As her foot touched the ground, the mud gave, so that she quickly found herself on her knees again. After a moment's pause, Erin began to scramble in earnest.

"Well, well," said Aiden.

Erin looked up to see the barely restrained laughter on his face. She glared at him. "It's not funny!"

"Okay!" He passed a hand across his mouth.

"Help me up!" she demanded.

He snorted through muffled laughter.

She placed her muddy fingers in his outstretched hand and scowled at the strangled sounds he was making.

He pulled on her arm but still she couldn't find secure footing and began to pump with her feet like the road-runner bird in the old cartoon.

Aiden exploded into uncontrolled laughter so that he lost his firm grip on Erin's hand.

Incensed at his hilarity of her situation, she gave a wicked little tug and with a loud whumping sound, Aiden came down beside her in the mud.

Winded, he was quiet for a second or two before he turned his head toward her. They regarded each other in silence. Erin's eyes were bright with indignation.

Perhaps it was the mud dripping from her nose and mouth that started it, but Aiden's face began a smile which soon turned into a deep belly laugh that shook his entire body. He lay back in the mud and flung his arms out, allowing the laughter to fill his tall frame.

Erin watched him for a moment before a grudging laugh began deep in her throat. Soon she was laughing with him and flung herself back into the mud so that they lay side by side looking up at the sky.

Shaking his head in disbelief so that the mud squelched against his ears, he asked, "What the feck were you about?"

"I was turning the field into a meadow like Gams wanted. I was going to throw the seeds around the field."

"Well, you certainly did that all right." This started another round of laughter in which they relayed the events each from their own point of view.

"Your pink wellie standing on its own in the mud."

"You, trying to pull me up."

"The noise you made when you landed beside me – whump!"

"You pulled me down, woman!"

"I may have," Erin looked over at the fence where the donkey and pony watched in perfect parody of an audience watching a movie. Erin giggled at the sight which set Aiden off again.

At last, when they managed to gain their footing and were headed back across the field toward the yard behind Gam's cottage, Aiden said, "This is how I remember you as a kid, not afraid of a bit of mud."

"Yeah, well I'd forgotten you could be fun to be around."

Aiden stopped walking.

"I have been grumpy, I know. It's the time of year that does it. So much going on with the sheep dipping, getting cattle to market and all the rest of it. I can be like a bear with a sore head."

"Once a year, hey?" She didn't say it but thought about her own moods that revolved around her monthly cycle. She'd been known to snap at work colleagues and even a few customers on occasion. Once a year didn't seem too bad when put into perspective.

Aiden was looking back at the field. "We should do something about this. Seriously, if you want to create a meadow here, let's do it."

"You'd help me, really?"

He looked down at her. "I could do that for an old friend." He wiped a splodge of mud from the end of her nose.

"I won't be here to see it flower though. I-I won't be here that long."

He paused a moment, considering this.

He then straightened up. "Right!" he said and turning, opened the gate so Erin could walk through.

## Chapter Sixteen

In the kitchen, Erin considered the events of the day before. That Aiden had been about to kiss her, she was in no doubt. Yet she couldn't in all good conscience allow a romance to begin that she couldn't follow through with. Certainly not anyway, from the other side of the world. 'It wouldn't be fair to either of us', she told herself.

Erin suddenly felt hungry for something sweet. "Hmm," she laughed, "Needing an infusion of dopamine maybe?" She paused while she considered this. "Is that connected with the need for sex? Or is it serotonin?" She gave up the task. Whatever it was, she needed something sweet for breakfast.

A pleasant memory brought a smile, of Gams preparing a steaming bowl of oats each morning. She would sprinkle brown sugar on top of the porridge followed by a dollop of fresh cream.

"Oh my gosh, Gams," Erin said to the empty kitchen. "I really miss your breakfasts. So delicious!" A moment later she announced, "I'm having that porridge today!"

As she prepared the oats, Erin pressed the button on the old radio Gams kept in the kitchen. It was tuned to a Gaeilge station. She was about to turn the dial to find an English speaker but realized she could understand some of the words. She lingered, her finger on the dial, finding comfort in listening to Gam's favorite station. One of the few words she could recognize was 'agus' which was repeated often as it meant 'and.'

'Le do thoil' was another term she recognized. It meant 'please' and she knew to pronounce it 'ledder hull'. Erin recalled Gam's method of teaching Irish. Erin might ask for something and Gams would raise her eyebrows and ask, "What do you say?"

The answer was always, 'le du thoil,' whereupon Gams would respond, "Yes of course mo stór," or conversely when Erin asked for more cream on her porridge Gams made her go through the whole rigmarole of saying le du thoil before telling her, "No! Too much cream is not good for ye."

There was also Go raibh maith agat or thank you. Gams would make her sound this out with Erin repeating between giggles, "guh-ruh-mah-a-gut."

Still smiling, Erin poured cooked porridge oats into a bowl, sprinkled brown sugar over it and plopped a spoonful of cream on the top. She paused for a moment with the spoon in mid-air while she inhaled the wonderful aroma of comfort food.

In a moment of spontaneity, she placed the spoon back into the bowl and poured a little more cream onto her porridge.

Closing her eyes, she brought the spoon to her mouth. "Mmm" she murmured appreciatively.

Before Erin could take another mouthful, she heard the sound of airbrakes in the lane outside, followed by a loud beeping that sounded like reverse signals accompanied by the more sighing of air brakes. She opened the front door to find a truck reversing into the driveway. Aiden leaned out of the cab.

"Don't leave your car there if ye don't mind. I'm taking this truckload through the yard to the north field."

"Oh sorry," said Erin. She recalled that Gam's farmyard was a right of way that farmers used occasionally.

She grabbed her car keys from the side table by the door.

"Could you open the gate for me?"

"Sure!" she said, peering at the truck. It appeared to be loaded with sheep which were all strangely silent.

Mykel and Beauty were standing side by side watching with interest from a safe distance at the far side of the yard.

Erin opened the gate and backed her car out of the way and watched as Aiden backed into the yard. He leaned out of the cab window and yelled, "Could you shut the gate after me?"

"Okayyy..." Erin's mouth twitched slightly as she walked over to shut the gate.

"And please don't bolt it. I'll do it as I go out again."

"Hey!" she yelled, arms on her hips and eyes glaring.

Aiden stilled the airbrakes and leaned out again. He lifted his chin in a 'What's up' motion.

"I'm not here at your beck and call. Get out of the truck and close the gate yourself!" She turned on her heel and stomped inside the cottage.

"What?" she heard Aiden call out. "I said please."

*197*

"Yeah? Well, go rabid maith agat yerself," yelled Erin and closed the front door with a firm hand.

Her porridge was cold, the cream melted and congealed into an unappealing mess. "Hmf!" she said and set it aside. Fuming, she rinsed the spoon under the tap and watched Aiden from the kitchen window.

He had secured the donkey and pony in the barn then backed all the way across the yard into the gate at the mouth of the north field. With a flick of his tanned arm, he dropped a ramp at the back of the truck. Immediately, sheep began to trot down into the field. They looked newly shorn and clean.

Aiden coaxed the last of the stragglers down the ramp by banging on the side of the truck and telling them "Come on out now. Come on."

One sheep held back but Aiden reached in with strong arms and pulled her out, gave her a pat on the rump and sent her on her way.

To Erin's surprise all the sheep ran into the center of the field and lay on their sides completely quiet.

They didn't move from this prostrate position until Aiden strode among them, clapping his hands together repeatedly. "Come away now, come away."

One by one the sheep obeyed his calm urgings. He remained there for several minutes, walking about and talking to them as they settled down to enjoy the lush grass.

"Huh!" said Erin. "The surprises never end in this place." She began to tidy the breakfast things away into the cupboards.

A little later she looked out when she heard the truck pass by the side of the cottage.

Mykel and Beauty were back in the yard. As usual, Beauty kept to herself whereas Mykel was right up against the fence with his nose through a gap studying the sheep, four of whom were equally fascinated by him and were busy nuzzling his nose and neck.

A short while later, there was a hesitant knock at the front door. When she opened it, Aiden stood a step or two back. If he could have held a cap in his hand, he might have. "Er, sorry," he began. "I didn't mean to take advantage of your good nature."

She looked at him but said nothing.

"Well okay, maybe I did … mean to." He grinned. "But I am sorry."

Erin was about to roll her eyes but when he grinned, she had a sudden urge for a spoonful of honey. She held the door open. "Tea?"

He followed her through to the kitchen.

Settling himself at the kitchen table, Aiden watched as she moved about the kitchen.

She poured him a mug and pushed it toward him. "I was thinking about Gams this morning,"

"Yes?" He picked up a teaspoon.

"Sugar?" She lifted the bowl of sugar and then put it down. Her hand closed instead, around the honeypot. "Or honey?"

"I'll do it." Without looking up, he added sugar to his tea and stirred it. "You were saying?"

Erin rolled her eyes at herself and put the honey down. She gathered her thoughts. "You know," she began. "Gams lived here all her adult life."

He sipped his tea and watched her over the rim of the mug.

"She made a choice to come here as a young woman." Erin reached for clarity. "I've never understood why she would do that. I mean, why leave her home and her family and presumably her friends to come all the way to Ireland."

"Didn't her parents pass away just before she made that decision?"

"That's true. They did." She poured tea for herself. "So maybe this was a kind of vacation."

"Time to mourn."

"Good point." She pointed a teaspoon at him before using it to stir her tea. "So, she may have come here just to get away from it all." Lifting the teaspoon to her mouth, she licked it clean of the honey she had used to sweeten her tea.

Aiden watched her, curiosity obvious on his face. "Well," he said, "that and the diary."

Erin stared at him, the spoon still in her mouth. Pulling it out with a plop like it was a lollipop she said, "You knew about the diary?"

"Um, sure."

"Why didn't you tell me?"

Aiden watched the teaspoon as Erin waved it about in the air. "Tell you what?"

Erin aimed the teaspoon at the sink and tossed it. There was a clang as it landed there. "That you knew about the diary."

He looked from the sink back to Erin. "You didn't ask."

Erin folded her arms across her chest and waited.

Aiden spread his hands in defense. "You never mentioned the diary."

Erin relented. "Oh!" She rolled a hand at him. "Well, go on …"

"Go on what?"

She wondered if he was being evasive or just obtuse or maybe both. "Aiden, tell me what you know about the diary ... and Gams ... and what the diary had to do with her coming here to Ireland."

"Ah!" he said. "Well, that's simple."

Erin raised her eyebrows.

Aiden continued, "She found Bridget Egan's diary among her parents' things."

"And whatever she found there made her pack up everything and leave?"

"I don't believe she meant to stay." Aiden mused. "Not at first. But she did say it was the diary that made her decide that in the end."

"She told you that?"

"She did." He sipped his tea.

'Sheesh, it was like pulling teeth. He's such a guy.' She smiled sweetly, trying to practice patience. "Tell me everything she told you, okay?"

"Oh! Okay!" He smacked his lips together. "Let's see... well, Maggie said she was struck by the memories Bridget had for Ireland, the nostalgia I suppose. It's what prompted Maggie to make the journey. But it's what she found here that made her stay."

Erin nodded encouragingly, trying not to break her calm outer demeanor with her internal lack of patience surfacing.

"It was the sense of permanence that she fell in love with. She believed Irish people know who they are and feel solid in their roots. Well, that's what she told me anyway."

Erin was intrigued. "And do you feel that Aiden, that sense of permanence?"

He looked startled, as if he hadn't given it any thought before, "I suppose I do."

"What does that feel like exactly?" She was curious. She hadn't felt that back home. At least, she didn't think she had.

Aiden took a breath. "If I had to define it," he looked at Erin who was leaning forward, her eyes wide. He began again, frowning in concentration. "Well, I'd say ... My parents were born here and their parents before them. I know my own family history, going back at least five hundred years and probably before that if I give it serious thought."

Aiden pushed a hand through his hair. "When I'm out working in the fields sometimes, I look up and I have the feeling I'm part of it. You know, part of the land." He shifted in his seat. "Sometimes ..."

"Sometimes?"

"There are times... when the breeze is soft and the bees are humming, it's almost as if the land..." He coughed as if embarrassed.

"Sings to you?"

"Yes!" He coughed again. "Yes... I suppose you think that's lame."

"I think it's beautiful." Erin reached out and put a hand over his, this calmed her instantly. "I've never felt that, but I wish I did."

Aiden nodded slowly. "Maybe you will when you find the village."

Erin gripped Aiden's hand. "The village where Bridget lived? You know where it is?"

Aiden brought his eyes up to meet hers. "I know Maggie went looking for the village."

She gripped harder. "But do you know where it is?"

"She never told me." He shrugged, looking down at their hands again. "And I never thought to ask."

"Oh!" Erin's shoulders slumped and she pulled her hand away. "That's ... too bad."

"I wish I'd pressed her for more details. But it wasn't really my business."

"Sorry Aiden." Erin was contrite. "You've been so helpful. More than you know."

Aiden took another sip of tea, using the mug to disguise a sudden bashful smile.

*****

After Aiden left, Erin wandered about the cottage, distractedly picking things up and putting them down again.

As she made her bed, she noticed the lilac and lavender potpourri on the bedside table. Picking it up, she sat on the edge of the bed and closed her eyes, inhaling the lovely perfume.

"Gams! Gams!" she murmured. "What a puzzle you've given me. I don't know how to solve it." Her eyes popped open. "But I know who might."

With a smile of triumph, Erin kissed the potpourri. "Thanks Gams!" She picked up the diary and headed for the car.

Erin drove over the bridge, noticing the level had risen so that trees growing along the banks were half submerged in the rushing water. "No wonder the field was so muddy yesterday," she grumbled but then smiled as she recalled the hilarious scene in the field.

Changing down into second, Erin idled briefly at the T-junction before right along the narrow road.

When she noted a car coming towards her from the opposite direction, she looked around for a place to pull in. There wasn't much room for manoeuvre. The oncoming driver who was on his cell phone, slowed down directly in front of her and held up one finger.

Thinking that for some reason, he needed to speak to her, Erin waited patiently for him to finish his phone conversation.

After waiting ten or fifteen seconds with no further movement, Erin began to move slowly forward although it was clear she would not be able to pass the other vehicle until it moved completely off to the side.

Again, the driver held up a finger, this time nodding at her presumably to let her know he had seen her.

Erin waited, the engine of the car idling in neutral while she wondered at the hold up.

Finally, the driver put down his phone, began edging toward the hedge and passed her slowly inch by inch.

Erin leaned out of the window, fully expecting words of wisdom that perhaps might indicate an accident up ahead or some other fortuitous event. The driver however, merely looked over as he passed by and said, "Ah sure, it's a lovely day now."

Stunned, Erin stayed where she was in the middle of the road while the other car revved up and disappeared around the corner behind her. There was nothing else for it but to laugh, push the gear into first and drive on her way.

When she reached the bookstore, Erin could see Maeve standing behind the till holding a phone near her face.

The bell rang as Erin walked into the bookstore. At the expression on Erin's face, Maeve quickly ended a call and put down her cell phone.

"What is it?" she asked. "What's happened?"

Erin held up the diary.

"Ouuu," Maeve's eyes danced. "Is that what I think it is?"

"Want to help me figure it out?"

"Love to!"

Erin placed the diary between them on the counter and bit her bottom lip. "I'm at a brick wall so to speak. I love reading about Bridget's life but ..." Her voice trailed off.

"But?"

"I still can't figure out where exactly the village is." Erin sucked in her breath, then let it out in a whoosh! "The village where Bridget grew up. I know for sure it's in the west, near Castlebar, but..."

Maeve studied Erin's face. "You're taking this far too seriously. Ye need to lighten up!"

"You don't understand. Look, it's all tied to my staying here. In Ireland I mean."

"You want to stay here?" Maeve grinned. "That would be altogether grand."

"Yes but ... under the terms of the will, I have to follow the clues in the diary to some conclusion that I'm not entirely sure of." She sighed, "And I can't figure it out on my own."

Maeve held up a hand. "Say no more. Haven't ye come to the right place?" She rubbed her hands together. "Now, what do ye know so far?"

Erin went over the details of Bridget's life as she knew it, along with her conversation with Aiden that morning.

"You're getting close, you and Aiden?"

"Are we?" Erin looked up at the ceiling as if the answer was written there. She frowned, not ready to think about it yet. She looked back at the diary. "I have to figure this out first."

"And then there's Finn..."

Something in Maeve's voice grabbed Erin's attention. "What?"

"Finn ... d'you like him?" Maeve seemed hesitant.

Erin's eyes narrowed. "Ohhh! You like him." It was a statement.

"Well ..."

"Why didn't you tell me?"

"I've known him a long time." Maeve looked down and then met Erin's eyes. "He's such a flirt, you know."

"You said that yesterday."

Maeve sighed. "Yeah …"

"Does he know?" Erin winked. "Does he know you like him?"

"No! He does not. And it's not me will be telling him." She pointed a finger at Erin. "Nor you I hope!"

Erin crossed her heart and held up a hand. "I promise he won't hear it from my lips."

"You don't mind Erin?"

"Hey! I just met him." She studied Maeve's face. "Aw … you *really* like him."

"I try to talk myself out of it, I do. But …"

"It's hard to talk yourself out of love."

"It is, so."

Erin opened her arms and hugged Maeve until she pulled away and said, "I don't want to talk about it anymore. It's almost a lost cause for I've no idea what to do about it, so." Maeve tapped the diary. "Anyway, let's figure this out, okay?"

"Okay."

They turned their attention to the diary.

*****

*We are visiting far to Dublin, the Missus and me. She is here to consult with doctors for she has a pain in her belly that will not go away.*

*The Missus keeps to her bed mostly and it is so very dreary tending to her in the half light of her chamber.*

*I so miss my weekly visits to Mam and Da. Often, I try to imagine what they are doing and if Mam is feeling the pain in her back.*

*And Terry ... Ah my dear Terry. I think of him when I compose myself for sleep at night. But sighing will not bring him near and so I try to push away thoughts of him. But still I cannot help myself and my worry returns unbidden.*

*I have written letters to Mam and Da and to Terry. As yet I have heard nothing in return.*

*The coach service delivers mail to Castlebar but delivery is dependent upon a kindly soul travelling in the direction of my village. Until I receive word, I must content myself in thinking them well and happy.*

*I imagine they have gathered in the turf, for the weather has been dry enough these past months. Surely it is already stacked against the cottage, drying and ready for the winter ahead.*

*One thing has concerned me and that is the newspaper which the Missus has me read to her every day.*

*There are reports of a lack of food but I think this cannot be true for the markets, when we pass by, are filled with fruit and vegetables of every kind.*

*Indeed I have observed cartloads piled high with the same foods headed for the docks for shipping to England. At least, that is what the Missus tells me.*

*I so look forward to the days when the Missus makes a great fuss about getting outside into the sunshine. I can scarce contain my excitement as I pull on a bonnet and assist the Missus out to the carriage.*

*Dublin is a grand city. The streets are so wide and there are so many exciting things happening that I can hardly take it all in.*

*I have never seen so many horse-drawn carriages and fine hats worn by the women who ride in them.*

*In the evening, the streets are lit by something called gas. I love the glow of them, for it is far superior to the oil lamps of Castlebar. I shall have so much to tell when I return home.*

\*\*\*\*\*

"Aw! Bless her." Maeve gave a mew of sympathy. "She's so sweet."

"Don't you just love her?"

"I want to adopt her." Maeve ran her fingers over the old pages and shivered. "It's like the past coming to life, isn't it?"

Erin nodded her head. "You have no idea." She almost told Maeve about her ghostly experience with the diary in Gams' cottage, but decided that perhaps it was too personal to share.

"I love reading about her adventures." Maeve reverently lifted the corner of another page. "But shouldn't we jump ahead to the end, find out where it leads?"

Erin gently put her hand over Maeve's. "No, we might miss a valuable clue. I think at this stage, we have to read it in sequence."

"You're right," Maeve relented. "Let's get on with it then." They bent their heads to the book and read on.

Quietly, Erin regarded her appreciation for her new friend, and the fact that she could share her adventure with someone, much like the Sam to her Frodo.

## Chapter Seventeen

The world has turned upside down, for the Missus is dead and I am returned to Castlebar with her coffin.

There is such a flurry of activity about the house for the funeral must be prepared.

There will be no wake as we know it in our village, as the Missus did not hold with the old ways. Instead, there will be the reading of the will with cake and sherry served for those who attend.

But as that will not occur for several days, I have begged time to visit my village. It has been seven long months since I have seen or indeed, heard anything from there. Christmas will be upon us within a few weeks and the ground is icy with the cold that comes in from the ocean.

*Cook had alarming news about the villages round about Castlebar. It is said that many good folk have become sick and some have even died and all because of a blight that has attacked the potato crop.*

*Cook said it was the rain that did it. Too much and too early so that even the sheep were falling over, their coats being so thick and wet that they could not right themselves but had to wait for shepherds to roll them over.*

*That such a thing would happen to sheep I can understand, yet I cannot imagine a whole crop of potatoes failing. There are potatoes stored in the pantry here at the house and the kitchen table all but groans from the food Cook lays on for the household staff, at least three or four times each day.*

*Mrs. Brophy the housekeeper said she heard rumours of the potato crop failing overnight so that instead of lush green potato leaves with their white flowers nodding in the breeze, there were only dark rotting plants to be found in the fields. She said it was as if they had been destroyed by sudden frost.*

*Still, as I said to Cook there will be oat bread to eat between the harvests so that people need not go hungry. And indeed what of the cow that many people in the country kept closeby. Most kept a pig but that was for payment of rent to the big house. But with a cow, at the very least they would have milk and cheese.*

*Cook was quiet a moment before she told me she wasn't sure of that because more people poured into the town every day and that from the looks of them, they were starving.*

*At this, I was more than ever determined to return home to my village immediately.*

*At my mithering, both Cook and the Housekeeper Mrs. Brophy have agreed that I may visit Mam and Da on the strict understanding that I am to return by tomorrow evening at the latest.*

*As it was already so late, they determined I may not leave until tomorrow morning.*

*I have come to bed but I am so very anxious that I am sure I shall not sleep this night.*

\*\*\*\*\*

The next morning Bridget was ready to leave the house before dawn. As the sun rose on the country lanes, she marched as fast as her booted feet would take her towards her home.

The first strange thing Bridget noticed was the lack of birdsong when any other day would have the air filled with the sound of trilling.

The second thing was the lack of people for usually at this time of the morning, the lanes would be at their busiest with the comings and goings of country folk.

No laborers whistled as they worked in the fields or called to each other in good-natured wit. It was as if the whole earth was suddenly bereft of life.

Breath catching in her throat, Bridget hurried her step. She passed several gráigeanna where, instead of the comforting welcome of turf fires curling up from each cottage, she was met only by an eerie quiet.

Some cabins and cottages looked as though they had been pulled down, their occupants gone. One such abode had been burned, smoke still emanating from its ruined state. Above all, there were no people that she could see as she evaluated her surroundings.

Riddled with alarm, Bridget began to run towards her own village. She urged herself on until at last, she stopped at the hazel trees and knew she was home.

Panting loud and puffing from the physical exertion, Bridget looked about with wild eyes. 'Where is everyone?' she wondered.

Heart in mouth, Bridget proceeded cautiously, dreading the unknown yet desperate to know the state of the place.

As she entered the street, she was shocked to see that most of the homes had been demolished to some degree so that the walls were not complete. Not one had its thatched roof intact.

She was transfixed by the scene. The hair on the back of her neck stood up in response even as her brain slowed down. She could not make sense of what was before her, nor could she move for several minutes.

The lack of childish laughter chilled her. No voices called out to each other. No pots were clanged in the making of the morning porridge. No old men sat in the winter sunshine and no chickens pecked in the dirt at their feet. The village was not only deserted but desecrated by what appeared to Bridget to be an unseen force.

She wondered if her parents were safe. This thought freed her body from its paralysis, and she began to run faster than before, desperate to see them.

Skirts flying about her ankles, she followed the track that led between the cottages toward the end of the village where the stream ran.

"Mam," she screamed as she splashed through, uncaring of the icy water as it dragged against her skirts. "Da, where are you!?"

That the cottage was empty, she could see before she arrived, for there was no door.

Bridget all but flew inside and looked in the corners as if by doing so, she could make her parents appear from the dust that gathered there.

Exhausted and disoriented, Bridget sat in the frozen mud at the entrance to her home. Tears ran down her face as sobs jarred her frame. She had no idea of what to do or how to make sense of it all.

At a sudden noise, she listened with head turned. Scrambling to her feet, Bridget ran toward the sound.

In one of the cottages, she found a man turning over the few belongings left within.

She stopped in the doorway, bringing a shadow across him. He in turn, fell back in shock at the sight of her.

Bridget could see the man was in fact Ted O'Brien. He was visibly ill, emaciated with a haggard face and eyes that stared. She pulled the piece of cheese and bread from her pocket that Cook had insisted she bring to sustain her on the journey. She held this out to Mr. O'Brien who grabbed it with trembling hands.

Stumbling to the corner of the cottage, he pushed the food into his mouth and swallowed piece after piece, not bothering to chew first. His eyes closed as the last of the food disappeared until Bridget feared he had fallen asleep.

She moved to rouse him. "Please!" she begged. "Where is everyone?"

He opened his eyes. After a huge sigh, he merely raised an arm and pointed, indicating the direction that led out from the other end of the village.

In her grief, Bridget cared nothing for the discomfort of the poor man but lunged forward and grabbed hold of his coat. "Eileen and Joe Egan. Where are they?" She shook him hard. "Where!?" she demanded.

Tears flooded Bridget's eyes as she waited with bated breath, hoping his next words would still her fear.....

"Dead," he whimpered.

Bridget stepped back. She pulled at her mouth with her fingers in distress, willing him to tell her what he knew of her family.

At last, he roused himself and said, "They were thrown out, like everyone else. But after dark, they crept back in. Himself closed the door and they propped themselves against the wall and waited for the end."

Almost choking in her grief, Bridget held herself together while she begged. "But they are not there. Where are they now?"

"Ah, they were found like that and buried down in the churchyard along with everyone else, in one big grave. Where—where my children and wife lay also."

Mr. O'Brien collapsed into pathetic sobs. Bridget looked at him in horror for a long moment before turning on her heels and running from the cottage.

She sped along the road that led past the little church beyond the village.

Above the well that was known to be holy, an ancient hawthorn tree spread its branches. The tree was used as a rag tree and was a place of offering to the saints of the well. Bridget knew that it had also been known in ancient days as a place of the goddess to whom similar offerings had been left.

She saw that the tree was overwhelmingly decorated with colorful remnants of brightly colored cloth, trinkets, and other things of value to the villagers, tenfold more than the usual. This was abnormal in itself and spoke a mute story of the horror that had obviously taken place over the past months.

As she approached the churchyard, her running feet faltered as she beheld a bewildering scene. The red skirt of a woman lay across a grave with arms reaching forward as if she had crawled there to die.

The smell was overwhelming and caused Bridget to gag. As she turned her face from the sight, she saw two others alongside the track outside the cemetery in putrefying degrees of death. It was as if, in their anguish they had tried to reach a place of holiness in which to take their final breath.

Bridget backed away and began to shake with fear. Swallowing hard, she gathered up her courage and stepped on, tripping over stones as if drunk with ale.

She looked about as she moved across the cemetery, trying hard to concentrate. There were no gravestones, no markings to indicate who had died recently.

In the corner, a huge mound of freshly turned earth lay spread across several yards of ground as if many bodies had been recently buried there.

Hand to mouth, the tears spilled over and through her fingers, Bridget threw herself upon the mound and stretched out her arms. "Mam!" she sobbed. "Da!" Over and over she cried until in her exhausted grief and despite the cold, she fell asleep.

When she awoke, the sun was high in the sky. Looking around, she saw where she was and finding her parents dead all over again, Bridget sobbed anew.

At last she looked up at the sky, wondering how it could be so bright and blue, and she so miserable.

A thought occurred to her. "Terry," she murmured. Rolling onto her knees, Bridget staggered to her feet and crossed the cemetery, skirting the dead with renewed hope. When she reached the road, she ran as if pursued by the devil himself until she reached Terry's village.

It was the same nightmare as before. Terry's cottage was half pulled down, its thatched roof burned and fallen through.

Nearby, one of the cottages was still intact. Its emaciated occupant sat unmoving in the dirt, one which Bridget did not recognise.

"Terry," Bridget gasped. "The family that lived here. Where are they?"

He raised his listless face to hers. He spoke slowly as if unused to the practice of speech. "Turned out by the landlord."

"Why? What had they done?"

"What indeed?" he said and shook his head as if he could not fathom the reason. He took a deep breath as if gathering his strength. "'Tis said they offended the good folk when young Terry accidentally broke an old limb from a faerie tree."

Bridget's started back in surprise for she had not heard about this event. It must have happened while she was away in Dublin.

Her rational mind told her that although it was both inauspicious and unfortunate, still it was an accident by the man's account. 'Surely,' she reasoned to herself, 'Punishment by the Aos sí could not spread its tentacles across half the county and beyond.'

"Please," she begged, "what happened here?"

In a sudden angry burst of energy, the man responded, "They roasted their rent pig and shared it with the village. When the landlord's agent came to collect the rent, there was none to be had from their cottage."

"Ah," she mustered, her reasoning satisfied while the horror and the question yet remained. "They were hungry." It was more a statement she made than a question.

The man seemed to take offense and said, "Where have you been girl? We have starved here these past months." He turned his gaze away, dismissing her.

"Please!" she begged again, "I need to know where they are."

He looked back at her, misery plain to see on his face. "They're gone from here. Sick with the fever so they were." He indicated the road. "Pushed out onto the road and gone." Taking pity on her he added, "Weeks ago it was. They left here weeks ago." He gazed at her for a long moment and then leaned back and closed his eyes, her presence forgotten.

*****

Maeve and Erin looked at each other, horror plain on both their faces.

"The poor girl," breathed Maeve.

Erin had been crying for most of the time so that Maeve had to take over the reading of the diary, all while rubbing her friend's back in sympathy.

"We should stop reading. It's too upsetting." Maeve looked about and handed a box of tissues to Erin who noisily blew her nose and then took another tissue to dab at her eyes.

"I had no idea," said Erin. "Was it really that bad back then?"

"Sure, and it was." She held up the diary. "Aren't you here reading the evidence for yourself?"

"It's just so hard to believe. And didn't Bridget say there was plenty of food at the markets in Dublin?"

"That was the thing of it," agreed Maeve. "There was plenty of food around but not for these people. When their potato crop failed, they'd no recourse because they depended on potatoes way too much.

Many of them kept a pig but that was to sell at the market when the rent was due for paying to the landlord. Without the potatoes and the pig gone already, they killed the cow and fished the streams, even killing off the birds and rabbits for food." She sighed, "And it wasn't long before that was exhausted."

"But there were forests, weren't there?" asked Erin. "Full of deer and I don't know, other animals."

"Is that what ye think?" Maeve shook her head. "Sure, the English had been decimating the forests since the 1500s. In any case, deer were the property of the landowner and punishable by law for the villagers to trap and eat them."

"They had no crops and no way to feed themselves."

"Starvation in the midst of plenty was how one report put it. Wagon loads of food transported along country lanes and the people starving as they passed by on their way to Dublin and the markets of England."

Maeve paused before continuing. "And then they were forced out of their homes because they couldn't pay their rent. And didn't the landowners want to breed cattle in place of all the little plots of land taken up by the tenants!"

"It's... so horrible." Erin slumped over, taken aback by grief for her people. "Gams never told me about this, I just... I didn't know!"

"People didn't talk about it. They still don't for the most part. It was traumatic, not only for the people who lived through it but for the entire country."

"It's too much to take in." She flopped back in the chair. "I need a cup of tea."

"Never mind tea," said Maeve. "We need something stronger than that."

She disappeared from the room for a moment and, just as quickly, returned, producing a bottle of wine from the fridge and two glasses from a small cupboard beside it.

"That will do!" said Erin.

*****

They spoke of other things for a while, unnerved by the history within the pages of the diary and unwilling to return to it until the wine softened the edges.

Unwilling to put it off any longer, Erin said, "We have to keep going but I don't think I can read without crying."

Maeve nodded sympathetically, "Okay." She took another gulp of wine, "I'll do it."

She lifted the diary onto her lap and read on.

# Chapter Eighteen

The kitchen was in a flurry of activity. It seemed the entire household of servants flowed in and out of the door that led above stairs.

Cook, wisps of red hair fallen from her cap and sweating on her brow, wrestled with a huge roll of dough at the great wooden table that dominated the center of the room. As she worked, she shouted orders at her minions who scuttled about the kitchen at her bidding.

Mrs. Murphy swept in and out of the door that led above stairs and barked orders in her deep voice that seemed in effect to create a sort of harmony with that of Cook's high-pitched tone.

No-one appeared to notice Bridget standing in the shadow of the outside door until Cook raised her head to blow at the wisps of hair. In doing so, she saw Bridget and stopped in the middle of a yelled instruction.

With a tip of her head and a sideways glance towards the little cubby where she made her lists, she indicated that Bridget should make herself scarce.

Obediently, Bridget slid quick as lightening across the back of the kitchen and into the cubby without drawing the eyes of the staff. Gratefully, she sank into a chair that was positioned behind the door. Lulled by the familiar comfort of kitchen sounds and smells, Bridget soon fell into a doze.

It was some time before Cook entered, pulling off her cap and pushing her hair back. She carried a dish of sweet pudding with wine sauce for Bridget, for she was a firm believer in the restorative value of good food. Seeing Bridget slumped in the chair and fast asleep, she placed the pudding on the table and shook her awake.

"Where have ye been?" she admonished. "Ye were told to be back here last night." Cook bustled about the cubby before something in the stillness of the younger woman's demeanor held her attention. She peered more closely at Bridget and saw that her bottom lip was trembling. "Whatever is the matter child?"

Bridget burst into noisy tears, explaining between sobs the events of the past few days from the loss of her parents to the disappearance of Terry.

Cook's face became as white as Bridget's. Frowning in sympathy, the older woman offered Bridget the pudding.

When that did not elicit the appropriate response, she put it back on the table and held Bridget close. She stroked the long brown hair for a moment before taking her by the shoulders and pushing her away so that they stared at each other eye to eye.

"Now!" Cook began. "Listen here girl." She gave Bridget a little shake to emphasize her words. "Ye need your position in this household more than it needs you. Pull yourself together. Time enough to grieve your own family when the Missus has been laid in her grave."

"Yes but …"

"Never mind, yes but. You've to put your own grief aside for the present." Cook knew the order of things and personal grief had no place in the running and order of a big house.

To separate herself from Bridget's pain she looked about the room and said, "'Tis uncommon busy I am with preparations for the funeral and the meals that will go with all the people coming and going from the house."

She tucked her chin into her neck to show her disapproval. "Godstruth, it will not be over until after the reading of the will."

She gave Bridget a little pat on the head as if to declare the matter of Bridget's grief over. "The worst of it all is not knowing who is to inherit the house and all that belongs to the Missus."

Cook drew herself to her full height and said with disapproval, "Himself is here already, the nephew. 'Tis thought he will inherit but not confirmed as yet. Mrs. Murphy tells me he is closeted with Mr. Doyle the family solicitor in the study at this moment."

She tutted and wiped her brow. "I am fit to burst with the uncertainty of it all. Once this week is over, t'will give us time to think again." Cook looked at Bridget at last. "Now! Wipe your face on your apron and give it to me for tis is fit to be thrown away tis so muddy." She peered into Bridget's face. "Can ye set yourself to rights now?"

Bridget swallowed and choked back her sobs. Eyes large in her pale drawn face, she breathed heavily in and out until at last, she gave a final sigh.

"'Tis lucky it will be if they do not notice ye were gone. Get yourself cleaned up and attend on Mrs. Murphy. I will talk to her now and smooth over the waters."

Grateful to Cook and mindful that she did at least have a place in the house, Bridget ran up the backstairs to the attic.

Washed and wearing a clean dress, Bridget paused as she passed the study door. She could hear voices within and recognized Mr. Doyle's voice for she had met him several times when he attended on the Missus. He was saying something about the Poor Relief Act."

Another voice, younger and one she supposed must belong to Himself said, "So that is the attitude, is it? Get the tenants off the land and the gentry are entitled to Government returns and land grants."

"I am afraid that is the way of it indeed," said Mr. Doyle.

"If that is the case, then 'tis glad I am, that I do not have such a fortune that gives me rights to land. For my good conscience could not bear to turn good people off their land, rented or no."

"Indeed!" said the other. "Indeed."

Bridget tiptoed away, deep in thought and trying to make sense of what she had heard.

When Bridget presented herself to the housekeeper, Mrs. Murphy opened the door and lifted her hands. "Bridget!"

She looked Bridget up and down. "Cook has just this minute apprised me of your circumstances." She bustled ahead into the room and Bridget followed. "I am prepared to waive your tardiness and not mention it to Himself."

She waited while Bridget murmured her thanks, for she was from Galway and thought herself above the rest of the staff.

"You are returned not a moment too soon for I have so much to think and do. It is quite put out I have been this past few days." She indicated for Bridget to follow to her desk.

"Now!" She indicated a list of names written on a piece of paper. "We have to write to all of these people immediately." She picked up the notepaper and handed it to Bridget. "Tis no time I have had for this task and you with a passing hand at writing letters."

She pulled out a chair. "Sit yourself down here and write an invitation to each of these people." She handed Bridget another piece of paper. "Copy from this." She sighed with relief as she said, "I thought I would have to do it all myself." As she turned to leave, she added, "They must all be written today and delivered before nightfall do you hear?"

"Yes, Mrs. Murphy," said Bridget and sat herself down. She was glad of the task as forming the letters and ensuring she did not make any errors, would keep her mind from wandering.

Later, as she sat with Cook in her cubby, Bridget told what she had heard at

Terry's village.

"I think it is why Terry and his family were evicted from their cottage. They were ill with fever when they were evicted." Bridget's eyes filled with fresh tears. The rush of the day being over, Cook allowed herself a moment of sympathy and patted the younger woman's shoulder.

"He may not be lost to ye child. Perhaps he will still turn up." Even as Cook offered these words of comfort, the words sounded hollow.

Bridget was quiet awhile as she contemplated the possibility. "I have no one in the world," she whispered.

"Ah, there now," Cook gathered Bridget into her ample arms and patted her back. In an effort to comfort her she asked, "Do ye have money saved child? Ye could always take ship to America."

She changed her tone at the sight of Bridget's shocked face. "Many an Irish man and woman have done it. A fresh start ye might say. Leave the dead to the dead."

At this, Bridget sobbed anew, "I have no money saved for I gave all to Mam and Da. Except these last months for I was unable to get it to them. Tis my fault they had no money for food." She sobbed against Cook's chest until the older woman's bodice was quite wet with tears.

At last Cook urged Bridget to bed. "Surely tomorrow will bring better news. Off you go now."

Pale and exhausted, Bridget headed for the stairs.

*****

*A wondrous event happened today.*

*Cook had admonished me to be grateful for my place here in the house. In truth I was trying to feel so, although I must confess, I was still wallowed in grief for my dear Mam and Da and my sweet Terry.*

*But then, Mrs. Murphy found me in the corridor.*

"Wisht now girl, ye look like a ghost. Get a hold of yourself for the family are waiting!" Mrs. Murphy waved her hand at Bridget indicating that she should follow her along the corridor.

"I am sorry. I do not understand." said Bridget, a crease forming between her brows.

"They are all seated in the library and here we are, delaying the proceedings." At Bridget's obvious confusion, Mrs. Murphy spoke slowly as if to a child. "The family are waiting in the Library." At this, she grabbed hold of Bridget's arm and hustled her along the corridor. "Tis the reading of the Will girl, have ye forgotten?"

"Oh but ... they won't need me in there."

"Struth! I have no idea why you are needed in there either, but so it is that I have been instructed to find you and bring you in."

The housekeeper pushed open the door of the library and walked in, Bridget in tow. A buzz of expectant chatter greeted them from the many people who seemed to have known or been acquainted with the Missus, for here they all were.

To Bridget's surprise, Mrs. Murphy stayed in the room, seating herself in one of the chairs near the back of the room.

Bridget nodded at Cook who stood at the back of the room with her back pressed against the wall and her chins tucked into her neck. She had taken off her cook's apron for the occasion.

Several of the well-dressed people in the room turned to look at Bridget who colored and veered away from their disapproval. Seeking comfort, she positioned herself against the back wall with Cook.

After a moment, Cook whispered, "'Tis a surprise to me that I am needed here." She glanced furtively about the room where ladies wore grand hats and men consulted their pocket watches. "Sure, and it will be a wonder if the tea is made and cake served in good time if I am not in the kitchen to oversee the proceedings."

Cook shook her head and folded her arms as she was wont to do when in a self-righteous mood. At that moment Mrs. Murphy turned and catching Cook's eye, frowned so that Cook dropped her arms back to her sides and sat up straight.

"Look!" urged Bridget. "Mr. Doyle is standing. Surely he will tell us why we are here."

The solicitor coughed discreetly and a sudden quiet fell over the room. All eyes were riveted on him.

"Thank you for coming here today."

A short but urgent buzz circulated the room for as anyone would know, the possibility of inheriting money made attendance a certainty.

In no particular hurry, the solicitor waited til the room was quiet again and began to intone the smaller legacies beginning with the servants of the house.

Mrs. Murphy had been left five guineas. She looked directly ahead when she heard this news, merely lifting her head slightly as if this were her due and not unexpected.

When Cook heard she had been left a similar amount, Bridget could feel her excitement as she looked up and around, a broad beam lighting her face.

To Bridget's surprise her name was called. "Bridget Egan," said Mr. Doyle. The imperious eyes of one or two in the room, looked Bridget up and down then turned away as if unimpressed.

The solicitor droned on as if reciting a prayer by rote, so often had he read wills in the company of such as were present that day. "Bridget Egan, you have been willed the sum of fifteen guineas, to be granted in cash, which sum is to be used in whatsoever way you deem most beneficial to yourself."

Cook's arm jostling hers, caused Bridget's teeth to chatter until she composed herself and firmly closed her mouth. She could scarcely imagine such a princely sum and was overcome as the Missus had never mentioned such an inclination.

Bridget thought of Mam and how she would have loved the telling of this moment. She would want to pay rent for several years ahead whereas Da would probably get that far-away look in his eye that came whenever he'd think of owning land. "Ah t'was no so long ago we Irish owned all the land between the sea and the ocean."

Her eyes filled up at the knowledge that Mam and Da would never hear tell of this day. Nor Terry either. Bridget began to whimper and was only brought out of it by Cook giving her a sharp nudge in the ribs.

When she looked up, the company had risen and were dispersing to the dining room. Several of the ladies looked Bridget up and down tight-lipped and disapproving, as they left. Bridget had no doubt they must be wondering how she could have the good fortune to be mentioned in the will.

Late that night after the maids had been sent to their beds, Cook and Mrs. Murphy sat down with Bridget at the big table in the kitchen.

"I've a mind to retire," Cook confided.

"'Tis dreaming you are, for that money will not last you long enough. Do you not have a fine job here and for many more years to come?

Himself has the house now. He will no doubt move in with his wife and children and your good services will be needed for many a year. No doubt he will show his appreciation and good faith by an increase in pay."

It was clear that Cook had not considered this for she said, "Ah! Well perhaps a new hat will suffice after all."

Mrs. Murphy nodded approvingly. "'Tis a wise choice." She turned to Bridget. "What of you now? Will you apply for the post of nursemaid or even governess to the children for I cannot think the new Missus will be in need of a companion. She is young and will soon have friends of her own."

Bridget shook her head. "Cook told me there are folk leaving for America."

"You would do that Bridget? All alone as you are and such a long way to travel."

"There is nothing left for me here."

Cook put her hand over Bridget's and tut tutted. Even Mrs. Murphy looked on with sympathy for Bridget had risen in her estimation now that she had a little money behind her.

"Surely it would be an adventure." Bridget's attempt at a smile was not convincing.

"I do know of folk who took the boat," Cook said. "My cousin said the charge is five guineas for steerage passengers.

"Five guineas?" Bridget was thoughtful. "I would have money left when I arrived there."

Mrs. Murphy was not impressed. "I think you should stay here and take your chance at governess."

"If I could work as a governess here, surely I could find work as such over there in America."

There was quiet in the kitchen. The two older women observed Bridget as she gazed off into the distance. No doubt they had their own thoughts of how they might use their money were they as young as she.

Although grateful, Bridget's mind was far from her newfound inheritance, and still dwelling in her recent events.

## Chapter Nineteen

"I don't know whether to laugh or cry," said Maeve. "It's too much to take in. All that grief and then a gift of money and wanting to take off for America."

"And who could blame her," added Erin. "I'm sure I'd want to do the same, get as far as possible from all that trauma."

Maeve poured them both another glass of wine. "What about Terry?" she asked. "Did she find him?"

"I don't know. I mean, all I know is what Gams told me."

"But didn't you say she was always telling you stories of ancestors?"

"She was." Erin thought back to those stories. "I don't recall anything about Bridget getting married."

"Well," Maeve pointed out. "I don't think people just lived together in those days without getting married, so…"

"Probably true."

"And here you are, proof of some kind of union between Bridget and whoever she married."

"But I have no idea who she married."

Maeve's mouth opened in astonishment. "How can ye not know who she married?"

Erin pulled at her earring. "How could I not know...?" Her voice trailed off. "How *could* I know? Do you know who your great, great, great grandmother was married to?"

"Well sure, and aren't the names passed down from one generation to another."

"I don't think it was like that in my family."

"Well isn't that the pity now!" Maeve regarded her friend in a fair imitation of that emotion, so that Erin began to feel uncomfortable by her apparent lack of family knowledge.

"Wait now," Erin said with a smile. "My grandfather's name was Joe."

"There you go," said Maeve. "That name was passed down. Old traditions die hard."

Erin considered her words. "I think I like that custom."

"Me too. It's kinda cool."

"My middle name is Bridget."

Maeve laughed and slapped Erin playfully on the arm. "You didn't tell me that."

"Well, middle names don't come up a lot, do they?" She shrugged. "I think it's why Gams told me stories about Bridget."

"And you look like her." Maeve nodded at the book between them. "You told me, same color eyes. And your hair too." She paused. "Don't you think that's special?"

"I do. Actually, I feel connected to Bridget. More so while I've been reading her story."

"That makes sense. Sure, it would be strange if you didn't"

Erin indicated the diary. "Let's keep reading."

"I was thinking the same thing myself, so." Maeve's tone was sympathetic as was the half-smile she offered her friend before reaching for the diary again.

Maeve turned the page. They both looked down in silence.

"That's it!" Maeve announced.

There were no further diary entries. She turned the remaining delicate pages as quickly as she dared.

They stared at each other.

"Now what?" asked Maeve.

"I don't know." Erin was at a loss to understand. "That can't be the end of the story."

"I'm sorry to say it but it looks like it is."

"Wow!" seemed a suitable response for the surprise and dismay that flooded Erin's thoughts.

"Well now, disappointing as that is, I have to ask, Is it enough?"

"For what?"

"To get you know, the will sorted out with Orla."

"Er ..." Erin was still shocked at the unexpected end of Bridget's story. "I don't know ... Maybe."

"Maybe? What else do ye need?" Maeve shrugged her shoulders and pointed at the empty page between them. "There is nothing else."

"True I suppose... but..."

"But?"

Erin looked up from her reverie. "I could still find out where Bridget came from. I mean, I want to see the village. I want to find out where it is and go there. I want ... I don't know what I want." She pulled at her earring. "But I think I'll know when I get there."

"Ah! Sure, I understand."

"You do?"

"Ye want to walk where she walked, stand where she stood."

"Yes!" agreed Erin. "That's it exactly."

"Wait now!" Exclaimed Maeve. "Didn't ye say Aiden knows where the village is?"

"No. Gams told him she went looking for it."

"Yes, but where did she go?"

"Well, that's the thing of it. She didn't say exactly.

"Ye don't need to know exactly where she went. Approximately will do."

"So, you're saying ..." Erin's voice trailed off. "What are you saying?"

"Where did she go from here? Before she went there, to the village."

"Ouuuu!"

"The middle place." Maeve leaned in so their faces were close. "And more to the point, did she tell Aiden where that place might be?"

"I said already. That trail is cold. All he knows is she went looking."

"Ah sure, it's because you haven't lived in Ireland long enough that you cannot think in a circle. C'mere to me now, for I'm thinking she told Aiden the place where she started looking."

Maeve sat back with a triumphant expression on her face. "And if she did, well we're off to the races!"

Erin sat up straighter. "It's worth a try!"

Maeve nodded her head in solidarity, a wise owl figure.

"I have to go." Erin almost knocked the chair over in her hurry to leave.

As she reached the door with the bell already tinkling, Maeve called out, "Are ye forgetting something?"

Head cocked to one side in obvious amusement, Maeve held out the diary.

Erin rushed back, a sheepish expression on her face. She grabbed the diary and held it tight to her chest. Turning, she ran out of the shop, the bell tinkling as she went.

As the door swung closed Maeve called, "Ah sure and you're welcome. What are friends for after all."

*****

It was late when Erin started the car and already dark. Erin drove like a native Irish driver, intrepid and courageous through the narrow winding lanes.

As she drew up beside Aiden's cottage, she was disappointed to see no welcoming light. He must have gone to bed.

"Darn farmers." She blurted. "They wake you up at dawn but they're not about when you need them at night …" She consulted her phone, "Quarter to midnight." She slumped over the steering wheel. She would have to wait until tomorrow.

That night, Erin could barely sleep for excitement. Knowing she might be close to solving the puzzle of the diary yet still not knowing what the answer might be, had her on tenterhooks most of the night.

To pass the time, she cleaned the already clean cottage, scrubbing the bathroom, the kitchen, the floors and emptying the dustpan until dawn began to peep through.

Erin checked the clock in the hallway at 4:30 am. She would leave it another hour before storming into Aiden's cottage. Settling herself into Gams armchair to wait, she promptly fell asleep.

It was almost noon when she awoke. Scolding herself for sleeping so long, she quickly showered and barely allowed time for her long hair to dry before rushing along the lane to Aiden's.

Not waiting to knock, Erin turned the handle of the door and flung it wide. She stepped inside, chest heaving as if she'd just run a marathon.

Aiden was seated beside the fire, a mug of tea in one hand and a sandwich in the other. He had just raised the latter to his mouth which had opened to receive it.

Momentarily halted in her quest, Erin narrowed her eyes and asked, "Is that what I think it is?"

He tipped his head. "It's a bacon buttie." He looked at the sandwich and returned it to the plate along with the mug of tea. "I blame Maggie! She converted me."

"Ah!" said Erin, her purpose diverted and almost forgotten.

Aiden pointed to the open door and raised his eyebrows. "You couldn't knock?"

"Oh! Sorry!" Erin remembered why she was here. "Did Gams tell you where she went?"

Aiden's brow furrowed. Erin tried to explain. "I mean, when she tried to find the village where Bridget lived."

Aiden looked perplexed. "I already told you. I don't know where the village is. She didn't tell me and I didn't ask."

"Yes! Yes! Yes!" Erin waved her hand impatiently. Then took a deep breath and spoke slowly.

"Think, Aiden." She held up a finger. "Where did she get the information she needed, to help in her search? Because it's not in the diary. The clue is in where she went after she left here."

"Ah now," interrupted Aiden. "She went to Castlebar."

"Castlebar, yes. But where in Castlebar?"

He shrugged. "She said something about finding some family in Castlebar."

Erin did a happy dance which comprised a series of hand flingings and twirling about which ended in her grabbing a surprised Aiden, pulling him to his feet and kissing him full on the lips.

Still in victory mode, Erin began to pull away when she realized Aiden had her shoulders in a vice-like grip.

She gasped in surprise and looked up to meet his eyes. The intensity there made her eyelashes flutter and her pulse race. Holding her gaze, he slowly leaned in and pressed his lips against hers.

When the kiss ended, Erin found herself in a moment of limp surrender. Placing a shaking finger over his lips she said, "I have to go." His grip tightened but she reassured him. "I have to go to Castlebar and I have to find Bridget's village."

Aiden's grip relaxed somewhat.

"I'll come back in a few days." She gulped and summoned her resolve. "We'll er, take this up then."

Before Aiden's kisses could change her mind, Erin ran to the car and roared off toward her own cottage, determined to leave for Castlebar that very afternoon.

Had she stopped to look, she would have seen Aiden watch her go, with a grin that stretched from one side of his face to the other.

## Chapter Twenty

Erin parked on the hill of a street at the edge of Castlebar. She had noticed an old stone building painted white with green trim and with a signpost to match that boasted O'Flaherty's B&B.

"As good a place as any to stay." She was stiff from sitting for so long, almost having to haul herself out of the seat.

Grabbing her overnight bag from the trunk, she draped a raincoat around her back to ward off the fine but steady downpour.

Erin stepped up to the door of the B&B and pressed the bell. Almost immediately a cheery face looked out.

"Hi, I'm Erin. I'm looking for a room."

"Well hello and good evening to ye. Ken O'Flaherty, that's me." He stepped back. "Certainly, we've rooms. Now, let's get ye booked in and I'll show ye the room."

Ken reached for Erin's bag which she gratefully gave up. "Have ye come far? Ye must be tired after your journey if ye have."

"A couple of hours and I am a bit, thanks." Erin admitted.

Ken soon booked her in and then walked ahead of her up the narrow wood polished staircase that twisted away out of sight.

The walls were painted bright green. 'Was the choice of paint meant to match the outside of the house?' she wondered.

"I've put ye at the front of the house with a fine view of the street."

Erin remembered her manners "Thanks Mr. O'Flaherty, that's kind of you."

"Just Ken will do. Well, here we are," he pushed through the half open door of the room and walked in, waiting there for her approval.

Erin looked around at the brightly painted room and the flowers on the windowsill. She smiled at him. "It'll do just fine."

Satisfied with her response, he turned to go "I'll leave ye to it. Would you like a cup of tea and a bit of soda bread with butter?"

"Sounds wonderful," she agreed. "Perhaps in an hour?"

"I'll send it up," he lumbered off like a big kindly bear, closing the door behind him.

Erin opened the window and looked out. It was early evening. It would be a good time to explore and get her bearings.

At the bottom of the stairs, Erin passed what must be the dining room, the clatter of cutlery attesting to dinner obviously being an option if she were to require it.

She opened the front door and stepped out into the street. Turning left, she walked briskly to the top of the hill and along the road between rows of narrow, two-storey houses.

Each was painted in bright colors without apparent thought for blending with that of its neighbor. Many of them were nestled against higher four-storey buildings, very charming and quaint.

The town seemed small enough so that Erin felt she could easily find her way back if she became a little lost.

Erin took the next turn which led along a street filled with little shops in varying states of closing after the day's work. A greengrocer was unloading a late delivery, the clattering of crates sounding loud in the quiet.

"Good evening" called Erin.

"It's a grand one," came the reply.

She smiled and walked on, eventually finding herself at the edge of a rich green lawn that spread across what appeared to be the town square. It was lined with flowerbeds and trees and dotted with streetlights of an older style, perhaps Victorian.

The houses surrounding the green were old but brightly painted. She looked down the side streets and wondered how she would find the family she was looking for.

The only information she had was the diary entry that indicated the Missus was the widow of a man by the name of Finlan and that they had lived in a house near the town square.

She had researched it but found no one in Castlebar by that name. Hopefully, a personal search would bring results although short of going door to door, she had no clear idea how she would go about this.

After a while, she returned to her room. An unappetizing cup of cold milky tea with a small plate of stale bread and butter sat untouched beside the clock-radio on her bedside table.

She poured the tea into the sink but hid the bread in a tissue and placed it in her bag to deposit in a garbage somewhere the following day. She didn't want the kindly Ken O'Flaherty to think she hadn't enjoyed and appreciated his kind offering.

Kicking off her shoes, Erin sank onto the yellow candlewick bedspread, lay back against the pillows and looked around the room.

The sun was low in the summer sky and set the flowered wallpaper to gold. "Such a very cozy room," Erin sighed and with happy thoughts of the grand day she herself hoped to find the following morning, she allowed her eyelids to flutter closed.

*****

As seemed to be the case with B&Bs, it was the smell of bacon that woke Erin.

She stretched long and lazy, enjoying the enticing aroma. Picking up her phone she glanced at the time. It was 6 a.m.

Breakfast was everything she had hoped for. There were thick slices of Irish bacon with eggs, sausage and fried tomato with lots of tea and toast.

There was also something called black pudding, which didn't look quite so appetising after Ken O'Flaherty explained that it was made from cow's blood.

"Er …" Erin's interest in breakfast waned immediately. "Maybe I'll just have a poached egg on dry toast."

"Suit yourself now. Will I tell Herself you'll be staying on again tonight?" asked Ken.

"I think so, yes."

"Having a little look around, is it?"

Erin replied sheepishly, "I'm trying to find ... you see ..."

"Looking for your ancestors?" Ken nodded encouragingly. "Sure, we have lots of visitors doing the same in the summer months."

"Yes. Well … They ... well she left here about the time of the Famine."

Ken's smile faded, "Ah, it was a bad time. What was her name?"

"Egan, like mine. I think the family I'm looking for came from just outside Castlebar. A village where other Egans lived."

"Hmm. I can't help you there."

"She worked in town here for a family by the name of Finlan."

His brows drew closer as he concentrated his thoughts. He shook his head. "The Finlans you say. Never heard of that name."

Erin's shoulders slumped. "Well, maybe I should start with Egans." She looked up hopefully. "I could google it but … I don't suppose you know of Egans in town whose family might have lived here for maybe a hundred years or more?"

Ken's eyebrows raised. "I'm sure there's a few Egans about the town of course. But as for how long any of them have been here is anybody's guess.

"My own family haven't lived here in Castlebar for more than thirty years so I'm no help to ye. I'm from further east myself."

Ken pursed his lips in concentration. "Now, ye might want to try the library. They keep land records and such." He pointed toward the window. "You'll find it down the hill and just across the square. They should be open at this time, so.

With a belly full of breakfast and with a strong sense of purpose, Erin crossed the square and went into the town library.

One of the librarians, Mrs. Noonan was a history buff and brought up a local search on the Finlan name. "What we can help you with is the head of each household as it was recorded at that time."

To Erin's disappointment, the search produced nothing by that name even though they scrolled back to the late 1700s and forward to the present time.

Biting her lip, Erin thought for a moment and said, "Could we try the name Egan. Perhaps if we could locate the village where Bridget Egan lived …" her voice trailed off. She wasn't sure what she would do if this lead failed.

Mrs. Noonan continued to be enthusiastic in assisting Erin. She soon found the households of several Egan families who were living in and around Castlebar in the mid 1800's.

There was a John Egan who had lived at number 25 Spencer Street. He had a house, yard and garden for which he paid fifteen shillings in rent annually to a landlord by the name of John C. Grosvenor.

Mrs. Noonan referred to another page. "Neither of those names are in the records now though and you have to understand, some of the houses are no longer standing but the streets are still there."

There was another Egan, also by the name of John, who had rented seven acres from a John Peirson and paid two pounds a year.

"This was probably a small farm," advised Mrs. Noonan. "You notice there was no street address, just an area name, Derrylea."

Mrs. Noonan referred to another screen. "From the ordinance map here, it looks to have been divided into what looks like small holdings."

There was another possible farmer, William Egan who had rented 33 acres in an area called Loughrusheen, for two pounds ten shillings a year.

Erin thought either of these might be possibilities and said so.

Mrs. Noonan pursed her lips and then explained that Derrylea and Loughrusheen were only a mile or so from the town whereas from what Erin had told her, it seemed Bridget had walked for a good ten miles.

"Even so, you'd be wandering all over the countryside trying to locate these old places and it may be that there's no buildings to be found any more, hardly worth your while."

Erin's spirits began to sink even further when Mrs. Noonan said, "Now that I think on it, I do happen to know of an Egan over there not far from the center of town. She scrolled through the records. "Yes, and here they are right back in the time you're looking at, mid 1800s."

Erin's heart began to race as Mrs. Noonan went on, "Of course, he's gone now but his wife is still there, old Mrs. Egan. She might be able to help you."

"That's wonderful." It was not the Finlan family she had hoped for but it was surely a good lead. "How do I get there?"

"Straight up the street here, second on the left is Spencer Street. You can't miss the house. It is a fine-looking piece of architecture."

*****

The town that had seemed quiet the evening before, was now packed with cars and trucks.

Pedestrians filled the sidewalks. The rabbit warren of streets led to more streets and alleyways going off from there. The town was filled with people milling around gazing into shop windows, wandering about with ice cream cones or meandering in and out of gift stores.

Erin was relieved to find the house quite easily. It was as Mrs. Noonan had said, an attractive home with gabled windows and ivy-covered walls. Erin took hold of the brass handle and knocked on the door, hoping this visit wouldn't turn into a dead end.

The door opened. A young woman stood in the doorway.

"Hello" said Erin "I was hoping to see Mrs. Egan."

"I'm Mrs. Egan," said the young woman.

"I think I'm looking for an older lady, actually."

"Ah, my grandmother. She's out right now and she won't be back until this evening. Is she expecting you?"

"No, but … maybe I could come back later today. I'm in town for only a few days and I'd like to speak to her while I'm here. I'm Erin. Erin Egan."

"I'm Saoirse Egan," said the young woman with no surprise in her voice. Erin wondered if other Egan's dropped by now and then in search of genealogy leads.

"How about 5pm? I'll tell her you called."

"That's great," said Erin, "thank you!"

'Well,' Erin told herself as she walked away, 'You've got yourself an appointment, hopefully with destiny.'

*****

To fill in time, Erin returned to the B&B. Stepping into the cool shaded hallway at the B&B, she could hear a woman's voice and Ken O'Flaherty's answering rumble of laughter. There was a delicious aroma of baking that made her mouth water. She followed the delicious smell and the sound of voices down the hall.

Knocking softly, Erin carefully opened the door to the kitchen and looked into a big comfortable room. In the center was a large scrubbed wooden table. On this, sat a mound of hot, fresh baked biscuits along with a bowl of creamy Irish butter.

Ken O'Flaherty sat in a well-worn rocking chair by an open range. He was sucking on a pipe that didn't appear to be lit.

Mrs. O'Flaherty, or so Erin presumed, was standing with her hands in a bowl at the kitchen sink and laughing merrily at her husband's remarks. She looked up and smiled when Erin opened the door. "Ah! And who is this now?"

"I'm sorry to intrude," Erin said. "I'm staying here."

The woman waved a hand. "Come away in. Sit down with us and help yourself." She gestured to the hot biscuits. "Diedre O'Flaherty."

Diedre went to shake hands but then realised hers were soapy and wiped them on a tea towel instead. "Tea is it? Or coffee you'll be wanting?"

"Nice to meet you," said Erin. "Tea would be lovely."

Taking milk from the fridge and mugs from the cupboard, Diedre said, "I do all the work around here. Himself has the fun side of it, so." Diedre beamed at her husband.

Ken smiled back good naturedly and adjusted the end of the pipe in the corner of his mouth. "Now!" he began. "You and I were speaking this morning about people living in Castlebar at the time of the famine. Well, I did a bit of a search of my own while you were gone." He reached for a small sheaf of papers he had printed off.

Erin nibbled on a hot biscuit as Ken leafed through the papers in his hand until he found the article he was after. "Here it is. It's from back in the day. Listen to this now." He cleared his throat and began to read aloud.

"An enquiry was held in the House of Lords in 1847." Ken looked up. "That's in London, so it is."

He continued reading. "The Sligo landowner was asked why he had evicted 40,000 people in the height of one of the worst winters, starving and penniless."

Erin gasped in disbelief. "And what was his excuse?" She reached out for the article, wanting to hold it in her hands to read the terrible story for herself.

She began to read. "The landowner replied that no one understood the Irish better than the landowners and the courts would do well to stay out of it."

Erin looked at the O'Flaherty's for their reaction. At the confusion on Erin's face, Ken tried to explain. "The Irish tenants and the landowners had one thing in common and that was their mutual hatred of each other." Ken shook his head in disapproval. "The tenants hated the landowner through fear, while the landowners despised the tenant farmers, seeing them as swarming, half starved, ignorant and Roman Catholics into the bargain. It's doubtful if such landowners considered the Irish as human beings at all."

"Wow!" said Erin, confused. "What gave the landowners such an attitude towards their tenants? Did they think they owned them?"

Ken nodded thoughtfully, "It was a complicated situation. Many of the tenants were dispossessed landowners themselves, cheated out of their land through centuries of penal law."

"Penal law?" asked Erin. "What's that exactly?"

"Oh, don't get me started." said Ken, throwing his hands up in mock despair. "I don't want to bore you with all that old stuff."

Erin's brow furrowed. "No really, I'd like to know."

Ken began slowly, as if reaching back into his memory for the things he'd been taught about that time. "They were here for seven hundred years, the English. They came to help get rid of the Danes, saw how beautiful Ireland was and decided to stay. Next thing we knew, their English Kings and Queens were giving away large parcels of Irish land to their own people."

Diedre caught Erin's eye and nodded her head. "It's true," she added. "Ireland was a land of small kingdoms at the time and by the time they managed to rally together it was too late, several centuries had passed and the English were firmly in control. They wanted all of the land so they came up with laws designed to rob the Irish of everything, including the culture."

"How can you rob a people of their culture?" asked Erin.

"Ah," sighed Diedre. "There were too many things went into that one and it's probably a story for another day, but that wasn't the whole of it. Not satisfied with taking away the religion and the land, the English brought out more laws to prevent Irish Catholics from being educated and even from speaking their own language."

Erin frowned in concentration. She recalled Gams speaking about this very thing and repeated her words now. "If you weren't allowed to speak the language, you would lose the poetry of the old stories and the link to your own family."

"You would indeed!" Ken slapped the arm of his chair. "And that's the truth of it. Sure, isn't it why you're here now, trying to connect yourself to your past?"

*****

At 5pm, Erin was shown into the front room of the Egan home by Saoirse. An elderly woman was seated in a comfortable armchair by the window. Saoirse introduced her as Mrs. Egan.

Erin was invited to sit down. She brought out the diary and over a cup of tea, Erin told the story of how it had been willed to her by her great aunt Maggie.

She told of her attendance at the clan gathering and how she had poured over the diary entries and consulted with friends, all of which had finally led her to Castlebar.

Mrs. Egan said, "And you think your ancestor may have lived and worked in Castlebar?"

"Well, I'm not sure," said Erin. "I'm just trying every available lead. That's all I can do, really."

"I wish my husband were still alive," said Mrs. Egan. "He loved history, you know. He would have enjoyed this discussion." She looked off into the distance for a moment. "My dear Finlan. I do miss him so…" She paused then, noticing Erin. "Why, what is it dear? You look as though you've seen a ghost."

Erin's eyes were indeed bulging, and her body was frozen so that the cup in her hand all but slipped from her fingers. Her breath coming in short bursts, she gasped, "Finlan Egan. Is that a family name?"

"It is, yes." Mrs. Egan was taken by surprise at Erin's sudden excitement.

"Of course. Oh, My Goodness." Erin managed to return the cup to the saucer before jumping up and hugging a surprised Saoirse and an equally shocked Mrs. Egan.

"Don't you see?" Erin laughed. "It is possible… that this is the place that Erin worked in!"

Mrs. Egan and Saoirse looked at each other in surprise. "You mean, here… in this house?"

Erin spread her hands, unsure whether to laugh or cry in her delight at this new information. "Yes. Maybe. Who knows? I'm just thrilled that there's a connection."

Both Mrs. Egan and Saoirse were enthralled and insisted on looking at the diary where they poured over the entries, carefully turning the pages so as not to damage them.

The older woman wagged a finger. "You know, I do think we may still have the accounts from those years." With an expression of happy triumph, she said, "We may find from there where Bridget's village was located."

"Really?" Erin could not believe her good fortune.

"I don't doubt it," said the old lady. "They'll be locked away in the cellars though." Gazing off into the distance, she added, "So many rooms down there and none of them in use for a long time now."

She looked back at Erin, "We use them for storage. I often wondered if I should give the old records to the library, but I just couldn't bear to part with them. And now here you are, looking for them."

Smiling at Saoirse, she asked, "Would you mind dear? Perhaps Erin would like to go down with you and help."

To Erin she said, "Be warned. It will be very dusty."

Erin was having trouble keeping her excitement under control. At this point she felt she would walk through fire to get at the records. A little dust was nothing.

Down in the basement, one tiny room after another led off from the large square kitchen back into the depths of the old house. In most of the rooms, a single light bulb hung bare and unwelcoming from the ceiling.

The rooms nearest the kitchen were obviously still in use as office space and pantries. Other rooms held old furniture piled on top of each other. Still further and the rooms were lined with boxes from floor to ceiling.

Finally, at the furthest end from the kitchen, a door opened into a small room of all.

There, boxes lined the walls as before, but they were stacked low and separated from the floor by racks made of wood.

"It's to preserve them you see," explained Saoirse when Erin bent to examine the racks. "These old houses can be quite damp."

Each box was labelled. Erin followed Saoirse around the room as they examined each in turn.

Saoirse tapped the boxes as she read off the labels:

1891-1900
1881-1890
1871-1880
1861-1870
1851-1860

She tapped twice on the last box, 1841-1850.

Between them, they pulled out the box and carried it to the kitchen where they set it on a big table in the center of the room.

Erin looked at her hands. They were as warned, quite dusty. She quietly wiped both hands on her jeans.

Inside the box, were books of accounts all diligently labelled for the various workings of a large house.

There was a book for gardening implements, including the price of each tool and also wages paid for each gardener.

Erin noted that a home address was recorded for each employee. Another book showed the annual reckoning of kitchen expenses as well as staff wages of all below stairs staff.

Finally, Saoirse lifted out a book labelled 'Above Stairs Accounts and Staff." She smiled and handed the book to Erin who gulped and set it down on the table with shaking hands.

Quietly, Erin asked herself, 'Could this be the end of her journey? Would she finally know the whereabouts of Bridget's village?"

Settling herself, she opened the book and looked inside the front cover. There in the beautifully formed penmanship of a housekeeper, was the information she had been waiting for

*Bridget Egan*
*Bar Cuill*
*County Mayo*

Erin sat back. At that moment, she felt her joy was complete. She looked up at Saoirse with tears in her eyes. "You can't imagine the journey it's been to find this... I can hardly imagine it myself."

Saoirse beamed back at her. "I'm glad we kept it then. Just for you. Like a gift from the past."

"A gift from the past," echoed Erin.

Taking her leave of Saoirse and Mrs. Egan with plans for staying in touch, Erin walked through Castlebar, the diary hugged tight against her chest.

She crossed the square in the soft glow of electric lights that were modelled on their original 19th century style. Pausing near the center of the square, Erin wondered if Bridget had crossed this very same square when returning to her work in Castlebar.

In that moment, Erin felt something brush her shoulder. Surprised, she looked around but there was no one in sight. Erin had a sudden awareness of a young woman close by and shivered as a tingling sensation ran along her arms and across her shoulders.

It was as if someone she cared for was very close. A warm knowing crossed her mind. She knew it was Bridget, felt it with every fiber of her being.

As suddenly as the experience came over her, it disappeared. Yet, the feeling of love that accompanied it, stayed with her.

As she prepared for bed that night, Erin intuitively felt that her experience with Bridget on this night heralded something so important that she was fairly buzzing with excitement.

She could scarcely bear to waste time in sleep yet when her breathing finally settled into a settled rhythm, it was of bluebells and summer sunsets that she dreamed.

## Chapter Twenty-One

"Bar Cuill?" The man looked down at the ground and nodded his head. "Top of the hazels. That's what the name means." He looked up at her then. "Exploring are ye?"

"Well, in a way I guess I am." Suddenly shy, Erin said, "My er, ancestors came from that village."

The man sighed. His voice was gentle. "You'll not find anything there now."

"I ... yes, I thought as much."

"It was a bad business back then. I heard the story from my grandfather who heard it from his. Sure, it was terrible what happened, and it wasn't just here. It was all over the West of Ireland."

Erin waited, content to let him talk her through the history.

"It was a terrible time altogether." He shook his head. "People crawling into the graveyards to die there, so as not to be a bother d'you see?"

He leaned against a gate that led onto farmlands, settling in to tell the story.

"Most of the families that lived here had nowhere to go when they were turned out of their cottages. Some were offered passage to other places, Canada and America.

"I heard of a family here, their daughter was offered passage to America – just one ticket. They say she was sent off to Cork on a wagon to join with other emigrants from the villages round about and all with their heads hanging low. Defeated in spirit they were at having to leave their homes."

He stopped talking and gazed across the field beyond the gate for a long moment before continuing. "Most of us lost family back then. A bad business it was, so."

Eager to learn what she could, Erin prompted, "What happened to the family, the one you just mentioned?"

"Sure, it's hard to know what happened to each individual family. But the story, as I heard it, was that after their girl left, they shut themselves into their home. They wanted to preserve their dignity d'you see. They shut the door on the world so they could die in peace."

Difficult as this was to hear, Erin blinked back the tears, not wishing to disturb his flow of what were probably third-hand memories.

The man shook his head slowly. "Who can say what happened to the family really? But I imagine it gave them hope, knowing they'd sent their girl off to a new life."

Erin opened her mouth to say that it was probably Bridget's family he was talking about but thought better of it. What difference could it make now for him to know that Bridget had left after her parents passed away and not before.

As if affirming his own words, he said, "They'd know it was too late for themselves. But I'd imagine it was a hope they could hold onto as they breathed their dying breath, that one child at least would get away from the curse that rode the land in those desperate years."

Erin thought of Bridget and how she must have felt when she learned her parents had starved to death while she was away in Dublin, and her with the money that could have kept them alive. Surely the memory must have stayed with Bridget all of her life.

The man seemed to want to talk now that he had begun. "Sitting up against the wall is how they were found, with their arms wrapped around each other for comfort."

Erin swallowed and bit her lip fiercely.

"These days of course, there are warning signs as there must have been back then, when a potato blight is coming. When early summer rains are too plentiful now, farmers will be out there protecting the potatoes by spraying the stalks against a possible blight."

He sucked the air in through his teeth. "Sure, things have changed a good deal since then and thank the good lord for it."

He offered to walk Erin to the village which was inaccessible by road. She thanked him politely but refused, saying she wanted to explore the place on her own.

Using the ordnance map she had acquired from the librarian, Erin opened the gate and walked across the field that was lined with green hawthorn hedge and beautiful in the morning sun.

She followed an ancient track that led through more fields with lazy-bed ridges raised high to carry the rain away.

The first indication that she had found the village of Bar Cuill, were the hazel trees that flourished up and down a hill interspersed with holly and the ever-present alder. This led into a valley of rich ground flora filled with woodland flowers.

Like a journey back in time, the forgotten village revealed itself little by little. Here at the base of the hill was a low wall, barely a foot high of gray stones cobbled together.

Erin picked her way along the base of the hill, following the trail of one ghostly rock wall after another. The ordinance map showed the existence of a well, but she couldn't see any sign of it.

There was a tight copse of hawthorn trees that looked to be in the approximate area of what might have been a source of water, at least according to the map.

At last, she spied an old graveyard next to a small abandoned chapel of which four walls still remained but without a roof.

As Erin explored the graveyard in which she knew Bridget's parents were in all likelihood, buried there.

The call of a robin broke the silence disturbing Erin from her reverie. She had the strangest feeling that she stood in a place that was between places. The horror that once was, buried now in the timeless perfection of a pretty postcard.

The robin hopped from one gravestone to another, none of them grand in a way that spoke of the importance of the deceased that might be sleeping there.

When the robin reached the outer wall of the cemetery, it sat awhile as if waiting for her. She followed where it led, more by instinct than any sense of intellectual judgement.

When she drew closer, the bird spread its wings and flew away, perching on a taller tree so that she could still see it through the overgrowth.

Erin walked from the graveyard onto a carpet of buttercups, primroses and dandelions that were sprinkled between low-lying, ivy-covered walls.

As she moved further in toward the place she had last seen the robin, these slowly revealed themselves as half tumbled cottages.

She found herself in a sort of street. It was overgrown by thistles and brambles. She was glad of the hiking boots and jeans that protected her from the worst of the stinging overgrowth for she could hardly pay attention to where she was walking, in the effort of trying to make sense of the place.

The robin was perched on the lower arms of an oak tree with wide-spread branches, its leaves rustling gently in the breeze of the Irish morning.

She could see from the layout that the cottages had been set out more or less in a line each side of this area.

It was as if the very land itself had reclaimed the village, hiding it from the casual eye by an overgrowth of bushes and trees. Yet in the sunlight the place revealed itself to Erin and as she turned back to look at the tree, the robin was gone, its purpose complete.

The tree and the village that surrounded it seemed suspended between yesterday and tomorrow, an empty shell of those who had passed from this forgotten place.

In the quiet of the moment Erin heard the tinkling sound of water and turned toward it.

When she reached the source, she found a stream that bubbled and gurgled over rocks and stones that must have sat just below the surface of the water for a thousand years.

Erin strained to see the cottage she yearned to find. She knew from reading the diary that it lay over the stream and beyond the trees but could not at that moment discern it.

She began to pick her way through the water, taking her time, careful not to slip on the stones that probably had felt no step in over a hundred years and more.

Hearing a plop, Erin looked about thinking she had disturbed a fish or perhaps a small animal.

Her boot slipped off the stone she had been about to place her full weight onto. As she struggled to balance, the cold water slapped against her legs right up to her knees, a kind of baptism.

When she looked up again, it was to a scene that moments before had not been there.

A young woman tread lightly through the wooded area. She wore a shawl over long full skirts which as she laughed and twirled about, lifted slightly to reveal a bright red petticoat.

The figure paused before a white-washed cottage with trim of red on the door and one tiny window. A curl of blue smoke floated lazily from its thatched roof.

The color left Erin's face as the young woman paused to look directly at her before disappearing inside the cottage.

Erin's first reaction was that of goosebumps which crawled up her spine and across her scalp. This was immediately followed by a sensation of joy and then relief that flooded through so that her breath came out in a huge whoosh!

Then, splashing, running, tripping, she called out, "Bridget!" Her boots wet-slapped against the grass as she followed the figure into the place where the cottage had been only moments before.

Surely it had been there. Hadn't she seen it with her own two eyes.

Running into the woods, she stepped uncaring through long grass and thistles until she stood within the space that once was a cottage.

Its walls now were barely three feet tall. Yet she had seen it as it was and knew it to be the home of Bridget.

She dug in her pockets for tissues to wipe her nose and tried to blink the tears away so that she could see.

There against one wall was the remains of an old fireplace. Perhaps it was just to one side that Da had held Mam in his arms one last time as they waited helplessly for the moment that would come, slowly, inevitably a last long sleep.

This was the secret that Bridget had carried with her into the new world; the secret that stopped her merry laughter so that she'd stare off into the past, into the memories of the loving family she had left behind.

No wonder she could never speak of this time. No wonder those brief recollections of the past were quickly followed by the gathering of children and grandchildren into her loving arms, holding them close and stroking their sweet faces.

What joy she must have felt that she had survived to see her descendants live and prosper in a land that had taken her for the talents she had to offer and not for what she had in her purse.

When Erin came out from the cottage, she could not bear to leave the scene that was so pretty in the morning light.

She walked over to the grassy banks of the little stream that sparkled blue as the sky.

She heard the water tinkling over the stones she'd crossed to reach the cottage. She listened to the wind as it sighed through the trees and the migrant sandpipers as they called to each other.

It was a sweet place now and sang of peace to her grieving heart.

At last, Erin walked back through the remnants of homes and reached the old track that led away from the village.

She thought she saw Bridget sitting on the back of a hay cart, desolation on her face as she stared back toward her home.

As Erin caught a glimpse of this with breaking heart, Bridget seemed for a moment to become aware of her presence.

Her face lit up in a smile that washed over Erin with all the love of a mother for her child and for the child of her child. It was a smile that was filled with hope for the future that lay ahead.

## Chapter Twenty-Two

Five years later, Erin stood in the place where she had last seen Bridget. She ran a hand gently over the bump in her belly. Aiden placed his large hand over hers. They smiled at each other and gazed at the village beyond the stream.

With government grants and sponsorships, the land around the area had been cultivated into a showcase of an Irish heritage village.

Permissions had been sought and the track widened to permit tours to trek across the fields from a small car park created down by the road.

A tour guide with a smile in her voice, led a chattering group through homes in various stages of renovation.

None of the cottages were complete nor would they be, out of reverence for what once was. But some had been half rebuilt to show what had been and the comfort that could be imagined there.

The ground between the two rows of cottages had been cleared and restored with a calculated replica of the grasses that might originally have covered it.

The old oak tree in the center of the green was said to be quite ancient. It could easily be imagined that the wooden bench which now sat beneath its branches, replaced a bench from an earlier time that had in its turn, given rest to the long ago occupants of this place.

The guide led her party out of one cottage and along the grassy track where she paused briefly before leading them into another home.

Her voice wafted across the green, bright and cheerful although what she was saying was not clear.

Erin imagined the guide would be at the point in her well-rehearsed tour, where she would explain that sheep occasionally wandered into the village and would often stay awhile to nibble on the green which helped to keep it trimmed.

She would give a lightened version of the events that had happened here, only delving into its depths if called upon by those who required a deeper explanation.

Some of those who came here sought the tranquility of such places that could only be found off the beaten track. Others came for the history and a look inside a village that was half forgotten until this point in time.

Still others came in search of their ancestral home such as it was. For here there were no manor houses to be found but merely the cottages of people who lived simple lives, yet rich with shared cultural history and quality of courage, hard-working every one of them.

Those few who bore a family history that intertwined with that of Erin, she liked to welcome personally. With such people she would listen to their stories and share hers, happy to weave the family tapestry with yet more beautiful threads that served to enrich the design still further.

She listened to children calling to each other as they played on the green or ran in and out of the cottages. In their youth and purity of heart, they were unheeding of the tragedy that had befallen this lovely village; and of their parents who tread softly with the knowledge of the place, where their children ran unaware.

Erin listened to the song that wove itself from the voices of the past and the laughter of the present. Her heart was glad that the spirits of the people who once lived here were no longer forgotten.

She recalled the envelope she had retrieved from Orla who had found it within a larger envelope on the dining room table.

It had been addressed to Orla herself along with a note to give it to Erin at the end of her search along with the check and the deed to Gam's cottage.

Inside the envelope addressed to Erin had been a note that read ~

*My Darling Erin,*

*If you're reading this, then I know you've found the diary and the village where our shared ancestor Bridget Egan was born and raised.*

*Such a terrible thing it was she must have witnessed, for it made her leave the island of Ireland to put an ocean between the past and the future.*

*How Bridget must have mourned for the country and the family she left behind. Yet she never burdened her American family with the telling of it.*

*Instead, she wrote her story into a diary and then closed it the day she left Ireland, never to open it to write in again, until the day that I found it after my own parents passed away.*

*And now my dear Erin, you've reversed her lonely journey and come home. You've seen the place where Bridget was born and raised and the little churchyard where her dear parents are buried.*

*This is not the end of the story as I'm sure you will have guessed from the old photograph I've enclosed with this note. Please forgive me for keeping that information from you, but I know that you understand that you might not appreciated this story the same way, had you simply been told all the details.*

*I hope you realize how important it is to understand the tapestry a family weaves, as their journey intersects with our own, to make the most beautiful of designs.*

*Although it is your choice, it is my cherished hope that you make your home here in Ireland. And one day, if you pay attention, the land will sing to you as it did to me and to all our mothers who came before us.*

*I am your most loving Gams,*
*Maggie Bridget Egan*

Accompanying the note was a photograph which showed an elderly couple, both with white hair.

They stared out at the camera with implacable expressions on their aged faces.

One small detail distinguished them from a thousand similar photographs of the time.

If the observer looked away from the faces and down, the couple could be seen holding hands, fingers entwined as if their lives were somehow wound together like threads of a cord that when combined, are made stronger.

On the back of the photograph, an inscription written in Indian ink read ~

*'Bridget and Terry, 1895.'*

Erin thought of the child growing in her belly. One day soon she would hold the babe in her arms and explain how their family tapestry was created. And then she would tell the child the story of her namesake, Bridget Egan.

# EPILOGUE

Erin, Mykel the donkey and Beauty the pony, stood side by side looking over the fence at the sheep in the meadow beyond. Erin's arm was coiled around the pony's neck.

Mykel biffed his nose against Erin's arm. She turned to look at him. Flies buzzed around his head as he biffed her again. "You know Mykel," she said. "You and I will have to learn to get along. I'm here for the long haul and you'd better get used to it."

Mykel merely snorted as if to say he'd consider the idea. Erin patted his neck and tried not to recoil from the flies he seemed unable to repel.

As Erin turned and walked back to the house, the donkey biffed her once more before trotting back to the fence where Beauty waited.

"I know you love me, really," Erin called over her shoulder. Yet when she entered the cottage, she closed the door firmly behind her.

# GLOSSARY

| | |
|---|---|
| Agus | And |
| Annals of the Four Masters | Chronicles of medieval Irish history |
| An Post | Postal Services |
| Aos sí | People of the mounds, known as Fairies |
| Arra | rish expletive: Really! |
| Bainne tuibhe | Old milk that's allowed to sour |
| Bar cúil | Place of the hazel trees |
| Bacon Buttie | Bacon sandwich - see recipe below |
| Bacstaí | Boxty - Irish potato pancakes |
| Bannock | Bread, similar to a scone - recipe below |
| Bastible | Iron cooking pot used over an open fire |
| Craic | Enjoyable conversation |
| Clover flavored butter | Refers to clover grasslands where cows graze, producing milk from which butter is made |
| Eoghan | Irish origin of the Anglicised name Egan |
| Fae | Faerie or those humans with ability to see or know the future |
| Fair Folk | Faeries |
| Gaeilge | Irish language |
| Geis | A vow |
| Good folk | Faeries |
| Gráigin | Hamlet or cluster of houses, not quite a village |
| Gráigeanna | Plural of Grágeanna - Hamlets |
| Is breá liom tú | Expression of romantic love, as in I love you |
| Léann ábhair | Barley Ale |
| Le do thoil | Please |
| Mo ghrá | My love |
| Mo stór | My treasure/my little darling |
| Other folk | Faeries |
| Peat logs | Decayed plant vegetation used as fuel |
| Poitín | Poteen/potheen Irish 'moonshine' an alcoholic beverage distilled in a small pot |
| Póit | Hangover - usually from drinking poitín |
| Prátaí | Potatoes |

| | |
|---|---|
| Rag tree | Often hawthorn trees on which rags or ribbons are hung as part of a healing ritual |
| Seanchai | Storyteller or bearer of old lore and folklore |
| Sídhe | A mound associated with faerie or the Tuatha de Danaan of ancient Irish times |
| Taoiseach | Historically, clan chief. In modern times, the term refers to the Prime Minister of Ireland |
| Tír na nÓg | Land of eternal youth - Irish mythology |
| Turf fire | Compressed fuel blocks made from peat that burn pungently |
| Wake | A celebration of the life of the departed |
| Wake Cake | Cake used at Irish wakes - see recipe |
| Wellies | Waterproof rubber boots, knee-high made |

ACKNOWLEDGMENTS

*Sariah for her tireless encouragement with and to, the creative process and her wonderfully designed book cover for this and all of my books*

*Coire Ansic writer's group for feedback on Irish customs, history and folklore along with encouragement and love*

*Ariel, Karen and Sharon for much appreciated feedback on reader expectation*

*Paul Cookson for his expertise and insights into wild life*

# OTHER BOOKS BY THIS AUTHOR

*www.CaroleMondragon.com*

### The Mists of Clonacool:
*An Irish Romance at Winter Solstice*

Deep in the west of Ireland under a full moon, beside a quiet lake on the road to Ballina, Kay McKierney reaches out to the Sídhe in a light-hearted plea for help with her failing relationship.

Kay unknowingly draws the attention of a Sídhe Prince of the Tuatha de Danaan. He recognizes the intricately designed Celtic necklace that Kay wears around her neck, gifted by him to Kay's great grandmother Caer over a hundred years previously.

### The Secret of Clonacool:
*The Romance in Ireland Returns on the Festival of Beltane*

Kay McKierney has returned to the west of Ireland with Liam and their daughter Aoife to live in their cottage on the edge of a meadow leading to a faerie circle, where strange things occur when the mist gathers beneath the moon.

Kay hopes they will live quietly so that she can protect Aoife from the unusual abilities that have begun to set her apart. But Aoife's budding powers cannot be hidden, and she is soon drawn to those who would guide her.

## The Key to Clonacool:
*The Irish Romance Continues on the Festival of Lughnasa*

Aoife, now a young woman, has consistently denied her heritage as a child of the Tuatha de Danaan. Faced with a challenge that threatens the island of ireland, Aoife realizes she must become part of the solution. To do this, she will have to undertake the journey Kay, Aoife's mother took fifteen years previously into the realms of Tir na Nog from where Kay never returned.

On the Night of Nights, under the Moon of Moons, Aoife gathers her courage to walk into the darkness of the portal, where she will confront both her past and her future.

To learn more about Carole Mondragon,
please visit

www.carolemondragon.com

Manufactured by Amazon.ca
Bolton, ON

40612073R00176